Left, Right aı

Someone has leaked a top secret Pentagon document to *The Monitor* newspaper in London. Who is the mole? Just the kind of person Defence Through Strength would like to see put behind bars, and their spokesman Paul Silverlight says as much in his regular column in *The World* next day. In the bastions of the New Right and the committee rooms of the Peace Movement, rumour buzzes. Will the leak set off the final holocaust? It seems as though it may . . . but by then, Silverlight is past caring. And in Fleet Street and Scotland Yard business is as usual, whatever the international situation. It is when Inspector Brian King of the Special Branch, rather than a CID officer, is given the Silverlight case that Andrew Taggart of *New Politics* smells something fishy and decides to do a little investigating on his own account.

From Cambridge, England, to Princeton, New Jersey, King finds he has to do without very much help from his friends—and Taggart had better keep well away from *his* . . .

RUTH BRANDON

Left, Right and Centre

F 85 57126

COLLINS, 8 GRAFTON STREET, LONDON W1

William Collins Sons & Co. Ltd
London · Glasgow · Sydney · Auckland
Toronto · Johannesburg

This one is for Carrie
and in spite of Lily

First published 1986
© Ruth Brandon 1986

British Library Cataloguing in Publication Data

Brandon, Ruth
  Left, right and centre.—(Crime club)
  I. Title
  823′.914[F]   PR6052.R264/

ISBN 0 00 231908 X

Photoset in Linotron Baskerville by
Rowland Phototypesetting Ltd
Bury St Edmunds, Suffolk
Printed in Great Britain by
William Collins Sons & Co. Ltd, Glasgow

PRELUDE

The editor sat fingering a bunch of papers, staring at them while the rest of that Tuesday's conference chatted and waited for him to begin. Finally he raised his head and said, 'Well, no question about today's lead. If it's genuine.' He turned to his deputy. 'Question is, can we believe it?'

'We've checked it every way we can. It seems real enough. And it's certainly believable.'

The editor sighed. 'I'm afraid it is.' He indicated the papers. 'What we have here, ladies and gentlemen, is what appears to be a leak from the Pentagon. I need hardly repeat that we've checked it as thoroughly as possible, but of course we have no idea who sent it to us—or why they picked us, come to that. Still, here it is.' He paused for a moment. 'It's real dynamite,' he said slowly. 'The only thing that worries me about publishing it is that it may turn out to be genuine dynamite. I wouldn't like to be known as the man who hastened the end of the world.'

The Monitor, Wednesday, 5 April
Late yesterday, an extraordinary document came into possession of *The Monitor*. We have naturally been at pains to ascertain its authenticity: it is, we have reason to believe, entirely authentic. In it, the Pentagon sets out the conditions under which the United States, now that it has achieved a satisfactory first strike capability, would launch a pre-emptive nuclear strike against Russia and the Warsaw Pact countries, or against any other countries which it believes to be holding nuclear weapons liable to be used against the interests of the United States and the free world.

The fact that this type of action is even contemplated of course directly contradicts stated NATO policy in which nuclear weapons are designated primarily as deterrents.

While NATO has not signed a 'no first use' declaration,

and it is known that NATO policy, given the present state
of its conventional war-fighting ability, envisages the use of
nuclear weapons in certain circumstances, the notion of a
pre-emptive strike to destroy the enemy's nuclear forces has
of course always been hotly and specifically denied. While
such denials, especially in the face of the known capabilities
of such weapons as cruise, Pershing and MX, have always
been treated with a certain scepticism in some quarters,
confirmation of such fears nevertheless puts the whole situation in quite a different light. We feel there are certain
questions which the public will now want answered as soon
and as clearly as possible. Has the British government (not
to mention the other member-states of NATO) been party
to this policy? If so, why has this been consistently denied
in public? And if not, must we not now question the whole
basis of our alliance with a Power which (to put it no higher)
deceives us on such matters, even while we act as its chief
aircraft-carrier? . . .

Extract from The World at One, BBC Radio 4, Wednesday, 5 April
SIR ROBIN DAY: The fact is, Minister, that a great many
people are going to be highly perturbed should this turn out
to be true. After all, quite apart from small matters of NATO
policy, such as whether or not we were informed about this
—and I'd like to return to that later—it surely puts us all,
the whole world, in the gravest danger?
MINISTER OF DEFENCE: I think, Robin, with respect, before
we indulge in hysterics and histrionics, we ought to concen-
trate on the first part of your question—should this turn
out to be true. After all, we all know *The Monitor*'s reputation
on this kind of thing. I'm not of course saying that they'd
print deliberate lies, but they do tend to rush into print
at the slightest suggestion—and no one will be very surprised that they relish an opportunity of this sort. I
notice they don't say what their authentication for this
is. Where did they get this document from? It's all very
well protecting sources, but it seems to me that unless
we know that—
SIR ROBIN DAY: With respect to you, Minister, you still

haven't answered my question. Should this be true, did you know about it?

MINISTER OF DEFENCE: Now you know as well as anyone, Robin, that there are certain aspects of NATO policy which, in the interests of us all, simply can't be broadcast wholesale. What I can say is, that I personally have the greatest faith and trust in our American allies, and nothing that has come to my attention over the past few hours or days has done anything whatever to affect that. And that's all I'm prepared to say.

SIR ROBIN DAY: Thank you, Minister. I'm sure we're all most reassured.

The World, Thursday, 6 April
SCAREMONGERING AGAIN—by Paul Silverlight
Perhaps the greatest proof of the strength of the NATO alliance is the way it survives even the almost daily battering it receives from within its own ranks. It is hard to believe that any newspaper behind the Iron Curtain would be allowed the freedom to publish the kind of obscene rubbish perpetrated by *The Monitor* yesterday.

It was obscene in the same way that all those films purporting to portray the aftermath of nuclear attack are obscene: they titillate and pander to a certain kind of depraved appetite. This political pornography is clearly highly gratifying to the perverted intellects of those who would go to any length to extend the shadow of the Iron Curtain over this country . . .

CHAPTER 1

Princes' College, founded in the sixteenth century in memory of the little princes murdered by Richard III (motto: The Meek Shall Inherit), is one of the sights of Cambridge. The Hall by Sir Christopher Wren, the Perpendicular chapel coeval with the college's founding, the graceful eighteenth-century courts, the famous gardens, attract flocks of tourists against whom notices are displayed in English and French (*Défense de marcher sur la pelouse; entrée interdite*) and ignored in all the languages of the globe.

Modern life inevitably makes its mark even on Cambridge, but Princes' resists it. One of the last colleges to admit women, it still steadfastly avoids the democratization of mealtimes. For the students, the Wren hall has been adapted to the cafeteria system, leaving the dwindling number of college servants free to cook and clean. The dons, however, do not take part in the distasteful process of queueing for their chips and mixing with *hoi polloi*, but still sit secluded at High Table where they are served food similar in essence to, but more classily presented than, that eaten by everyone else.

On this bright but chilly April evening, the late sun shone through stained glass windows and threw coloured light on to the already rainbow-hued heads of the eaters in the body of the Hall.

High Table, enlivened neither by coloured light nor red and green hairdye, presented a duller aspect. Conversation, too, seemed to have lapsed, or perhaps it was merely drowned by the noise level of the undergraduate eaters. They had been discussing estimates for the proposed new building, a matter of consuming interest to the Bursar but to very few others. For the most part, therefore, the senior members of Princes' ate in a silence they liked to think of as abstracted, but which to onlookers might merely have seemed glum.

The beef stew and dumplings were eaten and cleared away, and an elaborate bowl of what might have been trifle or blancmange was now presented, its top liberally adorned with whorls of whipped cream and decorations of angelica and candied peel. Sir Alan Jenkins, the Master, a noted international lawyer, cleared this decoration as a matter of course. He also took a little of what lay beneath. A visiting American scholar seated a few places away, was impressed. 'Wow!' he said. 'Does he always do that?'

'Always,' said Peter Conder. 'One can't really object, if one is dedicated to the preservation of privilege.'

'As you are?'

'Naturally. If one's against socialism and squalid equality, as I am, then it naturally follows that one's for privilege. Why be ashamed of saying so? One of the great gains, over the past few years, is that, precisely, one isn't ashamed. People are now able to say, quite clearly, all sorts of things which they'd have felt they ought to keep quiet about not so very long ago.'

'And you feel that's a gain?'

'Openness of expression is always a gain. Don't you feel? For me, it's always been one of the most attractive aspects of America,' said Conder, the University Reader in American Studies. 'That and the absence of hypocrisy about money. None of this feeling guilty if you're rich or privileged. You simply enjoy life more. Europe has much to learn from America, it seems to me.'

Around them discussion of the proposed new building appeared to have started up again. The Bursar, catching the tail end of Conder's remarks, turned to him and said, 'I'm glad to hear you're unashamed of privilege, Peter. I'm afraid that the way things seem to be shaping, the inhabitants of the new building won't enjoy quite the same living standards as you do. Aesthetically speaking, that is. Of course, they may feel that central heating offsets lino on the floor.'

Conder, who had one of the best sets of rooms in the college, especially notable for the beauty of the carving around the fireplace, said calmly, 'That's precisely the kind of thing I mean. I'm quite brazen in my shamelessness. In this as in so much else we Europeans must look to America.'

'Then I take it you don't approve of the Pentagon leak they ran in your *Monitor* newspaper yesterday,' remarked Gebhardt, the American.

Conder said, 'Disapprove! That's a very mild word for the way I feel. However, not all our press is as—well, traitorous, I feel, is not too strong a word for it. Did you see Paul Silverlight's piece in *The World* this morning?'

'Ah, Silverlight,' murmured the Bursar. Turning to Gebhardt, he explained, 'Silverlight and Conder here are great allies. You might call them guardians of the purity of thought on what is known as the New Right. Not that you could call this place a nest of socialists, exactly,' he went on, indicating the other senior members, 'but when in doubt we consult the oracles.'

'What puzzles me,' said Gebhardt, 'is how *The Monitor* got hold of it. Why them? Why not the *New York Times* or the *Washington Post*?'

Conder said, 'I don't suppose we shall ever know. Whoever did it will be lying low, you may be sure of that. I should have thought, as an American, that you'd be more perturbed,' he added rather severely. Severity came easily to him. He was tall and thin, with a long, thin-featured face and black-rimmed spectacles; his brown hair was cut rather clerically. In his gown he cut an altogether clerical figure, which might have been a consciously assumed affectation: he was a recent Catholic convert, and very zealous.

'Oh, I'm perturbed all right—if it's true. I mean, if it is, that's curtains, isn't it? For us all.'

Conder was saved from replying. The Master, having finished his meal, rose, and High Table filed out ceremoniously in his wake.

CHAPTER 2

The leaked paper and Paul Silverlight's response to it were also under discussion that night in another part of Cambridge—at the Dawes' house.

How many Dawes were there? Nobody had ever been able to say, exactly. Cambridge teemed with them—always had done and, it seemed, always would do. Indeed, it seemed sometimes as though everyone one spoke to was in some way related to them—if not an uncle, aunt or remote cousin, then at least by marriage. Economics, physics, biology, psychology—in all these fields at least one Dawes was, or had been, pre-eminent and at least three more were coming up fast. Each individual Dawes modestly insisted that this was nothing more than coincidence, and that there was no particular advantage in being a member of the family. However, any Dawes in academic life assumed that he could and would, if he so wished, become a professor—an assumption which was usually justified, since it was shared, subconsciously, by a large proportion of the academic world. There was also an assumption, where Dawes were concerned, of liberal politics—the very brand of automatic liberalism which most annoyed people like Peter Conder. 'For as long as I can remember,' he had remarked recently, 'all undergraduates wanted to end up being like a Dawes. However, I think I am justified in believing that things are changing now.'

John Dawes, Emeritus Professor of Economics, lived in Herschel Road, on the west side of town. It was a street of large Edwardian houses with white-painted windows, quarry-tiled pantries and enormous gardens. They were the kind of houses that, elsewhere, are nowadays almost always split into flats. In Herschel Road, however, many still remained in single-family occupation, more or less modernized, the old ranges now replaced by Aga cookers, wood-burning stoves set in the fireplaces.

The house, with its many bedrooms and echoing bathrooms, had obviously been designed for a large family. These days, however, the only permanent inhabitant, apart from John and Esme Dawes, was their daughter Charlotte, who was currently unemployed and was trying to decide what she should do next.

Although there were only four of them—the three Dawes and Charlotte's boyfriend Martin Davies—they were eating in the dining-room. Esme Dawes liked her dining-room, and saw no reason to change the habits of a lifetime simply because most of her family had left home. She was small and slight, with white hair cut short and darting brown eyes. Her speed of reaction contrasted with her husband's vagueness. He was tall, with wispy brown hair, a face of great benignity set on a gangling body. Was it possible that one so clearly without malice could also be intelligent? John Dawes's enemies doubted it and ascribed his professorship to his name. Certainly it always came as a surprise when a sharp remark emanated from so seemingly unlikely a quarter. This, he had found throughout his life, was a considerable political asset.

The talk at table naturally turned to the next Saturday afternoon, when the Peace Movement was organizing a large Easter rally. John Dawes was gloomily counting up the number of such events he had attended. 'At least twenty, more likely twenty-five. And where's it got us? Things get worse all the time and here we are still holding rallies.'

'Well, we've got to do something,' said Esme, who had obviously said the same thing before (at least twenty times, possibly twenty-five). 'It relieves us and annoys them, which is something. Have some more soup.'

'Somebody did do something,' said Charlotte. 'Didn't you see yesterday's *Monitor*? That should swell the ranks a bit.'

'Nothing much new in that,' said her father. 'It's been clear from the outset what all these new weapons are for. As for their world-view, I was talking just recently to a banker from Kentucky. A really charming fellow, and quite liberal, if you can imagine such a thing as a liberal banker from Kentucky. We were talking of this and that and we naturally got around to just this topic—under what circumstances America would feel justified in starting a war. He said, well, if it looked like our oil supplies would be cut off. He was quite surprised when I pointed out that they don't own the oil—that of course from their point of view it's highly desirable that the Saudis or whoever should sell it to them, but in the end they've no divine right to it. After all, that's imperialism, isn't it? There's a difference between wanting something and being justified in walking in and taking it. He was amazed—he'd never thought of it like that. I found it deeply depressing. If people like that—good, educated people—really think that way, then there's no hope for any of us. It's this habit of thinking they're entitled to anything they want.'

'Comes from the way they're brought up,' said Esme. 'Probably to do with the way they're potty-trained.'

'Still, to have it spelt out like that,' said Martin. 'This is what these weapons are for, and these are the circumstances under which we'll use them—when they're publicly denying it all the time. What was it? Middle East oil—European sovereignty—Central America—'

'The usual scenarios,' John pointed out. 'I doubt if they'd bother to wait for the eventuality, myself.'

'Still, I bet someone's gnashing their teeth,' said Charlotte. 'Did you hear the Minister on the news? He didn't have a thing to say. All he could do was hint that it was all a hoax and we all know *Monitor* readers love a hoax.'

'Of course they're gnashing their teeth,' said Martin. 'Didn't you see Silverlight's piece in *The World* today?'

There was a silence around the table. Esme said brightly, 'Well, if everyone's had enough soup I'll get the chicken. I think there's another bottle behind you, John.' They were drinking excellent claret. It was all very well being a social-ist, thought Martin, if you were as rich as the Dawes. Their money was reputed to come from inspired speculation by an economist Dawes, also impeccably left-minded. This lifestyle of easy comfort had attracted more than one student to Academe, only to find that it was not attainable on an academic salary.

'But did you see it?' persisted Martin. 'After all, he's a mouthpiece for that lot, isn't he? And it was nothing but abuse. I mean, he is capable of reason—isn't he? I thought he was supposed to be rather bright. So clearly someone's got them where it hurts.'

'On the contrary, I would say that's about the level of most of that young man's academic dealings,' said Dawes, with a sudden bitterness in his voice quite new to Martin. He then launched into a long story about an article in which he, among others, had been misquoted, misrepresented and almost actionably slandered by Silverlight. Dawes had re-plied, but had not been allowed to see proofs of his reply, which turned out, on publication, to have been altered, cut, and otherwise tampered with in such a way as to nullify all his most damaging points.

'And I notice,' Dawes went on, 'that whenever he reviews

a book, the review is invariably followed by a letter from the unfortunate author complaining about just the same sort of things—misquoting, distortion, you name it.'

'Doesn't he ever give a book a good review?'

'I've never seen one yet,' said Esme. 'Leg or breast?'

Silverlight, however, was not to be banished so easily. For the rest of the evening he hovered over the conversation, an unseen presence from whom everyone seemed to wish to keep their eyes averted but which, for some reason, could never be forgotten.

When Martin got up to go at the end of the evening, Charlotte said, 'I'll come with you. I feel like a walk.'

The evening was blustery and rather cold. The stars shone out of a clear sky on to quiet streets: the undergraduates had left for the Easter vacation. Charlotte huddled into her coat. They walked in silence down West Road, past the looming tower of the University Library—'this monstrous erection,' as a pre-Freudian Queen had remarked when she opened it.

Charlotte said, 'So you didn't know about Jenny.'

'Jenny? Your sister?' Martin was aware that Charlotte had a sister of this name, although he had never met her.

'Yes.'

'Married to Bob Chantrey, isn't she?' Chantrey Martin did dimly recall, a figure from his undergraduate days. He was then notionally engaged on some interminable PhD, as so many people were in those spacious days, and would hold court in the University Library tea-room, a black-bearded, sandalled figure, guru of the factionalist Left. Chantrey always knew the ins and outs of the internecine wars which went endlessly on between members of the far Left, and which preoccupied them quite to the exclusion of the fight against reaction. Reaction then was personified in the Labour Party. Oh, the dear dead days, thought Martin.

'Sort of.'

'Sort of?'

'Well, they're not divorced.' Charlotte glanced at him, then went on hurriedly, looking at the ground, 'She left

14

him. For Paul Silverlight. Then he dropped her. She's in Fulbourn now. She's a junkie.'

'Silverlight!' Well, that certainly explained the strangenesses of that evening. Fulbourn was the local psychiatric hospital. Most of Martin's acquaintance seemed to have passed through there at one time or another. 'So that's why your parents hate him so. I assumed it must be his views, but it seemed a bit extreme, even for that.'

'From one extreme to another,' said Charlotte. 'Perhaps that's what sent her over the edge.'

'How did she know him, anyway? I wouldn't have thought they'd exactly move in the same social circles.'

'Oh, they've known each other for ever, Bob and Paul. They were up here at the same time, both in the Labour Club. That was how they met Jenny. Our house was the committee rooms, they were always in and out. Then Paul changed sides. Perhaps that's when they began to hate each other. They're both very violent. I mean, intellectually. Physically, I wouldn't know, though I must say, I've sometimes wondered. Anyway, I expect it gave Paul a tremendous kick, taking Jenny off Bob. We've always assumed that's why he did it.'

'But what about her? You don't credit her with much of a mind of her own.'

'She doesn't seem to have one. Perhaps that's part of the trouble. One thing you have to say for people like Bob and Paul, they're never in any doubt. Perhaps that's what she liked. I've never been able to make out quite what else it might be,' said Charlotte.

They crossed Queens' Road and stopped on the Silver Street bridge, hypnotized by the chilly gleam of the dark river. Martin said, 'Do you ever see Bob Chantrey these days? His path and your father's must cross a good deal, mustn't they?'

'Poor old Bob,' said Charlotte. 'Paul Silverlight really seemed to haunt him. Took effortless firsts while Bob really slogged away. Pulled all the girls without even really wanting to. I always felt that Bob must have been rather pleased when Paul changed sides. I mean, that was that. He must have thought so, anyway. At least he'd never need to see him again. And then—well.' She paused, thinking. Bicycles passed them noiselessly. 'I believe he and Daddy see quite a lot of each other,' she added. 'He's very active in the Peace Movement, and he's on the editorial board of almost everything. You know the kind of thing. Does extra-mural teaching. I don't expect his lifestyle takes a lot of keeping up. It certainly never used to.'

'Poor old Chantrey,' said Martin.

'Poor Jenny,' said Charlotte.

New Politics, Friday, 7 April,
A PALPABLE HIT—by Andrew Taggart
Most people will by now be aware that *The Monitor* last Wednesday published what, if it is true, was a scoop of monumental proportions—a document apparently originating in the Pentagon outlining US plans for a pre-emptive nuclear strike on Russian missile bases, together with the political conditions under which such a strike might be considered. This is, of course, something of quite a different order from the existing NATO refusal to sign a 'no first use' agreement on the pretext of overwhelming Soviet superiority in conventional forces.

As might be expected, the establishment is now engaged in a massive wool-pulling exercise. The Minister of Defence implied that the document was a fake and the whole thing a got-up alarm. The Prime Minister, taking her cue from this, has refused to make a statement to the House on the grounds that there is nothing to make a statement about. Paul Silverlight, one of the New Right's more voluminous apologists, assures us that the document is a mere pornographic fantasy.

Do not, however, be deceived. Behind the scenes all is not sweetness, light and airy dismissal (though a few dismissals may be in the post at this moment). In Washington, various sorts of uproar have ensued. Perhaps most indignant is the editor of the *Washington Post*, who not unreasonably expects his highly-paid staff to be on the receiving end of any leaks of this sort which may be going.

16

The Pentagon, naturally, is denying everything, as is the White House. The line is that war games with a wide variety of scenarios are always in progress, and that some dummy has confused speculation with policy. According to this line, what *The Monitor* has bought is mere Monopoly money.

Most people, however do not believe this. There has for some time been rumour of a spectacular change of policy recently effected on the nuclear front: it is generally accepted that this is it.

Meanwhile telephone lines between Downing Street and the White House have been busy. The Prime Minister is bitterly complaining that once again Britain has not been taken into the confidence of her closest ally, and what will happen when it comes to the crunch? (Only the Prime Minister seems to be unaware of the answer to that one!) The President is busy pouring on the soft soap and reassuring everyone that he does not plan to end the world just yet.

At any rate, we should all hold on to our hats (and proof them against fall-out). There are signs that several of the scenarios mapped out in the document as likely triggers are about to erupt into crisis before long . . .

CHAPTER 3

Judith Croft sat in the Museum Tavern drinking vodka and tonic and glancing at her watch from time to time. Each time she did so she felt annoyed with herself. What did it matter what the time was? What did it matter if someone was late for a lunch date? She had to have lunch somewhere, and it wasn't as if she was in any way attached to Andrew Taggart. Besides, he was always late. She should know that by now. She glanced at her watch again. Forty minutes: it was ten past one now and the place was jammed. If he'd come when they arranged there might have been a chance of getting a table, not to say some food, but now, not a hope. Really, it was too bad. She would give him another five minutes and then leave.

Naturally, at fourteen minutes past he turned up, quite unapologetic. 'Unavoidable delay,' he said cheerfully. 'D'you want another one of those?'

'I tried to keep a table, but you can see, not a hope,' she said.

'Safety in numbers. Two vodkas and a tonic, please. And we'd better have some food.' His small, mackintoshed, straggly-bearded figure deftly inserted itself beside her and blended into the background. Taggart was not a man you would notice if you were looking for a dangerous intruder. He would pass easily as a rabbit going about its lawful business or a man about to mend the hole in the road he had just skilfully manufactured.

He peered suspiciously into the cheese and chutney sandwich he had just bought. Judith said, 'What d'you expect to find in there?'

'You never know where they put their bugs these days. It struck me the other day that the ideal bug would be one you ate and carried around with you. If it struck me, it struck them.'

'What goes in must come out.'

'True, but it's useful while it's around. I don't think there's one in this sandwich, though.'

'Everyone I know thinks their phone is tapped,' said Judith.

'They're probably right,' said Taggart. 'Mine is, and I expect yours is.'

'I doubt it. But one would lose an awful lot of face admitting it.'

They ate for a while. 'Well,' said Taggart, 'and what gems do you have for me today?'

'Not a lot. I hope your other sources manage better than I do, generally.'

'A little here, a little there.' He gestured. 'The important thing is knowing who to go to for what. I pride myself on the variety of my team. When do you have your final meeting?'

'About tomorrow? Tonight.'

'Well, you probably know this, but in case you don't,

keep a lookout for a nasty little organization calling itself Defence Through Strength.'

'Oh, my dear brother's lot,' Judith said dismissively.

'Your brother?'

'Yes, didn't you know? I always assume everyone does. Paul Silverlight.'

'Silverlight? Is your brother?' Taggart echoed her with the delighted incredulity of one who has just found a large gold nugget. He paused for a moment, digesting this new information.

'Write it down if you like,' Judith suggested.

'No, no, I won't forget,' he assured her seriously. Then he added, 'Just because he's your brother, don't make the mistake of underestimating him. They've got some very nasty tricks up their sleeve. I haven't been able to find out exactly what—they may not know themselves, yet. Didn't when I spoke to my source, anyhow. But they're out to make trouble for you. Hey, Judith,' he resumed in a social tone, 'tell me about yourself. I mean, we've known each other quite well for a long time now and I really don't know a thing about you.'

'You subtle creature. You mean, what background could possibly have produced both him and me?'

'Oh, you're so intelligent,' he said, screwing up his face as he chewed the lemon from his vodka. 'I'll get some more of these. You be thinking.'

'I don't need more vodka and I don't need to think, to tell you the family history,' she assured him. 'Our father was a small businessman. In blouses. Not very successful. Jewish—that accounts for our extraordinary name. Sounds better in German.'

'Silberlicht?'

'Silberlicht. What a linguist. Our mother was upper-middle-class English. They met during the war when Daddy was in the Army. Paul takes after her—blond and Aryan. I, as you see, take after him. Dark and yiddy. I suppose, now I come to think of it, that that's what happened politically as well. I believe our mother's family is very proper. I don't know for certain—we never met them. They disapproved of Daddy in a spectacular way. So *déclassé*. Jewish they might be able to take—after all, there are some awfully clever ones, aren't there? Professors and scientists and things. Musicians, even. But blouses, that was really too much.'

'Sounds really chippy.'

'Oh, the chip potential was enormous—and utterly fulfilled, as you see.'

'You mean, you're both reacting.'

'No, no, I'm just sensible. Paul's the one who's reacting. Well, I suppose we both felt we had to make our mark. To prove something to our mother's family? I don't know. I suppose they utterly approve of Paul. Or do you think he's a bit much, even for them?'

'I don't know. I've never met them.'

'No, well, you see, nor have I.'

'Are both your parents dead?'

'Yes, that's why Paul can pretend they never existed. Blouses isn't really his scene at all.'

'Nor yours,' Taggart pointed out.

'No, that's true. But I'm not ashamed of it.'

'Tell me, did they get on, your parents?' Taggart wanted to know.

'In a way. They found each other tremendously sexy, I think. But looking back, I should say Mother rather resented that. She liked to think she was in control of what went on, and here was the central thing in her life utterly out of her control.'

'Did she like you? Did you like her? It doesn't sound as if you did, much.'

'No, she liked Paul and Daddy liked me. But she died when we were quite young. Paul was fifteen and I was twelve. That was another chip for Paul—the wrong parent died. Daddy went on with the blouses long enough to put us both through college. Then he died, too.'

'Very convenient of him.'

'Oh, he was always a most obliging man.' Judith shrugged and glanced at her watch. 'So you really can't give me any more idea of what they're cooking up in Defence Through Strength?'

'Oh, I think it'll be more heat than light, in the end. These things usually are. Counter-demonstrations are always at a disadvantage—they're not the ones with the initiative, are they? But they're a spiteful lot. Keep a bit of an eye out, that's all.'

They got up and walked out into Great Russell Street. Taggart turned towards Gower Street and immediately, somehow, disappeared. Judith wandered for a while in the other direction, past the joke shop and the Chinese crafts emporium, relishing a few moments of unaccustomed freedom. For once, no one had any idea where she was. But it couldn't last. Nick was waiting for her with the children— he had to be back at the office by two-thirty. She sighed, and turned in the direction of Euston, towards Islington and home.

CHAPTER 4

Defence Through Strength was having a working lunch that Friday. They were all busy men (Defence Through Strength had no women members, a situation which they publicly regretted but which somehow never changed) and could not afford to waste chunks of a valuable day. Their Secretary, Damian Tranter, had found a couple of nice girls who did excellent cordon bleu lunches which they brought in all ready to serve, and which gave the members of DTS an opportunity to sample the selections of the Shelter-Owners' Wine Club, one of Tranter's more imaginative business excursions. Today the menu consisted of smoked salmon mousse, with which they were drinking a delightful Saumur, followed by bœuf Stroganoff, to go with which several bottles of Gruaud Larose 1978 had been standing open in the office since eleven o'clock.

Round the table sat Tranter, the athletic product of the British public school system, ruddy-faced, with that baby-fine straight hair peculiar to Englishmen which drops out so quickly at the onset of middle age; Alfred Edson, MP, holder of a safe Conservative seat in the House and currently a junior Minister in Defence; Paul Silverlight, tall and blond, at present enthusiastically eating the smoked salmon; a man they all knew as the Commodore, an ex-RAF-type who now ran a flying school near Guildford; and two or three other enthusiasts who always appeared at DTS lunches, mainly, Tranter suspected, for the food.

Tranter seated himself at the end of the table, by the window overlooking Whitehall. DTS, though emphatically not government-funded (it was the Government that was always emphatic about this), rented a suite in a building containing a number of government offices. Questioned about this, Tranter always replied, 'Well, hardly any offices don't belong to the government these days, do they?' It was understood that this was a state of affairs of which, incidentally, DTS (or its members in their private capacity) disapproved, but one has to make the best of circumstances as they exist.

'Well, gentlemen,' Tranter said. 'If you don't mind, we'd better get down to business. There's a lot to discuss.'

'I don't mind telling you,' said Edson, 'that people are pretty hopping mad at the Ministry. And in Downing Street. I don't know what our friends across the water think they're up to, but to hand the lunatics a whopping piece of propaganda like that—at a time like this—'

'You mean with this march tomorrow,' said one of the nameless supporters, drinking deeply.

'I mean a bit more than that,' Edson said. 'I expect it'll swell the ranks and all that, but quite frankly, that's more a matter of propaganda than anything else. I mean, clearly we'd like them to disappear off the face of the earth—we keep saying they have done, after all, and with the help of your excellent organization—' he nodded to Tranter—'that day will be speeded. But they've been having marches for longer than some of you have been around and it hasn't got them anywhere yet. Easter and Autumn, CND has a little march, or a bigger one, does a little scaremongering and subsides for the summer holidays or the Christmas break. But from their point of view the timing of this one is a little fortuitous. I'm sure you're all aware of what's going on in the Middle East at the moment. It looks very much as though the Strait of Hormuz may be definitively blocked by Iran if the Iraquis go on the way they are—'

'And then how will Iran earn any foreign currency?' Tranter asked. 'They may be mad, but surely they don't want to starve.'

'Iran is run by the mullahs, and mullahs aren't governed by logic. And if the Strait is blocked, so is America's oil. And if that goes, as the world now knows—'

'But that was merely a war-game scenario, surely?' said Silverlight.

'That's the line, of course,' said Edson. 'But I can tell you in confidence that it wasn't. It was the real McCoy. And of course the Pentagon are doing their nut. What was going to be a nice clean strike, minimum casualties, minimum fuss, cutting the bear's balls off once for all—well, the whole situation has to be entirely rethought. And of course it makes everything immensely dangerous. After all, the Russkies can read just as well as the rest of us.'

'Judging from the state of our intelligence,' said Silverlight, helping himself to some Stroganoff, 'they've known everything there was to be known in that department for years anyway.'

'That's not the point,' said Edson irritably. 'Just talking about things brings them to the boil, as you very well know. Anyway, the timing simply couldn't be worse. Happening now, it gives the loonies much more leverage than they've had before. So your work, my friends, is doubly important.'

'Well,' said Tranter, 'I'm sure everyone's taken that in, eh, lads? So maybe we'd better get down to details. Commodore, I take it everything's organized in your department?'

'Absolutely,' said the Commodore. 'Usual routine.' He grinned. Twice every year, the Campaign for Nuclear Disarmament provided the Commodore with an excuse to enjoy himself otherwise quite unavailable in his humdrum routine. Over the marching tens of thousands he flew as low as the law allowed—and sometimes lower—trailing an enormous banner behind his single-engined trainer. The wording of this banner varied from year to year.

'What's it to be this year?' asked Tranter.

'I'd show you, but it's rather large, of course. It says SUPPORT THE KREMLIN JOIN CND,' said the Commodore modestly.

'Sounds excellent.'

'And another thing, some of the television chappies are going to be filming from helicopters, so I've let them know, and they're going to get some real close-ups.'

'Excellent, Commodore, you really do us proud. What about on the ground? Smithson?' One of the supporters looked up from his cups and explained how he was organizing a rota of speeches from the roof of the building, which would be amplified to assault the ears of the masses marching along Whitehall below. 'You should see the amplification,' he said, and his voice filled with awe. 'Fellow from a pop group came along and helped. It's enormous. We shall have to wear ear muffs or we'll deafen ourselves.'

'It looks as though we're amply supplied on the brute force side, then,' Tranter said. 'Short of an army of skinheads I can't quite see what more we can do in that direction, and one would like to think we were above that, for the moment at least. So how about the silver tongues? Silverlight?'

Silverlight stopped eating and gazed around the table with the unconscious superiority of one who knows he possesses, not just the best, but possibly the only intellect in the room. This feeling was quite justified in the case of almost all his present audience. Tranter was always aware of a sensation of vague resentment in Silverlight's presence, but, unused to introspection, could never pinpoint it. Edson quite frankly loathed the conceited little pup—loathing not lessened by the uneasy awareness that Silverlight was, indeed, far superior to him intellectually. But brains, as everyone knows, are far from being the only thing that matters in politics. People quite without brains can, and often do, attain to high office. Edson, who had his own modest hopes, was inclined to think that too many brains could even be a positive disadvantage. They made people uneasy.

'We're having our own gathering in Trafalgar Square,' said Silverlight. 'After all, this publicity cuts both ways. It focuses on us as well as on them. I'm speaking, and Edson here, and the lady from the WRVS and—oh, a star-studded list, I assure you.' He smiled confidently. 'They're on the wane, you know. We're what's new these days—such a contrast, actually having something new to say. I can't emphasize too strongly the appeal of that. I was hoping to persuade Peter Conder. After all, he's our *éminence bleue*— you might say—'

'And will he?'

'Still making up his mind.' Silverlight chuckled. 'It's a bit naughty to say this, perhaps, but I do get the feeling he's a little bit, well, suspicious of people who are involved in practical politics. You know, theory's all very well, indeed, nothing could be more important, but one has to admit that practice is more fun. Well, you could say we here are a living testimonial to that. So Peter likes to keep a little bit aloof, just to emphasize the importance of pure thought. But I expect he'll come round in the end.'

'Well, you should know,' said Edson with a slight edge to his voice. 'You're the expert on thought. We all rely on you these days to keep us abreast of what the PM is thinking.'

Silverlight smiled and said, 'Oh, I wouldn't go so far as to say that.'

Tranter said smoothly, 'Talking about practical politicians, I hope MI5 and the Special Branch are keeping an eye on the loonies. Fair means as well as foul, eh?'

'Don't you worry about that,' Edson said. 'You'd be surprised what they come up with.' He turned to Silverlight. 'Your family and friends are going to be pretty well-represented tomorrow, aren't they, Paul?'

Silverlight flushed. When he lost his air of detachment, a resemblance to his sister flickered across his face, in feature so different from hers.

Tranter said, 'What on earth are you talking about, Ed?'

'Oh, nothing. It's not important. Paul knows what I mean.'

There was a pause. Silverlight shrugged and poured another glass of wine. Edson, looking modestly pleased, laid down his fork. Tranter, looking round, said, 'Well, if we've all finished, perhaps we should have some coffee.' He rang a small silver bell, and one of the nice girls came in with a coffee-pot. She smiled brightly as she collected the plates, and Tranter smiled back. This, after all, was what Defence Through Strength was about, was it not?—preserving old standards and defending them against those who wanted change and destruction for change and destruction's sake.

CHAPTER 5

The co-ordinating committee which was to finalize the arrangements for tomorrow's march was meeting in the Campaign offices on the second floor of a dingy but ca-pacious building not far from Holloway jail. The building was one shared by a good many similarly-inclined organiz-ations and was largely financed, not by Moscow, as the popular press and a good many politicians frequently averred, but by a trust set up by an impeccably capitalist and extremely rich Quaker.

The Committee sat around a rather dusty office in a large variety of chairs. From time to time the telephone would ring: arguments with the police were still going on, at this late stage, about the final route for the march. A route would, presumably, be agreed—eventually. If not, the march would still go ahead—many of the participants were already en route, aboard the coaches that would drive them overnight to London—but there would be unpleasantness and arrests.

The Minister of Defence had recently gone on record characterizing all participants in the Peace Movement as agents of Moscow or its well-meaning but misguided dupes. Looking around the room, Judith tried to decide into which category tonight's participants fell. Richard Essex, the chairman, a Quaker doctor: *prima facie*, a dupe, but considering his position, probably an agent. Chantrey—agent. Dawes —a man of his intelligence was unlikely to be a dupe, even though well-meaning: an agent, then. Herself—well, she knew she wasn't an agent: therefore, a dupe. On second thoughts, though, she plumped for agenthood as altogether less demeaning. Mrs Malahide, the calm, plump secretary, was, if an agent, remarkably well disguised. She had even voted Conservative once. Of course, that would be just what a well-prepared mole would be instructed to do. The delegates from the youth section were agents without question—they probably wouldn't have questioned it, either. Several of the committee had belonged to the Communist Party at one time or another, though only one was currently a member. These were all agents. One had once, somehow, caught a glimpse of his police dossier, which omitted the fact that he had been a Party member but mentioned that he had once contributed to a magazine, one of whose editors had been the notorious Palme Dutt. He was a nuclear physicist, a professor at some Northern university. No wonder this government was so opposed to the education system, staffed as it was by Moscow agents.

The meeting seemed interminable. Judith looked gloomily down the list of points still not covered and glanced at her watch. Ten o'clock. Seemed? It *was* interminable. They had begun at six-thirty and still not got through half the agenda. It was occasions like this, Judith thought, which turned one against democracy. At the other end of the table Bob Chantrey was arguing a point of tactics. Bob was a man for action. Mere demonstrations, he believed, got nobody anywhere.

'Well, where has it ever got us?' he demanded now, pounding the table with his fist. 'You tell us, John. You've been in it from the beginning. Twenty-five years, man and boy. Have things moved on a single millimetre? I'll tell you,' he went on, waving aside the proffered response to this rhetorical question. 'They've moved all right, but in the wrong direction.'

'So what do you suggest?' wearily asked a voice from across the room.

'I think we should go in and demolish those bastards in Trafalgar Square, for a start.'

'And a fat lot of good that would do us,' said Richard Essex crisply. 'For one thing, the police won't let anybody in there. For another, it seems a bit ironic to make arguments for peace by bashing people's heads in. It may relieve your feelings but it doesn't do anything for us.'

'Let's blockade Downing Street.'

'It's been decided,' Richard said patiently. 'Nothing like that.' He sighed. 'Listen, my friends, this is ridiculous. We've been through all these things before. We're all tired and tomorrow will be a long day. This is not a meeting about policy. Let's just get through all this as quickly as we can and then we can all go home.'

Half an hour later, the meeting came to an end. Everybody got up with sighs of relief. Judith, collecting her belongings, saw John Dawes approaching her. 'Just time for a quick drink,' he said.

'Well,' said Judith reluctantly, glancing at her watch. 'I shouldn't, really.'

'Of course you should. You need it. Anyway, I need it,' said Dawes persuasively.

Bob Chantrey came up to them. 'Coming for a drink?' he said to his father-in-law, who looked chagrined.

'That's just what we were saying,' Judith said with some relief. This was a tête-a-tête she had been hoping to avoid. For some time now, John Dawes had been hopelessly and romantically in love with her. It had been a while before she had let herself realize this. Naturally, they were thrown together a good deal, as all the committee were. Life was an endless round of speaking engagements, conferences, propaganda activities: those who were prepared to engage in all this found themselves doing so full-time and, often, side by side.

It is strange, thought Judith, how we are governed by our expectations. Schoolboy love was the last thing one expected —the last thing she expected—from an emeritus professor

28

and dedicated politician, a father-figure of the movement, like John Dawes. If it had been anyone else, she would have acknowledged it earlier. It was true that for some time he had seemed suspiciously ubiquitous—always beside her on the train, in the pub, at the welcoming dinner; always ready to offer a lift, happy to make a detour for her convenience, eager to help her with tricky points of politics . . . She had put all this down to his natural good nature and thought no more about it. *Amitié* slightly *amoureuse*, perhaps. But *amitié amoureuse* is an impermanent state if it precedes *l'amour*. Inevitably the moment had come when she could pretend no longer because he would pretend no longer . . .

It was in Paris. They were both delegates at an international conference of disarmament movements, staying, for once, not in someone's home, but in a small hotel in the Rue Bonaparte. After the evening session Dawes suggested dinner.

What could be pleasanter? They wandered along the boulevard and turned into the Quai des Grands Augustins, enjoying not only the evening—it was September, still and warm—but the fact, for once, of not talking about final catastrophe. They found a small, unpretentious-looking restaurant and went in; ordered, and sat back in pleasant expectation. John stared at her across the table, a curiously vulnerable look on his clever, mild face.

'You know what I'm going to say to you, Judith.' And of course, as soon as he said this, she did know, in the way that one always does know these things without ever having formulated them to oneself before. He said, 'I'm terribly in love with you. I have been for months. I simply can't think of anything else.'

'Don't be silly,' she said in what struck her as a terribly schoolmarmish voice. 'You think of other things all the time.'

He shook his head. 'You know what I mean.'

She wanted to say, Poor Esme: does this often happen? But somehow she couldn't. It was too detached, and she didn't feel altogether detached; and too patronizing, and she certainly didn't feel patronizing. So she said, 'I can't quite see what we can do about it,' thus instantly involving herself with that fatal 'we'.

'I know one thing we can do,' he said.

At this point their food arrived, so she was absolved from making an immediate response. But the reprieve was not long-lasting—how long does it take to eat a steak? As she ate, she was wondering what on earth she would say. It wasn't that she was not fond of John—she was, very. Nor did she find him repulsive, though he was considerably older than any man she had ever gone to bed with. The prospect, however, was in some way appalling. She said, 'Don't you think my family has done enough harm to yours already?'

He looked puzzled for a moment, then laughed. 'I always forget you're related to Silverlight.'

'His sister.'

But he was not to be so easily deflected. 'Say you will, Judy, say you will. Just this once. It would make me so happy.'

Just this once, indeed! He should know better than that— undoubtedly did know better. But it put her in an impossible position. After all, why on earth not just this once? She was hardly a sixteen-year-old schoolgirl (not that sixteen-year-old schoolgirls would hesitate for a second, these days). Just this once then, it had been—no possible occasion for a repetition, or even a discussion, of that night's further activities having, to Judith's relief, so far presented itself.

Nor would it present itself tonight, either, thought Judith with relief as she followed the two men out of the dusty office where the committee always held its meetings. As they filed down the narrow, lino-covered stairs (would any organization with which she was involved ever possess an office that was not up two or three flights of such stairs?) she studied Bob Chantrey's back. He presented a curiously outmoded figure, she reflected. Big black beards, bluejeans and lumberjack shirts dated one irretrievably: a guru of the late 'sixties or early 'seventies. At least he did not wear his hair shoulder-length and gathered into a rubber band. How petty I am, she thought. A petty bourgeoise. My brother would be proud of me.

They did not linger in the dark street, now damp and slippery under a fine drizzle, but went straight into the pub next door. In this part of north London, it was hard to find a building that did not have a pub next door. This pub had a mixed clientele: black, Greek, Irish, some cockney; the Peace Movement made a middle-class island.

The public bar was crowded: a darts match was in progress. They made their way through into the saloon, which contained a small number of port-and-lemon drinking ladies. Chantrey said, 'I'll get them. Usual?' and went over to the counter, returning with three pints of bitter. Judith said, as usual, 'I can never manage a pint. Sorry.' Chantrey said, as usual, 'Well, I'll finish what you can't manage.'

They discussed the meeting and hoped the weather would clear up for tomorrow. Other members of the committee drifted in for a quick one before closing time. Dawes joined in none of the chat but sat staring morosely into his drink. Chantrey said, 'That bastard Silverlight and his merry men will be out in force tomorrow.'

'Ignore them,' Judith said. 'It's the one thing they can't bear.'

'I'd like to kill him. I know he's your brother, Judy, but I would.'

'You aren't alone,' said Judith. 'I expect John feels the same.'

'No, no,' said Dawes. 'Killing people isn't my line.' He returned his gaze to his drink. The publican switched the light on and off and called, 'Drink up, please, gentlemen.'

When they emerged from the pub, the rain was falling harder. Chantrey said, 'I've got a car. Can I drop anyone anywhere? Judy?'

Judith looked round for Dawes, to say good night, but he had disappeared. She glimpsed him rounding the corner at a pace little short of a run, his head hunched into his shoulders. Feeling guilty, she walked with Chantrey to his car, a filthy VW Beetle, the floor covered in a litter of toffee-papers.

31

'Given up smoking?'

'Trying. That's why I'm so fat.'

He drove her the short distance to Islington, where she lived in a graceful square—oval-shaped, actually, but still called a square—which had been 'coming up' for as long as she could remember. It was still not visibly further up than when she had first known it, but house-prices had certainly risen. You could tell the newly middle-class houses by looking into the basement areas. Steps down, plants, and cork flooring visible through an uncurtained window indicated good pickings within. All the local burglars knew this, and all the owners of the cork floors knew they knew it. They thus faced a terrible dilemma: should they betray the æsthetic standards of a lifetime and put up net curtains? Most stuck to their principles and were regularly burgled.

Nick, Judith's husband, was in the sitting-room, reading the paper, the television on in its corner. He looked faintly annoyed, as usual. She paused by the television. 'You watching this?'

'Couldn't be bothered to turn it off. Saved the world?'

'No, that's for tomorrow.'

'Jonathan was sick this evening,' he said. 'Hope he's not in for another tummy upset.'

'Oh dear.' She immediately felt guilty and worried, as no doubt he had intended. And why shouldn't he so intend? She remembered when the boys were babies how she had tried to indicate in every way she could that he, dealing with the mere world of commerce, was the one with the easy life. It had irritated him then, and it irritated her now.

'You're rather late.'

'Oh, you know how these things drag on.'

Nick Croft was an architect. Unlike Bob Chantrey, he had kept sartorially up with the times: hair clipped short, sharply-cut suits. He was proud of Judith, admired her energy and liked having a wife people had heard of: in that way, he was not petty. But her life inevitably thrust the burdens of domesticity on to him, and this he found less agreeable. Their sons, Ben and Jonathan, were three and six respectively.

She said, 'I'm supposed to go to Brussels next week.'

'What for?'

'There's a conference of the European movements. I did mention it, actually.'

'Maybe, I don't remember. Next weekend?'

'Yes.'

'Well, you'll have to refuse, won't you?' It was an agreement they had: she would not accept weekend engagements unless they included the children. This did not sound like one for the children.

'I really ought to go.'

'No doubt.'

'Well, I'll think about it.' She sank wearily on to the sofa, feeling that she had had enough of discontented men for one evening. This, however, was hardly a complaint she could voice to her husband, who had returned reproachfully to the paper. 'Looks as if your brother's set to make a jackass of himself tomorrow,' he observed.

'Mm,' she agreed, and thought, Oh, don't I know it. She wondered, for the hundredth or thousandth time, how Paul could say and write the things he did. Did he really believe that stuff? He was not a fool—far from it. Perhaps he liked power and saw this as his way towards it. She had heard that he had the ear of the Prime Minister these days—a fact which said little for the Prime Minister, in Judith's opinion. Well, maybe he tickled the Prime Minister's fancy, should she possess such a thing. Pretty he certainly was— more than she had ever been. Fair hair, clear grey eyes, tall, slim, graceful—Paul had never had trouble in getting any woman he fancied. In her opinion he should go on a great deal less about principles and morals—two concepts which tended to recur rather frequently in his pronouncements. He should go on a great deal less, full stop. Oh, to hell with him. To hell with them all. 'I'm having a bath and going to bed,' she announced, and left the room in search of unconsciousness.

Daily Telegram, Saturday, 8 April—
Hostilities between Iran and Iraq took on renewed force

yesterday when the Iraqui forces, in a surprise attack, recaptured the Iranian town of Khorramshahr on the Persian Gulf. Details are not yet known but rumours are circulating of some hitherto unknown new weapon having been used in this attack.

Sources in Teheran are hinting that if Khorramshahr is not quickly retaken, Iran will close the Strait of Hormuz. This would have the effect of cutting off a large part of the oil supply to Europe and the United States. The hope in Teheran is that if this were done, the United States would be forced to take action in the Gulf to restore the status quo . . . (editorial p. 15)

A DILEMMA FOR NATO

Once again the Middle East is the focus of the worried attention of the world. The closing of the Strait of Hormuz, should Iran decide to take this step, poses a terrible dilemma for the free world. If the flow of oil through the strait is stopped, then prospects for many nations in the West are dire indeed. The situation would be especially severe in Japan, a very large proportion of whose oil imports are channelled through the Strait.

What, then, is to be done? All eyes are turned on the Sixth Fleet, which is fortuitously (as it turns out) conducting exercises in the Indian Ocean. Recent rumours about United States intentions in a situation such as this open up, it must be admitted, alarming prospects. Yet what is to be done? Are we to sit back and allow the Soviet Union to capitalize on the disarray of the West (as she most certainly would)?

One thing is certain—nothing could be more irrelevant to the issue than demonstrations such as that planned for today in London . . .

BBC news, 7.0 a.m., Saturday, 8 April
It has just been confirmed by sources in the Middle East that Iran has moved to close the Strait of Hormuz . . .

CHAPTER 6

It was appropriate weather for the end of the world. The sky was livid blue, streaked with black rushing clouds. Trees in the centre of squares stood out black, and children's swings clattered against their frames in the wind.

Despite the weather, London felt as if it were gearing up for a party. The entire city seemed to be making for the Embankment. Tubes and buses were filled with punks, rockers, grannies, pushchair-laden families, eyeing each others' badges and banners and experiencing the satisfying glow that comes of being one of a large, like-minded crowd. People held anxious conversations about the international situation, but even this could not dispel the gaiety.

As midday approached, the streets leading to the river began to fill up. Banners with rainbows jostled banners with doves. On Blackfriars Bridge, the Small Heath Workers Revolutionary Party merged imperceptibly with Abergele Against the Bomb. Stewards urged people to move away from bottlenecks. Small children seated in pushchairs amid a forest of alien legs began to cry. Badge-sellers moved up and down the ranks. Authors of factional pamphlets jostled each other and thrust their wares into passing hands. Bands struck up, as did solitary jews'-harpists. Agitators for a free Ireland shouted slogans, almost drowning out agitators for a free Palestine. Time passed. It was one o'clock, then two. More and more people were arriving, and nobody within sight was moving, although the march was billed to move off at twelve-thirty.

Charlotte and Martin stood on the bridge. It was two-thirty. They had eaten their lunch, and Charlotte needed a pee. Sternly she turned her mind from her bursting bladder. They were hemmed in on all sides: it was impossible to move. In front of them, a woman shifted her baby from shoulder to shoulder. It began to play peep-bo with Charlotte, who rather awkwardly played back: she felt ill-

35

at-ease with children. The baby, knowing nothing of this, giggled and went on playing while its mother rather desperately looked round for a break in the crowd. None appeared. A black cloud moved into the patch of livid blue overhead, and the first drops of a shower began to fall. Their touch reminded Charlotte of her bladder, and she wondered if she could somehow make her way to the railings and pee into the river. But at that moment a shudder of excitement and relief was felt in the crowd. There was movement. They were starting off at last. Slowly at first, the pace gradually picked up as the line spread out until it was possible for everyone to go at his or her own pace. The Small Heath WRP unfurled their banner, elaborately lettered white on red. A middle-aged woman, glancing up and realizing under whose ægis she was marching, moved delicately backwards.

Charlotte and Martin had come on one of the Cambridge buses, but had got separated from the rest, who now were nowhere within sight. 'I'm sure we should have been nearer the front,' Charlotte grumbled.

'Why, what difference does it make?'

'None, really, only I don't want to miss Daddy.' John Dawes was one of the afternoon's speakers. 'You know how it is,' Charlotte said apologetically. 'Family loyalty. Atavistic, really, but I know he'd be sorry if we missed him.'

Above them a number of white and red police helicopters were circling noisily, joined every so often by a small plane trailing a banner. People craned to read it: SUPPORT THE KREMLIN JOIN CND. They waved, but the Commodore, intent on his mission, did not wave back. At Temple station, Charlotte rushed in to the Ladies. About a hundred other people had had the same idea, but there was nothing to be done: she waited, dancing from foot to foot, and eventually emerged, relieved. They rejoined the march and found themselves marching now under the elaborate banner of the Milton Keynes Peace Campaign, a large rainbow with trees. 'Think how long that must have taken to make,' Charlotte said, awed. 'Nothing else to do in Milton Keynes,' Martin explained.

They reached Whitehall. A terrible din assaulted their

ears. People seemed to be speaking from the roof of one of the buildings, but the amplification was so enormous that their words were quite extinguished beneath it. A brass band started to play loudly. It was raining again, but people hardly noticed: the euphoria of the march enveloped them like a huge umbrella. Word passed along the column that there were a quarter of a million, three hundred thousand, half a million people on the road. 'But the cops will say it's a hundred thousand and the Government will say it's an insignificant minority,' said Martin, shrugging. He wished he could have more faith in the effectiveness of mass movements. If he had, he would certainly be a happier man now. But what, he wondered, did they propose to do at this stage —get together and catch the bombs in an enormous blanket as they fell? They were now nearly at Trafalgar Square. 'Didn't I read that your friend Silverlight was having a little rally of his own here?' he said.

'I thought so,' said Charlotte, and they craned to see what support Defence Through Strength could muster. As far as they could make out, however, nobody except pigeons was in the Square at all.

In fact, they were wrong: at that very moment Alfred Edson was addressing two hundred supporters positioned out of sight of the marching thousands, on the other side of Nelson's Column. (It had been decided that this would be the best policy, both so that the faithful could be spared the depressing sight of endless columns of misguided marchers and so that the speakers, not being visible from the march, would be spared the otherwise inevitable jeers and catcalls and would be able to make their point in relative peace.)

'At this moment,' Edson was saying, 'make no mistake about it, we are in the gravest peril. The situation in the world is becoming more dangerous day by day. In such a situation, what do we need? My friends, what we really need is to stick to our allies. We need our allies now as rarely before. We need to show the enemy that we are strong and determined. As we are, most of us! A stupid minority would have us, to quote the words of, you will remember, Aneurin Bevan—hardly a reactionary, even in their terms!—go

37

naked into the conference chamber. And into the theatre of war!' He paused to draw breath.

The two hundred applauded, but their applause was inaudible to the marchers streaming past the other side of Trafalgar Square. Judith Croft, resisting Jonathan's demands that she carry him, craned to see if she could catch sight of her brother, but he was not visible.

'Mummy, I'm tired!'

'Sorry, darling, you'll just have to keep going.'

'Why can't I go in the pushchair? Why is it always Ben?'

'You're too big for pushchairs now. At your age!'

'But I'm tired!'

'Shut up, Jonathan. Have some chocolate. I'm looking for something.'

'What?'

'Your Uncle Paul.'

'He's not here. Where's the chocolate . . . ?'

By the time Charlotte and Martin left Blackfriars Bridge John Dawes, near the head of the line, was entering Hyde Park.

The park looked enormous. Endless green spaces stretched in front of the speakers' platform with its amplifiers and the tent where the better-known could get drinks and meet the press.

Dawes glanced at his watch. Quarter to three. He was not due to speak until about four o'clock. Overhead, a short shower had now given place to a large stretch of blue sky. He arranged his waterproof cape on the ground near the park entrance being used by the marchers, got out his sandwiches, and settled down to watch.

It was an extraordinary sight. At the start of the morning, the party had been overlaid with a certain nervousness as people reacted to the morning's news. But as the day went on and the world with it, defiance and gaiety displaced panic. An enormous display of street theatre, constantly moving forward, stretched as far as the eye could see. A group of gesticulating skeletons was followed by Uncle Sam on stilts, sixteen feet high. Painted musicians capered behind gorgeous banners. Gradually the park filled up. By a quarter to four, when he began to make his way towards the platform, the green space in front was almost filled, so that what appeared to the speakers was a sea of banners and umbrellas, as the rain came down once again. Dawes was assailed, as he had been at intervals throughout the day, with a sense of overwhelming futility. Too late, he thought, too late. Still, might as well huddle together for comfort.—And was this what he was going to say to the assembled masses when his time came? It was hardly the required message of uplift. Indeed, most of the day's speakers seemed (not unnaturally) to have been affected by the same uncertainty. It was hard to know quite what note to strike. Should one go on to the defensive, justifying events such as today's despite their seeming ineffectiveness in making the world safer? Several speakers had struck a slightly defiant note, the gist of what they had to say being that someone had to try, at least. At the moment a Member of Parliament, the shadow spokesman on defence, was talking about proliferation. 'I'm afraid the genie may be out of the bottle already,' he was saying. 'I'm afraid it may already be too late. But one thing is certain. While the superpowers have the bomb and keep it and make more and more bombs, what possible authority have they to tell anybody else they mustn't have it?'

There was silence as the crowd digested this thought. Dawes approached the tent. A group of musicians was playing nearby, forming a ring within which people were dancing. Someone in a skeleton suit—black, with bones painted front and back, and a skull mask—put out a bony hand and drew him into the circle. 'Come on in, John Dawes,' he said. 'Come and dance.'

Dawes was startled, but not amazed. He appeared often on television and spoke at numerous meetings: it was not surprising that he should be recognized in a gathering such as this. He glanced at his watch. 'Plenty of time,' said the skeleton, and started to dance.

Dawes felt faintly claustrophobic. Was it his imagination, or was the circle of musicians moving inwards? The dancers, it seemed to him, were crowded closer and closer together.

39

Suddenly he felt what seemed to be a sharp blow in the back. The musicians stopped playing; before he quite realized what was happening, they and the dancers, with the skeleton, had melted away into the crowd. Dawes felt a great pain and weakness. His knees gave way beneath him: he seemed to be fainting. People rushed towards him. He heard someone say, 'Isn't it John Dawes?' and then lost consciousness.

Within seconds of Dawes sinking to the ground he was surrounded by policemen. There was, naturally, no shortage of policemen on the scene. All police leave had been cancelled and the route of the march had been lined by police every foot of the way. More police had walked with the marchers; still more had barred access to sensitive spots such as Downing Street and the streets leading from Piccadilly to the American Embassy in Grosvenor Square. Now at last they had something to do. They clustered round, holding the fascinated crowds and the circling press away from the celebrity tent where Dawes had been carried, and asking everyone who had seen anything of what had occurred to stay around and be ready to answer questions. Flashlights popped and television cameras whirred. The organizers of the rally conferred about what was to happen next. Would it be best if everything simply went ahead normally, as if nothing had happened? Everyone agreed that this would be the best thing, if the police would permit it.

The police could see no alternative but to permit it. People were still pouring into the park, and if the rally were suddenly broken up there would be chaos. So it was that most of those in the park had no idea, at the time, of the drama that had taken place: they were simply aware of the wider drama they themselves were helping to create, amid the dreadful threat which dominated them all.

The Crofts reached the park around four o'clock. They spent a while wandering around enjoying the sideshows— a group of morris dancers was performing near Park Lane, some bands were playing, there was a mime, and some street theatre; and some more time greeting acquaintances they had not seen for years. Then, full of party spirit, they made their way towards the platform. Judith was not herself speaking, but she had a ticket for the tent. She wondered vaguely what had happened to Dawes: surely he should have been speaking about this time? He was one of the movement's most able orators, and surely he would have been asked to speak during this peak period, when almost everyone had arrived and people had not yet begun to leave? But all they had heard so far was a succession of indifferent poets and party politicians. They were aware that a great many flashbulbs seemed to be going off in the vicinity of the platform, and that even more police than usual seemed to be positioned there, but that was nothing astonishing: perhaps there would be a decent coverage in tomorrow's papers, for once.

When they got to the tent, however they found it surrounded by an impenetrable barrier of police. 'Sorry, miss,' said a large sergeant—a curious mode of address, Judith reflected, considering that she had two children and an obvious husband-figure in tow. Then she felt annoyed with herself for so much as noticing such a detail. Whatever the mode of address, the policeman remained impassable. 'No one's allowed in there.'

'But I've got a ticket,' Judith explained. 'I'm one of the organizers.'

'I don't care who you are, miss, no one's allowed in. There's been an accident.' Someone, he explained, had been hurt. Who, and how, he would not, or could not, say.

It was at this point that Charlotte Dawes and Martin Davies arrived. They had got to the park somewhat later than the Crofts, and had been at pains to ascertain whether or not John Dawes had yet spoken. Most people seemed to think he had not, although the public address system was such that it was impossible to be certain. However, as Dawes's speaking style could generally overcome even the most static-ridden amplifier, the consensus was that he had yet to appear. When, therefore, five o'clock arrived and he had not yet done so, Charlotte and Martin made for the platform to find out what had happened. They arrived

41

just as the policeman was giving Judith his unsatisfactory explanation for the strange state of affairs prevailing around the tent.

The two women greeted each other with relief, familiar faces in this unfamiliar situation. They could draw no more information out of the policeman. Either he knew no more than he had told them or he was unwilling to expand in front of the large crowd which had, inevitably, collected, drawn by the flashbulbs and the wall of police. Rumours were, of course, circulating in the crowd, the consensus opinion being that there had been a murder, though who had been murdered no one could say. At this moment a press photographer came out of the tent, escorted by a policeman and accompanied by a protesting journalist waving his press card.

Judith called, 'What's happened?'

To which the journalist obligingly replied, 'Someone stuck a knife in John Dawes.'

Newsflash, BBC TV, 7.33 p.m., Saturday, 8 April
We interrupt programmes for a newsflash. Reports are coming in of what appears to be a nuclear explosion in Iran at the town of Qum, south of Teheran. No more is known at the moment. We will of course keep you informed as and when we receive more news about this.

Nine o'clock News, BBC TV, Saturday, 8 April
You may already have heard that, earlier this evening, a nuclear bomb was dropped on the town of Qum, to the south of Teheran in Iran. The bomb was delivered by an Iraqui TU-22 bomber. It is not known whether the bomb was originally intended for Teheran itself, and was diverted possibly because the city's defences were more formidable than had been expected, or whether Qum was chosen as the target being the home of Ayatollah Khomeini, one of Iran's main decision centres and one of its holiest places. No pictures have yet arrived from Qum, but first reports indicate that destruction of the city is almost total and that very few people living in the vicinity can expect to survive. Here

is our defence correspondent, Christopher Wain.

WAIN: The world has been wondering for some time whether Iraq had a nuclear capability. That question is now fully and terribly answered. When the Israelis bombed the Tammuz-1 reactor in 1981, many people assumed that they had success-fully stopped the Iraqui nuclear programme, or at least set it back many years. However, even at the time many people wondered whether the fuel itself had not been got safely away in time, and there were rumours that it was being stored in some unspecified place against future needs. Evi-dently these rumours were well-founded . . . As the Iranians try to pick up the pieces after this appalling shock, the world is asking itself three urgent questions. First, is Iran, too, nuclear-capable, and if so, will it try to reply in kind? Second, has Iraq any more bombs up its sleeve? And third, will the superpowers now intervene to prevent this Middle Eastern holocaust spreading until it engulfs the rest of the world?

CHAPTER 7

'I don't know if this knifing was anything to do with you,' said Edson furiously down the phone to Tranter the next morning. 'If it was, I certainly don't wish to be informed. But all I can say is that somebody has given the other side a whopping great boost, that's all. Didn't even have the nous to do the job properly. Just made sure they got all the publicity they could possibly wish for.'

'Now hold on, Ed,' Tranter interjected. 'You were there Friday. Did we ever mention anything like this?'

'As though things weren't delicate enough,' Edson swept on, 'with this bomb. Here we get a chance to discredit them completely, once for all, and some bloody fool goes and spoils it. I wouldn't be surprised if it was that cleverdick Silverlight. Do you know what I heard? His sister is that woman Judith Croft. Did you know that?'

'Silverlight was in Trafalgar Square,' said Tranter. 'You

know that. You were there too. Look, about this bomb,' he went on, eager to say his piece before Edson rang off, which he sounded as if he might do at any moment. 'What are we doing about it?'

'What d'you mean, what are we doing about it? It's nothing to do with us. We aren't doing anything about it, and judging by the way things have gone in the past, we shall only find out if anyone else is doing anything when they've done it.' Edson was a Little Englander rather than an Atlanticist.

'But couldn't we send an observer? What I'm thinking is this,' Tranter said portentously. 'It's an unequalled chance to test some of our theories. And hardware. We could send in some of our survival gear and monitor it. And test some methods. How about it? Can you fix it for us?'

'You are about the last people they're going to let in there,' snapped Edson. 'And frankly, on yesterday's showing I agree with them.'

'But Ed, we never—'

'I suppose that even you would not discuss a murder attempt during lunch in front of a Minister of the Crown.' And Edson ang off.

Tranter looked crossly at the receiver in his hand. It might have been Silverlight, at that. Croft his sister—he seemed to remember hearing something to that effect before. And wasn't she supposed to be Jewish or half-Jewish or something? That would mean of course that Silverlight, too . . . Well, he did lack a certain decent reticence. You can't hide your ancestry for ever.

Tranter sighed. More than anything else he wanted to get out there and have a look at Qum. He had a pet theory about the uses of ferrets in these situations which he very much wanted to put to the test. It would also be nice to see for oneself that it was perfectly possible to survive a nuclear explosion. It was, of course, already proved that the whole place didn't come to an end as soon as a bomb went off. Here they were. Life went on as normal.

The Sunday papers had certainly featured the rally largely. Together with the bomb, it had made the front page

44

on more or less every one—an unprecedented achievement. The *Mail on Sunday* had parallel headlines: BAGHDAD NUKES QUM and RED PROF KNIFED AT RALLY.

The rest of the Sunday papers echoed this, with varying degrees of politeness. In some, the fact of a nuclear weapon actually having been used, with its various attendant corollaries, occupied the entire front page; others judged that a spectacular attempt at murder in a suitably nuclear context, even though unaccompanied by sexual assault, would be more to the taste of their readers. But all ran these two stories, perhaps because they in a way complemented each other. After all, the professor had been knifed in the act of trying to prevent what has taken place at Qum . . .

He had been knifed; but by great good fortune, he had not been killed. The knife had missed the heart by only three millimetres, but it had missed, and Dawes was now in University College Hospital, with queues of policemen and journalists waiting outside his door for the moment when he might recover sufficiently to tell them what had happened. For the moment, all that was known was what could be described by those few spectators who had happened to be watching at the moment when the band stopped playing and melted away into the crowd, accompanied by the skeleton and all the rest of the dancers—all except John Dawes. And what could they say—what, indeed, could anyone say, Dawes included? The band, the dancers, the skeleton, had not been in any way noticeable among that crowd. As for being recognized—sooner find the proverbial needle in a field of haystacks. Everyone had been milling around, almost everyone had been wearing more or less strange garments: there must have been at least a hundred in skeleton costume alone.

> 'It ain't no sin
> To take off your skin
> And dance around in your bones . . .'

And what could be easier than to resume that skin when the bones were no longer needed?

'Hardly a triumphal aftermath,' said Nick Croft. He pointed to the centre pages of the *Sunday Review*. 'I see your brother's sounding off again.'

Judith took the paper. Under the headline STRENGTH IS OUR ONLY DEFENCE Paul Silverlight drew the moral he took to be obvious. 'Of one thing we can be quite sure. Iraq would never have perpetrated this outrage if Iran, too, had possessed nuclear weapons.'

'How does he know they haven't?' Nick said crossly.

'Presumably he thinks that if they had they'd have done some bombing of their own in return.'

'He thinks everyone should have one, does he?'

'Everyone worth preserving,' his sister qualified. 'Though I don't expect he thinks the Iranians were really worth preserving. He's a philosopher, you know. They like to keep real life separate from the life of the intellect. When he draws a moral it's intended purely as a moral.' Then she burst out crying. The boys, who were spooning down shredded wheat, looked on aghast. Ben also began to cry. Jonathan said, 'Why is Mummy crying?' Nick was shocked, too. He was usually the one near tears while Judith, apparently immovable, churned on.

Why am I crying, Judith wondered. Is it because the world is about to end? No: that was too general a calamity. Is it because I have spent my whole adult life trying to achieve one thing, and failed? That was certainly a distressing thought, but that was not why she was crying. It was more that nobody, and nothing that anyone did, seemed any longer to be of the slightest importance. So somebody had tried to kill John Dawes, who a few months ago had been in bed with her, who was her old friend, who was the inspiration of the movement to which she devoted the best part of her life. So what? Compared to the annihilation of an entire city, it seemed scarcely to matter. Yesterday Qum, tomorrow the world. It sounded like an advertising slogan.

Martin sat in his room in Princes'. He, too, was reading the *Sunday Review*. What ought he to be doing at this point, he

46

wondered? Building a refuge of doors and books beneath the nearest staircase? Bringing out two weeks' supply of canned food and a shotgun to ward off unwelcome visitors? It was manifestly too late to persuade the great powers to divest themselves of nuclear arms, and even if they did, the small powers clearly would not hesitate to use theirs—had not hesitated, indeed. Paul Silverlight's piece in the *Review*'s centre spread made these very points. Had the world then come to this, that he found himself agreeing with Silverlight? Not entirely, he was relieved to note. For whereas Silverlight drew the conclusion that the only hope lay in Defence Through Strength, Martin thought there was no hope and no defence, through strength or anything else. It might be too late already. How much megatonnage was needed to cause nuclear winter?—surely not just one bomb! No, it must be more than that: after all, there had been Hiroshima and Nagasaki, and here we all still were. But bombs now were bigger than bombs then . . .

The telephone rang. It was Charlotte. 'How are you?'

'Terrible. You?'

'Worse. Mother's in London with Dad and Jenny's here for the day. Can we come and see you?'

Martin was curious about Jenny. They had never met. When he thought of her as Mrs Chantrey he had pictured her as an earnest lady of the left, possibly a repressed feminist (any feminist who married Chantrey would be repressed) eschewing glamour and tending to a low-fat vegetable diet, possibly salt-free. Their home would un-doubtedly smell of beer and pipe-smoke: did she preserve a small corner of it free of those two all-pervasive scents? Since the revelations about Silverlight and Fulbourn, however, this image had somewhat blurred. It was hard to imagine anyone who could move from such a one to such another. The only certain thing was that she must have a liking for political excess—a nearly unimaginable characteristic, thought Martin.

They arrived at two o'clock, immediately after lunch: clearly Charlotte did not find the undiluted company of her sister easy to take. Meeting Jenny at last, Martin could see why. She was not like his fantasies: she was not like anything. She was null. She was rather fat, and her complexion was muddy and spotty. Occasionally the flicker of a resemblance to her father, her mother, her sister, crossed her face, and it was possible to see that she might once have had a life of her own. Clearly she had no such thing now. As for her thoughts, there was no telling what they might be, for she did not speak. Politely, Martin addressed remarks to her, but she would not reply. She seemed indeed quite unaware that she was being addressed. Yet she was not deaf, for she started at the sound of a bell; and she was so solidly there that it was impossible to talk across her indifferently—about the political situation, for example, which (Martin found) occupied his mind to the exclusion of almost all else. Was this, then, the Messalina of the extremists? When she left the room in search of a lavatory Charlotte whispered, 'She's rather depressed, poor thing, at the treatment they're giving her.'

They went for a walk, and Charlotte conversed brightly. Their father had recovered consciousness. What did Martin think of the international situation? Had he read today's editorial in the *Review*? He had; what about it? 'It's a miracle,' said Charlotte. 'They're on our side at last.' In what way? Martin inquired. 'Why,' she said, 'they're against nuclear weapons. They think they're a bad thing. Hadn't you noticed? It's like—oh, wasn't it William James who described it? First they think your idea's mad. Then they say everybody's known that all the time. And then they say they thought of it themselves.' She gave a hysterical little laugh. 'Only now it's too late.' Occasionally she addressed Jenny directly, but got no response. 'Mother will be so sorry to have missed you,' she said. 'She was hoping she might catch you tonight or tomorrow morning, but she's staying in London to be with Daddy as much as she can.'

Would any mother, Martin wondered, be sorry to miss so desolating a sight? Martin and Charlotte wandered ahead of Jenny. 'If I were your mother, I think I should want to kill them,' he said.

'Kill who?'

'Chantrey. Silverlight.'

'Yes,' said Charlotte, 'I expect she does. But one can't kill everyone one feels like killing. It's just one of those impossible dreams. Besides, these days, what's the point? No need to worry about killing anybody any more. It's all going to be done for us.'

BBC World Service, 3.30 p.m., Sunday, 9 April
We are interrupting programmes to go to the newsroom.

News is just coming in of what appears to be a nuclear explosion in the centre of Baghdad. It is unclear who is responsible, although it is assumed that it is probably Iran. However, nobody has yet claimed responsibility. As yet, there are no estimates of damage or casualties, although it is probable that both will be very grave.

BBC World Service, 6 o'clock news, Sunday, 9 April
It is now known that Iran was responsible for the nuclear bomb that exploded in Baghdad earlier today. Teheran has announced in the last hour that it was a retaliation for the nuclear attack by Iraq on the Iranian holy city of Qum yesterday. There was puzzlement in international circles at first because no Iranian planes were seen over Baghdad at the relevant time, and indeed, such has been the damage done by Iraq to the Iranian airforce that it is very doubtful whether Iran now possesses planes capable of penetrating the Iraqui air defences. However, it was explained in Teheran that the bomb was delivered by a suicide squad driving a truck. This may also explain the delay between the first attack and the retaliation.

At least one hundred thousand people are already feared dead from the initial blast and firestorm. Destruction of the city centre was almost total, and was made even worse because of the fabric sunroofs which cover so much of the area and which burned immediately. As with Qum, the area is at present so heavily contaminated with radiation that it is assumed that very few of those still alive near ground zero will survive in either case.

Urgent consultations are at present going on between the United States and the Soviet Union in an attempt to prevent the conflict worsening.

CHAPTER 8.

'Well,' said Jane Addison. 'Ought I to cancel, I wonder? It does seem in rather bad taste.'

Jane was having a party. Jane gave a good many parties: she always enjoyed her own parties more than she enjoyed other people's. At one's own parties, she pointed out, one was entitled to break in on any conversation. And she gave good parties, and people were always happy to come to them. This was certainly true. Jane was literary editor of the *Sunday Review*: authors, reviewers, publishers, all welcomed the chance of being entertained by her (so much cheaper than entertaining her!) She lived in a charming, pastel-coloured house in Primrose Hill. Her children, who were now nearly grown up, lived on the top floor, and her divorced husband lived nearby and was a frequent visitor (to the chagrin of his present wife, who also resented the fact that her house was not so grand as Jane's).

Jane's daughter Joanna, making mayonnaise for the potato salad, said, 'Frankly, I don't see that you having a party makes any difference one way or the other, Mum. You may as well go on with it. Think of all the telephoning you'd have to do otherwise. Anyway, what would you say? I'm not having the party after all because they're dropping atom bombs on each other in the Middle East. Be honest, what do you or your posh friends care about the Middle East?'

'I didn't know you cared about it that much.'

'I don't, but at least I'm honest about it. Anyway, half of them would be sure to turn up anyway, and then what would you do?'

So it was that a few hours after Jenny Chantrey had left Princes', Paul Silverlight was knocking on Jane's dark blue door.

The door was opened by a man Paul did not know. It was now nine o'clock, and the house was filling up. The door-opener waved vaguely behind him. 'She's in there,' he said. Silverlight gave the little jerk of the head with which he acknowledged people he did not know and went on into the house.

The day before, Jane Addison's party would have felt like the essence of the moment, if your moments were those defined by the Sunday papers. Today, however, it had a slightly dated air. This was because everybody, as if by some unwritten law, was not discussing politics. This was for roughly the reason that Judith Croft had burst into tears that morning. If one was to start on that, then nothing else was worth thinking or talking about, and then what was the point of coming to a party? So, almost unconsciously, Jane's guests talked of just those things they would have talked about at any other time, thus leaving a gaping hole at the centre of every conversation. The one exception was Alfred Edson, who, being a politician, had no other topic of conversation. He overcame the delicate problem by discussing it purely in terms of personalities. At the present moment he was discussing Damian Tranter with Peter Conder.

'I sometimes despair of Tranter. Heart's in the right place, of course, but not a great deal up here, know what I mean?'

'Oh, I do,' said Conder, whose exact opinion of Edson might have been expressed in just those words.

'Know what he said to me this morning?'

'No.'

'Wanted to be transported out there, I don't know quite how he thought it would be arranged, some sort of magic carpet, to try out some mad idea he has about ferrets.'

'Ferrets?'

The word echoed across the entrance-hall, reverberating in one of those momentary silences which sometimes occur in a roomful of people.

The entrance-hall was paved with black and white marble tiles and the sitting-room, now beginning to fill with people, was silvery green. It suited Jane, who was an ash-blonde and looked delicate. (She was not delicate.) She waved at Silverlight from across the room, and came across holding out a glass of champagne, managing deftly to kiss him without spilling it. 'Paul, how lovely to see you.'

'Glad you think so.'

'Modesty doesn't suit you,' she said, and led him across to the group she had been talking to. 'This is Paul Silverlight,' she said. 'He's simply brilliant. Have you read his novel? *The Lives of Henry Buckfast?*'

'I've read the reviews,' said a large man standing by the window. 'Or were they reviews by you?'

'Either or both,' said Silverlight. 'I wouldn't bother with the novel if I were you. I don't think I'm one of nature's novelists.'

'No, that was what the reviews said,' the man agreed.

'I see myself rather as an intellectual agitator,' Silverlight offered.

'Ah,' said the man, and stumped off. Silverlight's Adam's apple moved convulsively, a sign that he was nervous.

'Take no notice,' said Jane. 'I thought that was a brilliant piece today.'

'Got it rather wrong, though, didn't you?' said a small man with a ragged black beard who had been listening to these exchanges. 'I mean, they did have a bomb after all, didn't they? So your logic rather falls by the wayside.'

'Oh—Andrew—' Jane seemed slightly embarrassed. 'Do you know Paul Silverlight? Andrew Taggart.'

'Delighted to meet you,' said Taggart. 'I was having lunch with your sister only the other day.'

'Really?' said Silverlight.

'I didn't know you had a sister,' said Jane.

'I can't remember when I last saw her. We don't have a lot in common.'

'Oh, I don't know. I should say you were very alike in a way,' said Taggart. 'Opposite sides of the same coin, sort of thing.' He turned to Jane and explained, 'Mr Silverlight's sister is Judith Croft.'

'I know the name—'

'The forceful lady behind the Peace Movement.' Silverlight looked furious. Taggart said, 'I don't know why you're so embarrassed. One can't help one's family, and anyway, she's very intelligent. A credit, I should say. But to return to our muttons,' he went on cheerfully, as if they had been his muttons in the first place, 'The deterrent doesn't seem to deter after all, does it?'

'I don't suppose they thought they had one,' said Silverlight coldly. 'No one else did.'

'What I've been wondering is why they decided to do it now,' said Taggart. 'After all, this war's been going on for years, hasn't it?'

'Not the faintest idea,' said Silverlight. 'Why talk about it? We can't do anything.' The atmosphere of the party was beginning to affect him.

'Can't we?' said Taggart. 'I thought you were the man who could do something. Aren't you supposed to have the ear of the Prime Minister? Isn't that what I read? Or aren't we supposed to mention that? You must have more idea than most about what's going on.'

'I'm afraid that in the present circumstances the Prime Minister is almost as much of an onlooker as anybody else.'

'There I agree with you,' said Taggart, 'and for the first time in my career I'm genuinely sorry for it. The thought that we have to depend for our continued existence on that bunch of maniacs—'

'Politics are so gloomy,' said Jane. 'I know they're inescapable, but do we have to talk about them all the time? Why don't we just drown our sorrows?'

Silverlight said, 'It depends whether we can face them down.'

'I would say it depends more whether that supposed Pentagon leak really was policy, or just a hypothetical scenario,' said Taggart.

'And if it was policy?'

'Why, then the fingers will be on the buttons at this very moment, won't they? Even if it wasn't, it'll have scared the shit out of the Russians, so I expect the fingers'll be on the buttons anyway. Whoever found that piece of paper and sent it off may turn out to have been the pivotal figure in world history. The pity of it is that nobody will be there to appreciate it.'

Jane said, 'Paul, there are a whole lot of people who want to meet you.' From across the room, Peter Conder waved. He occasionally reviewed books for Jane's literary pages. 'That is certainly more the complexion of person you'd like,' Taggart agreed. He raised his empty glass, bowed ceremoniously to his hostess, and said, 'It's always so instructive meeting your guests, dear Jane.'

The party proceeded on its way, as a hundred parties had proceeded before it. The obliteration of Qum and Baghdad, though it left all Iran and Iraq mourning, had no effect on Primrose Hill. In the square outside, car doors slammed and strollers strolled in the suddenly mild air of the April evening. Jane's two children, who abhorred their mother's parties and had been spending the evening with friends, came home, looked in, politely said hello to their mother's friends, and locked themselves into their top floor with relief. Her ex-husband and his new wife looked in but left after a short time. They arrived too late to see the children, which pleased the new wife, who found them rather intimidating, and declined Jane's invitation to seek them out in their top-floor stronghold. Literary critics discussed the authors they were currently slaughtering. Authors avoided those critics who had been unkind about their latest books. Guests looked over the shoulders of fellow-guests with whom they were conversing to make sure nobody important had entered or left the room while they were otherwise engaged. A fattish, rather pasty girl who had just arrived engaged an art critic in conversation. She seemed to know very little about art: he hadn't caught her name. While she asked him earnestly, 'But can you really feel that what you do is worth doing?' he looked desperately round for an escape route. One presented itself. 'Excuse me a moment,' he said, noticing that a prominent gallery-owner had just arrived. 'There's Daz.'

He hurried precipitately away. The girl looked round the room. She seemed to be looking for someone, but maybe that was merely in order to avoid the demeaning situation of being at a party such as this with no one to talk to. Conder was standing nearby and was for the moment disengaged, but he did not approach her. Doing a strange girl a good turn was not his style. The sight and sound of Silverlight holding forth on the other side of the room appeared to be the final straw as far as the girl was concerned. She melted away unnoticed, as she had arrived. She might even have been invited. Parties like this were not for girls like that.

Taggart, too, was left standing. This was not really his kind of party. He followed Jane's ex-husband and his new wife in leaving early, having first made sure that there was no one there who might possess nuggets of information to his advantage and with whom he had not already conversed. He was a man who lived for his work: it was his hobby and his consuming interest. People wondered why Jane invited him to a gathering of this sort. In fact they had known each other for years and had even (briefly) been lovers—a fact which Jane did not broadcast, but which had left her with an affection for this rather disreputable figure which surprised even herself. It did not surprise Taggart. Nothing ever surprised him, or not for more than the fraction of a second.

By one o'clock, despite the fact that there was some wine still undrunk, most of the guests had departed. Somehow the evening had not gone with quite the usual swing. The impending threat of nuclear war might not be talked about but it could not be forgotten. It was definitely lowering to the spirits. Jane herself was not unaffected. The thought of spending the night alone, surrounded by debris, was intolerable.

Silverlight was standing by the window studying his glass. Jane said, 'Don't go yet, Paul. I feel I've hardly spoken to you all evening. You know how it is at one's own parties, one has to be continually moving around and one never really gets to talk to anyone.' Her cat, a small, slinky tabby, came up and rubbed itself against their legs. 'You see,' she said, 'it must be the end. Prune always knows when everyone's finally off, don't you, Prune?' Silverlight, who hated cats, shuddered slightly and distanced his leg from the feline presence. 'I'm going to make a cup of coffee,' said Jane. 'Would you like one?'

They sat in Jane's quarry-tiled kitchen, drinking coffee. The last guest had by now departed. The cat came in and sat companionably on the tiled worktop, keeping them company.

Silverlight said, 'Isn't that rather unhygienic?'

'I suppose so,' said Jane. 'Buzz off, Prune. Don't reveal our shameful secrets to Mr Silverlight, or he'll put us in his next novel.'

'I don't expect I'll be writing any more novels.'

'No? What a shame,' said Jane abstractedly. It was clearly not as a novelist that Silverlight interested her. She said, 'Is Judith Croft really your sister, or is that just one of Andrew's little embroideries?'

'Yes.'

'She is?'

'Yes.'

'Oh well, we won't talk about it if you don't want to. I met her once or twice, that's all. Rather liked her, actually. She doesn't live so very far from here, you know.'

'I know.' He looked at her, obstinately mute. She, too, said nothing, too curious about this discovery to help him any further. His Adam's apple jerked—nerves which could have been brought on by the situation or the topic of conversation. There was a silence. Finally he burst out, 'Blood isn't thicker than water, you know. We're not at all alike. I don't like her and she doesn't like me. And you can imagine, in my present position it could be a terrible embarrassment to me. I enjoy the confidence of—well, people in very high places. I shouldn't like to see that undermined.'

'But surely they know all about it? Don't you have to be positively vetted and x-rated before they even let you set foot in Downing Street?'

'I don't have an official position,' he said stiffly. 'It's purely a matter of friendship and confidence. And you can

56

imagine what people in those circles think of my sister and her crowd.'

'Worse than the Russians,' laughed Jane.

'Precisely,' he said, not laughing. 'They are the enemy, in their way.'

'And are they worried, in Downing Street? About what seems to be going on?'

'Here?'

'Everywhere.'

'I think they're quietly confident that things will turn out all right.'

'Not moved to the bunker yet?'

'Not this afternoon,' he said, taking evident pleasure in being able to relay this up-to-date information. 'At any rate,' he went on, a slight note of desperation in his voice, 'you can see why I don't want the press to get hold of this.'

'Poor Paul, they have got hold of it,' Jane laughed. 'But maybe events will eclipse your family affairs. At any rate, it looks as if your views are prevailing at the moment, whatever the press does. I haven't noticed anyone nuclear disarming recently.'

Silverlight finished his coffee. 'I must go now,' he said.

'Must you really?' She held out a hand. 'Why?'

The hand put Silverlight into a quandary. If he ignored it he was making as much of a positive statement as if he took it. He did not feel inclined to take it. On the other hand, if he failed to do so he would undoubtedly alienate Jane, and she was a powerful woman. She could help him or she could do him a considerable amount of harm. Such are the difficulties of being a public figure. Reluctantly, he took the hand in his own. She smiled at him warmly. 'I've always fancied you,' she said. He smiled back. The smile was rather uncertain. In a man generally so very certain of himself, Jane found this endearing. It was also, she thought, encouraging. Part of the reason she found him interesting was that it was generally rather difficult to imagine him in such an essentially undressed situation as the bedroom: his armour, literally and metaphorically, seemed so chinkless. He was such a dandy, tall and slim, his suits cut just so, wide silk ties perfectly judged, thick fair hair perfectly cut; opinions all of a piece, perfectly thought out, incisively expressed. The thought of luring such a person into abandonment was an appealing one. Jane was not the first woman to sense this challenge and respond to it in this way. But she had never met Jenny Chantrey. (Anyway, even if she had, what woman does not feel that she will do better than the abandoned wife or mistress? And Jenny, now, was not a beautiful sight.) 'Why don't we go to bed?' said Jane. 'You can stay the night.'

'I've got a lecture in the morning.'

'Go to it from here.'

'There are some notes I must pick up—they're at my flat.' Jane looked cross. Paul said, 'I could leave early.' They went to bed.

At about three in the morning Jane said, 'I just remembered. There was something I wanted to ask you.'

At that moment Paul said, 'I'd better go.'

'All right.' Jane wondered if she should make soothing noises such as, 'It'll be better next time,' or, maybe more tactfully, 'It'll be even better next time.' But she was not sure whether she wanted a next time. This was partly because Paul seemed quite unaware that there was anything wrong with this time. He went to the bathroom, came back and sat on the side of the bed to pull his socks on. He said, 'That was very nice.'

'Oh, good.'

He put on his pants with dignity. She knew the answer to one question, at least. Even in the throes of passion, or lust, his armour did not desert him. The naked Silverlight had not appeared that night even though all his flesh had been exposed. He put on his shirt and knotted his tie carefully. 'You said there was something you wanted to ask me,' he said politely.

'Oh, yes. I'd nearly forgotten again. Look, did you do it? I'm dying to know.'

'Do what?'

'Knife John Dawes, of course. I somehow thought it must have been you.'

Silverlight sat down on the bed again, startled. 'What an extraordinary thing to say! Why?'

'I don't know,' said Jane thoughtfully. 'It seemed the sort of thing you might do. A romantic without feeling.'

'Well, thank you! Actually, I'm not sure that isn't a contradiction in terms,' Silverlight said stiffly. 'Since you ask, I should think Dawes would be more inclined to knife me.'

'Oh? Why?'

'It's a long story and I'm not inclined to go into it,' said Silverlight quickly, obviously regretting this indiscreet opening. The cat, which had been curled in the corner of the room, as was its habit, jumped up and stretched. Silverlight started. 'Has that been here all the time?'

'I expect so. Why? D'you mind?'

He did mind. It seemed somehow obscene, to have been watched by a cat. He could imagine being a voyeur, but did not like the thought of being the object of voyeurism. He put on his jacket.

'Will you get a taxi?'

'I've got my car.'

'Well, goodbye, then.'

She heard him go downstairs and shut the door quietly behind him. He had not, in fact, answered her question.

CHAPTER 9

Peter Conder was sitting in a seminar room deep in the bowels of University College. It was below ground level, so that although the day was brilliantly sunny the room was sunk in the gloom of fluorescent lighting. The chairs were of that convenient but singularly ugly design which incorporates a sort of writing-desk into one arm. The room was dingy and rather dusty: it needed a coat of paint and a thorough cleaning. But recent cuts in university funding precluded much of either. Conder sighed. His rather long nose twitched at the end: dust affected him these days. Thank goodness Princes', at least, was able to keep up its standard of cleaning and decoration.

The hands of the clock on the wall moved with a slight click. Half past ten. Conder wriggled restlessly in his chair, and the ten or so young men or women occupying the similar chairs set in a rough circle in the middle of the room broke off their various conversations and glanced at him questioningly. 'What do you think we should do?' he enquired. There was silence, as there invariably is when a question is addressed to several people simultaneously. 'Is he usually late?'

'Never has been before,' offered a young man dressed in bluejeans, politely removing the cigarette from his mouth before he spoke. 'Perhaps he's ill.'

'He seemed perfectly all right last night,' said Conder impatiently. He had heard rumours about Jane Addison's insatiable appetites, and would have expected better of Paul than to succumb to such obvious and unbridled advances. Women had little subtlety, he thought.

'Maybe he's got a hangover.'

'He's extremely conscientious as a rule,' said Conder. 'I don't think that would stop him coming to a seminar, or sending a message at the very least.'

'Shall we try and phone him?' suggested one of the girls. 'I've got his number.' It was agreed that this would be a good idea, but when she returned, she shook her head. 'No reply from his flat.' Conder wondered whether to suggest that they try Jane Addison, but felt this would be irresponsible. He ought not to broadcast Silverlight's lapses simply because he himself happened to have noticed them. However, he could try himself. Saying, 'I think I know where he might be,' he left the room. But Jane was unable to help him. 'He seemed all right when he left here,' she said. 'I haven't heard from him since. But then I wouldn't expect to, really.'

'It was a delightful party,' said Conder. 'Thank you.'

'I'm glad you enjoyed it. I thought you looked a bit gloomy.'

'With the international situation as it is, who isn't gloomy?' observed Conder. 'Sorry to have bothered you.' He rang off and returned to the seminar room. Silverlight had still not appeared. They decided to abandon that morning's seminar on The American Political Scene Today, in which Conder was to have delivered a critique of a paper by Silverlight, and instead held an informal discussion on The Function of the Presidency. Like parties, academic life cannot let itself be disrupted by mere world events.

On the midday news it was announced that the foreign ministers of the Soviet Union and the United States were meeting at the United Nations in New York to discuss the situation in the Middle East. A professor, an expert in Russian studies, gave it as his opinion that the Soviets must be very tempted to do nothing and allow the capitalist economies of the West to dry up with their oil supplies. 'In a sense, it is against all their natural interests to intervene,' he said. 'This isn't Russia's problem.'

'Unless the nuclear war spreads,' said the interviewer.

'Unless, indeed, the nuclear war spreads. And if we are to believe recent leaks, then unless they can reach some agreement, nuclear war is likely to spread.'

'Are you referring to last week's so-called Pentagon leak?'

'That's exactly what I am referring to.'

Other opinions, the news went on, were that the leak might have been instrumental in precipitating the use of the bombs themselves—or at any rate, the first one. Saddam Hussein, the Iraqui dictator (the reasoning went), might have taken it as a reference to his own store of nuclear weapons, and determined to use them before they could be 'taken out'. And once he had used his bomb, then it was inevitable that the Iranians would use theirs, if they had one. Which, to most people's surprise—including, presumably, Hussein's—they did.

If the Russians and Americans could reach some agreement then the situation might be kept under control, the news went on. Nevertheless, there had been a run on such items as white paint, buckets and tinned food, and companies providing fallout shelters were doing record business. In the senior common room, Peter Conder observed to a colleague that Silverlight, who had still not appeared, was probably closeted at No. 10 Downing Street. 'I believe he is one of her close confidants.'

'But surely this is a matter for the inner cabinet?' said the colleague sceptically.

'Oh, well—I believe there are other factors,' murmured Conder meaningly, and raised an eyebrow. The end of his nose wriggled in distaste. The colleague also raised an eyebrow, but in disbelief.

'I didn't think his tastes ran in that direction. As for her, I imagine she's got other things on her mind, wouldn't you think?'

'Don't ask me,' murmured Conder. 'I've never met her. But I imagine a woman's still a woman, even if she's a prime minister. And, conversely, a prime minister's still a prime minister, even if she's a woman.'

His interlocutor remained unconvinced. 'Well,' he said, 'we'll see when he turns up this afternoon, won't we?— unless it's all too deathly secret to mention. Do you suppose he's been allotted a place in the bunker?'

'Probably.'

'Do you suppose they have double bunks there?'

'I doubt it,' said Conder. 'The last thing they'd want to risk there is procreation, I should imagine.'

The afternoon came and went. There was no sign of Silverlight. Yet another seminar room full of people waited and was disappointed. 'Don't you think it's a bit worrying?' someone asked Conder.

'Faintly,' agreed Conder, who was not used to worrying about anybody or (his domestic life being taken care of as it was) anything. 'But I don't see what we can do.' Nor did anyone else, so they did nothing. Worries about Paul Silverlight joined that multitude of slightly pleasurable *frissons* which would give then an appetite for dinner in spite of everything that appeared to be happening in the world.

Jane Addison was also trying to contact Silverlight. When he had left her that morning she had felt nothing but relief and had sunk back gratefully into her solitary pillow. She saw no reason ever to meet him again, except by accident. Ships pass in the night: there need be no fatal collision. Given the choice between Paul Silverlight and her cat Prune as an evening's companion—and should this relationship persist the choice would clearly have to be made—she unhesitatingly chose Prune. One could not live a completely solitary life, but one made one's mistakes, and these days, there would be no disastrous consequences. (The way things were going, she thought bitterly, there need be no consequences at all, consequences requiring time to manifest themselves.)

At breakfast-time she was particularly glad he was not there. Breakfast that Monday was a late and lingering affair at Jane's house. The schools were having their Easter break, and Sunday papers do not work on Mondays.

Joanna and Sam, Jane's son and daughter, showed no desire whatever to enter the glamorous media world inhabited by their mother. 'God, Mum, your friends are pricks,' they grumbled as they shambled into the kitchen at ten o'clock, thus dismissing their mother's carefully-chosen guest-list representative of the cream of literature, politics, Academe . . . 'Is it true,' Sam wanted to know 'that that creep Paul Silverlight was here? We heard someone say he was.' 'How can you have people like that in the house?' asked Joanna. 'If there's a war now it'll be because of people like him.' They would not argue about this, taking it as read by any intelligent person, but went on to quiz their mother about her supplies of white paint, tinned food, Elsan fluid and cyanide pills. Ought they to be cleaning out the cellar?

'It's very damp down there,' objected Jane. They brushed this objection aside. Dampness, they pointed out, might be a positive advantage. Not that they need worry anyway, living in the middle of London. They would be fried, blasted, atomized and radioactivated in the first seconds. But one ought to take reasonable precautions. They thought cyanide pills were the most important thing. So did Jane, but she had none, so they agreed to compromise with aspirin. 'We'd better rush out and get some while there's still any in the shops,' they said, and did so. They returned loaded with useful items including plastic bags (to help the aspirin do its job) and tapes and batteries, to while away the hours in the cellar. They did not know whether EMP would affect their tape-recorder, but were prepared to take a chance. They had bought all this on Jane's credit, they explained, since one might as well hang on to one's cash for immediate use: who knew if there would be a future anyway? Then they rushed upstairs to play their new tapes, leaving their mother sunk in depression.

This did not lift as the day wore on. It was a beautiful day. The sun shone down, daffodils glittered in gardens and window-boxes, the first tulips glowed red against the intense green of young leaves. Under the pale blue sky the trees seemed visibly to burgeon: yesterday's bare branches swelled into bud and would be in leaf by tomorrow. Jane wondered gloomily how much of all this would be left by this time next week. The midday news chronicled the remorseless slide towards—who knew what? Paul Silverlight, maybe, thought Jane. She dialled his number. No reply. Of course not: she remembered that he had said he had a lecture this morning. She would try again later. She did so. Still no reply.

By the evening she was in that state of semi-panic which is so familiar a feature of many relationships. The day which had begun in relief at the thought of never seeing him again drew towards evening in a fevered desire to speak to him at all costs which took on a momentum of its own quite unconnected with anything she might wish to say. She dialled his number every half-hour. No reply. Once it was engaged: excited, relieved, she tried it again five minutes later, once more without reply. His telephone must have been ringing for someone else.

When by eight o'clock she had still not succeeded in contacting him, she told herself that he must have spent all day wherever he was lecturing and then gone straight out to dinner. She would try again much later.

She did so, but to no avail. By about two in the morning she was in a sweat of totally illogical jealousy. Their love-making had accorded her no pleasure, but the thought that he was now with someone else—and what other possible explanation could there be?—was intolerable. She could not sleep. When finally she did so, she was tormented with nightmares in which his face dissolved into atomic explosions and then reassembled, fearfully burnt away.

Next morning, Tuesday, April 11, Paul Silverlight's cleaning lady arrived at his flat as usual at nine in the morning. She picked up his bottle of milk and let herself in with her key. The newspaper was still lying on the mat, overlaid with the day's post. Putting these on the hall table, she went into the kitchen, stowed the milk in the fridge and put the kettle on for a cup of tea. Then she went into the living-room to start clearing up.

Silverlight's flat was the converted top floor of one of the enormous houses which line Fitzjohn's Avenue in Hampstead. The thickness of ceilings and walls means that these flats are pretty well soundproofed, but the charlady's scream was such that it brought the downstairs neighbour running up to see what could be the matter. She opened the door shaking, and led the avid neighbour (he was an Indian medical student whose flatmates had all left for work) into the living-room. There sat Silverlight, slumped back in an easy chair, a plastic bag over his head, his hand languidly stretched towards a cup containing dregs of coffee which stood on an occasional table beside him. He was quite dead.

CHAPTER 10

Tuesday, 11, April
So this, thought Brian King, is what they call anomie.

King was part of the graduate intake into the Force. He had done a sociology degree at Leeds before beginning his duties as a community policeman. His tutor there, he recalled, had made quite a speciality of anomie—had written a book about it, hadn't he? King had never quite known what it meant until now. In times like these a policeman's lot is not a happy one, he thought. When the most serious crime of all is in preparation while the world looks on helplessly, individual peccadilloes—individual serious crimes, even—lose their importance. What does the odd rape or murder matter in the face of the end? What on earth was he doing at the office, even? Shouldn't he be at home with his wife and children, tending the garden, savouring these last days . . . ? He pictured the scene. The reality, unfortunately was not as idyllic as the thought. His son would be spending the day, as he spent all days when he was not at school, lying on his bed wearing headphones and drowning in sound. His daughter would be obsessively playing computer games. His wife—well, who knew where his wife might be? He did not inquire how she spent her days. Not that he suspected anything in particular, but he had the definite feeling, when he was at home, that she had evolved her own routine in her own world and that he was not part of it. Well, you can't have it all ways. You can't both have a job that is liable to call you out at any time of the day and night and have a perfect home life. In choosing the one he had realized he was probably sacrificing the other. He had an overdeveloped social conscience, as Janine had now tired of telling him. He dated the decline of their marriage from the time when she had stopped nagging him about never being home, which was about the same time he had ceased to worry about what she did when he was not there.

He switched on the radio which sat on his desk, a miniature Cassandra. Bad news again, no doubt. Everywhere in the building one could hear the murmur of radios as people tried to keep abreast of their possible fate.

In fact, the news did not seem quite so terrifying today. As far as could be made out there was a pause in the headlong rush towards obliteration. The Soviet foreign minister was addressing the United Nations and meeting his

American counterpart; the two leaders were apparently in constant communication. The American President had told the world that 'nobody wants Armageddon to erupt on account of some stupid fanatics,' and this, although unlikely to please the fanatics in question, was something with which everyone else could agree. Let us hope, thought King, in common with other anxious listeners all over the world, that words will be translated into action. The American fleet had arrived at the Strait of Hormuz, but for the moment they were simply lying quiet and doing nothing. No more atomic bombs had yet exploded. The first photographs and reports from Qum and Baghdad were beginning to filter out. They were appalling beyond imagination. Pictures and accounts of Hiroshima and Nagasaki had not inured the world to such sights. Anyway, it was more than forty years since that had happened, and most of the world's present population was not yet born.

It was not known whether any outside scientific observers would be allowed in to inspect the damage, though such facilities were urgently being sought. As one interested scientist put it, 'We don't often get an opportunity like this and we'd sure like to make the most of it.'

There was, unfortunately, no evidence that the Iranian or Iraqui governments shared this sense of scientific priorities. Both nations were in deep mourning, and were also feeling an acute sense of national paranoia. Far from being crushed by their trials, the fondest wish of each, so far as it could be made out, was totally to crush and destroy the other. The world was holding its breath, and King's telephone was, he realized, ringing. It might have been ringing for some time.

It was the Assistant Commissioner. Was King busy? Then would he come and see him now?

When he came in, the AC held out a dossier to him. 'Sit down, King,' he said. 'Take a look at this.'

The subject of the dossier was Paul Silverlight. King glanced through it. The AC said, 'He was found dead in his flat this morning. We've been asked to take the case.'

King said, 'I'm sorry, sir, I can't see quite why. I mean, obviously he was mixed up in politics, but it looks as if it was almost certainly a family affair to me. There seem to be any number of people with perfectly good, normal reasons for hating his guts.'

The AC said, 'Well, I can only tell you what I've been told, which is that this is one for us. Obviously you'll conduct the investigation as you think best. Just begin at the beginning and see what you come up with.'

By the time King reached Silverlight's flat, a sprinkling of journalists had begun to gather around it. 'All right, gentlemen,' he said. 'Nothing much here for you. We don't know any more than you do. Less, very probably—he was one of you lot, wasn't he? We'll tell you when we've got anything.'

'If we're still here to write it down,' said someone.

'If we are,' agreed King, who found that his anomie had, snarklike, mysteriously vanished away with the onset of action.

The flat was as the cleaning lady had found it. It was a pleasant place, light, warm, quiet. It was not, as many bachelor apartments are, an empty frame, as if the vital parts of the owner's life are spent elsewhere. One might not share his tastes (Schopenhauer and sado-masochism on the bookshelves, ikons and a rather elaborate portrait of Silverlight himself on the walls) but they were definite. The portrait showed a slender young man with a narrow, intelligent face and thick blond hair, his style of dress considered to the point of foppishness. King studied it with interest, but the painting was not good enough to tell him much about the sitter other than that he had been vain, or affluent, enough to commission it. It stared down at its original, now sprawled stiffly in an armchair waiting for photographer and fingerprint men before he could be tidied decently away.

Finally everything had been done. No angle unphotographed, no surface undusted with powder. The remains of Paul Silverlight were removed and King was left in possession, temporary proprietor of all he surveyed.

A curious job, mine, he mused, but eminently suitable for

a sociology graduate. From the general to the particular. As a community policeman he had been concerned with corporate bodies, like ants' nests: now, in the Special Branch, he delved deep into the lives of individual ants.

He looked around him. This particular ant had appreciated comfort. Thick rugs on the floor, an Eames chair by the window. The place seemed unnaturally silent. The Indian student, like everyone else in the house, must now have gone to work. A girl walked her baby in its stroller along the pavement far below. The traffic along Fitzjohn's Avenue was heavy, but the sound was muffled by double glazing. All the place needed was cork walls and it would have been hermetically sealed against the world.

King sat down in the chair and reopened the file the AC had given him. Reading through it at his leisure, he was once again puzzled by the fact of this case having been assigned to him. When there is a simple explanation for something, then that is usually also the correct one. If he had been Dawes, Mrs Dawes, Chantrey, he would have wanted nothing more than to kill Silverlight; and there were a good many other people who could have cherished little affection for him. It would have been the easiest thing in the world for him to have pushed one of them just a little too far, and that was doubtless what had happened. Still, with the world apparently headed for disaster, he might as well be doing this as anything else. It was too late to start worrying about catching spies, that was for sure. So let's get on with it, he thought.

Now where would he keep his papers and correspondence? In his desk. No desk in here. King got up and began to wander round the flat.

Although large in area, it had not many rooms. There was a kitchen, bathroom, living-room, which was where he had been sitting, bedroom and study. The study contained a filing cabinet and a large roll-top desk. Both were locked. King felt in his pocket for Silverlight's keys and found what he wanted: one for the cabinet, one for the desk.

He began with the desk. It had drawers on either side of a kneehole and the familiar array of small pigeonholes under the rolltop. The drawers contained paper, carbon, envelopes — the familiar necessities of office life. Silverlight, it seemed, still used a typewriter: it sat on a table near the desk. Well, thought King, at least I shan't have to go through endless discs to see what's on them. He started to comb through the pigeonholes. Strange how guilty one still felt doing this kind of thing, even when the person was dead — especially when they were dead.

The desk contained three rows of pigeonholes, the top ones very small and used only for things like paperclips and spare pens. Silverlight was evidently a methodical man: the pens were arranged neatly, felt-tips according to colour, a compartment for fountain-pens, pencils from HH to B.

In the next row were recent bills, paid and unpaid. These might have been revealing, but they were not. Gas, electricity, telephone, credit cards — the usual things. No obvious extravagances, no last reminders.

The bottom row contained what King had been hoping to find. Personal correspondence, invitations, even a few photographs. He took these out and studied them. Silverlight, he knew, had been thirty-six, so these must have been taken over the last ten years. An attractive, rather confident-looking young man, the confidence gradually turning into arrogance as the years went on. Some groups from what was presumably Cambridge, at parties, in college courts. A couple with a rather pretty girl, slender, long brown hair down her back, laughing, their arms around each other. Jenny Chantrey? It seemed likely, since there were no signs of any other attachments. One, rather faded, of a middle-aged woman with one of those blonde, rather dried-up, closed English faces. His mother? None of any other members of his family. A few more recent portraits, the kind of thing used for the back flaps of book covers.

The correspondence was not particularly revealing. It was mostly of a business or semi-business nature: requests to lecture, to participate in seminars, acknowledgements of articles received. There was a note from somebody called Art from Princeton, apparently referring to a recent visit. King made a note of this, and of the sender's address. He turned to the invitations. Not displayed on the mantelpiece, he noted; either because nobody came here to view them or because their recipient preferred to keep his invitations to himself: either way, a rather exaggerated, or at least unusual, eye to privacy. There were a lot of invitations, reflecting Silverlight's multifarious interests: to literary parties, to political parties, to a feast due to take place next week at Princes' College. Hard to say which, if any, of these were from personal friends. King noted Jane Addison's name as the giver of the most recent of these. He turned to the filing cabinet.

This turned out uninteresting, from his point of view at least. Nothing in it but copies of articles, a book in preparation (The Death of the Left), lecture notes. He closed it and relocked everything. Then he returned to the living-room and the Eames chair to make a list of the people whom he would go and see first.

CHAPTER 11

The pathologist's report was short and simple. Silverlight had died between 5.0 a.m. and midday. He had been drugged with sleeping tablets, traces of which had been found in the coffee dregs, and then smothered with the plastic bag. Only his own fingerprints were to be found on the cup, and there were none on the bag. It might have been suicide, but in that case Silverlight's prints would have been on the bag. King digested this information and set out on his first visit.

Bob Chantrey lived in Wandsworth, in one of the maze of roads between Clapham South station and Wandsworth Common. King, a North Londoner himself, could not understand how a civilized person could bear to live in this anonymous wilderness, so far from anywhere. He checked with his A—Z. First right, fifth left.

Identical streets of identical semi-detached houses. Just the place for a revolutionary.

King opened the gate and picked his way along an uneven crazy-paving path towards the front door. On either side, the neighbours' gardens were trim and neat, havens for orderly lines of bulbs set around carefully squared patches of front lawn. The Chantrey demesne, by contrast, was definitely ragged, scrubby grass with the odd daffodil appearing as if by mistake. Just before King reached the door, it opened and a matchingly scruffy young man emerged who looked at him questioningly—but not very questioningly, as if unknown visitors were no unusual occurrence in this household: the only oddity being the wearing of a suit. 'Is this Mr Chantrey's house?' King asked. The young man said it was, and that he was in it. He then proceeded on his way.

The door was ajar. King rang the bell. A telephone started to ring inside. A voice—Chantrey's?—shouted 'Come' and then answered the phone. King went in.

The telephone was in the hall, on the floor by the stairs. A man was sitting on the stairs talking into it. This was presumably Chantrey. He was big and burly and dressed as a Canadian lumberjack. It was hard to distinguish his features, as they were mostly covered by a thick black beard, beneath which a small area of ruddy cheek and bright grey eyes could be discerned. He waved at King, gestured towards the telephone with a despairing lift of the eyebrows, and signalled that he would be free shortly. The conversation, which seemed to be about a meeting due to take place that evening for which speakers were urgently needed, came to an end. King brought out his identification, but Chantrey had barely time to glance at it before the telephone rang again. This conversation appeared to refer to the one he had just finished. The speaker question seemed to have been partially solved. Chantrey replaced the receiver and looked at it suspiciously. For the moment, it remained silent. He took King's ID and studied it closely. 'Well,' he said, handing it back, 'and to what do I owe this doubtful pleasure?' His voice, beneath the beard and the lumberjack outfit, was purest public school.

King explained that Paul Silverlight had been found dead.

'And I suppose you want to know if I killed him. Better come into the kitchen and we'll discuss it over a cup of tea.' He handed back the ID and led the way towards the back of the house.

The kitchen backed on to a conservatory filled with thriving, indeed rampant, greenery, so that light filtered dimly through on to the piles of washing-up. Chantrey put a kettle on, and soon the atmosphere was further thickened by steam and smoke from a pipe which he continuously lit and relit. He said nothing while they waited for the kettle to boil, merely stared at King through the fug. After a while this got rather annoying. King cleared his throat, brought out a notebook, and said, 'Well, sir, just for the record, perhaps we could begin by your telling me just what you were doing Sunday night and Monday morning.'

'Certainly,' said Chantrey obligingly. 'Nothing like getting straight down to business, is there? Sunday night I was at a meeting of the Iraq Solidarity Committee. That went on till about midnight. Then I took some people home. Then I came back here and met the lodger and we had a whisky. Then I went to bed and got up around eleven. I'm not what they call regular in my habits these days. I was woken up by the phone, as usual. Should have been giving a class. I didn't kill him. Anything else you want to know?'

'I should like to know anything you can tell me,' said King. 'About Silverlight.'

'Haven't seen him for years. Not since he dropped my wife in the waste-bin.'

'Would you like to tell me about that?'

'Not much,' said Chantrey heavily. 'But I will if you feel it'll be helpful.'

'I think it may.'

'Have you met Jenny?' asked Chantrey. 'No? Hang on a minute, I'll get a picture of her.' He went out of the room and came back with a photograph. It was the same slim, long-haired, laughing girl who had been on the photograph with Silverlight. 'When you see her,' said Chantrey, 'you'll understand why I feel the way I do about that bastard.'

73

'I understand your wife left you for Silverlight some time ago.'

'Five years ago, poor silly cow. I told her at the time she was a bloody fool. Leave me if you must, I said. I'm not in the business of tying anybody down personally any more than I am politically. But not for him! I suppose if you want to make sure a woman does something, all you need do is say that kind of thing at a time like that. But I knew he'd be no good for her. He was no good for anything. He was a twisted bastard.'

'What exactly do you mean by that?'

The door opened and a young man came in. 'This is John,' said Chantrey. 'Part of my alibi, among other things. John, this is Detective-Inspector Brian King who is asking me questions about Paul Silverlight. Somebody killed him. I am telling him what I know, which isn't much, but it passes the time. We'll be through in a minute, I expect.'

'OK,' said John, and left.

'I let rooms,' Chantrey explained. 'It seemed ridiculous to live all alone in a place like this.' He looked round the room and seemed depressed by what he saw. 'You should have seen this place when Jenny and I were together. It was a really nice place.' He waved his hand towards the window. 'She was a great gardener. Made it really beautiful. It looks a terrible mess now. You wouldn't believe what it used to be like. D'you know, I found mould growing on some of the washing-up the other day.'

'Miss the little woman's touch?' King said.

'You're right, I expect that was one reason she left,' said Chantrey, with a sensitivity to nuance King found surprising. He went on rather abruptly, 'You were asking me about Paul. We've all known each other for years, you know. Met at Cambridge. We were all there about the same time.

'All?'

'Me. Him. We were undergraduates together. His sister. That's Judith Croft.'

'The CND woman?'

'That's the one. I imagine Paul finds—found—the

74

relationship most embarrassing. He always did find Judith a bit embarrassing, I felt. She's very unsubtle, really. Wears her heart on her sleeve, and it always is her real heart. A lousy politician, really. Whereas he—well—whatever he says you can bet he's thinking the opposite.'

'An excellent politician, in other words.'

'You said it,' said Chantrey. He turned his attention to his pipe, which had gone out again. Must spend half his life tamping and lighting matches and puffing, thought King. Time-consuming toys, pipes. Of course, with that image, only a pipe would do.

'You were all friends?'

Chantrey nodded. 'We were all in the Labour Club. That was how we met Jenny. Everyone in the Labour Club knew the Dawes. We all went there Saturdays. It was a sort of institution, and it was a nice place, and John and Esme were our friends. And then of course there were the girls— though I suppose Charlotte can't have been more than about thirteen. You know, it was a really nice alternative to the Red Cow on Saturday nights, or even the Inkspots in the Rex ballroom. There, you see, that dates me.' He laughed. 'But even then one felt somehow—well—Paul was interested in all that for different reasons. It was useful to know John. It might be useful to get off with his daughter.'

'Well, it was, wasn't it? And he did, didn't he? Eventually.'

Chantrey shrugged. 'Take it like that if you want. But I think you know what I mean. It all depends what you call things, doesn't it? If you call it detachment, it sounds like a jolly good thing. Objectivity—something we all need. But you can carry it too far, can't you? No good being detached if you can't ever be attached. That way you don't know what you're being detached from. Well, Paul was like that. I shall never forget one evening—it was in the summer sometime and, we'd all gone to some pub on the river, the usual lot, Paul and Judith and Jenny and me and a few others, and we'd had a few. It was a lovely night, and we'd taken our drinks outside and it was only just starting to get dark. I remember turning round and seeing Paul. He was standing a bit apart from the rest of us, watching us as though we were zoological specimens. I suddenly thought he really hated us. Really hated everyone. He certainly behaved as if he hated poor Jenny.' He shrugged. 'I don't know if that's any help. It's about all I've got to say. Now do go away and leave me in peace, there's a good chap. I don't want to waste what may be my last hours on earth thinking about Paul Silverlight.'

BBC News, 4.35 p.m. Tuesday, 11, April
We interrupt our programmes for a newsflash. News has just been received that after a series of urgent meetings and consultations between the American and Russian foreign ministers, between the foreign ministers of Iran and Iraq and between the Heads of State, agreement has been reached for an immediate ceasefire. All sides have stated their hope that this may pave the way to an agreement which will lead to a permanent ceasefire in the area. Here is our diplomatic correspondent, Christopher Davies.

DAVIES: The conclusion of this agreement marks something of a diplomatic breakthrough, in that it involves a joint Russian-American initiative. I understand that America and the Soviet Union have each guaranteed a massive response against Iran, Iraq or anybody else who breaks the future nuclear peace. Meanwhile, an international peace-keeping force, also armed with battlefield nuclear weapons, is to be deployed in the area . . .

ITN, News at Ten, Tuesday, 11, April
We have just received the first pictures from Qum, which was destroyed by a nuclear bomb on Saturday. Before showing them we feel we should warn viewers that they are extremely horrifying. People who are easily upset may prefer not to watch. The bomb exploded at Qum is estimated to have been roughly the size of the Hiroshima bomb, an extremely small weapon by today's standards. The bomb exploded in the centre of the city, near the mosques and holy buildings for which Qum was famous. These buildings

are all totally destroyed. The day was quite clear, so that the effect of the explosion was maximized. It is estimated that an area of ten square kilometres around the centre of the explosion has been reduced to rubble and ashes by blast and fire damage, and hardly anybody who was in that area at the time of the explosion has survived. This accounts for more than seventy per cent of the population of Qum. As you can see, even people living on the outskirts of the city, at distances of four or five kilometres from the centre, sustained very severe burns. The death toll is likely to rise considerably, as the effects of radiation, which will be considerable as the weapon was exploded on the ground rather than in the air, have not yet fully manifested themselves . . .

Editorial, The World, Wednesday, 12 April,
So agreement in the Gulf has for the moment been reached and the world can heave a sigh of relief as the immediate danger of nuclear war recedes. It may be that the Iraqis have done us all something of a service in bringing home in the most inescapable way both the extreme horrors of such a war and our perennial closeness to the brink. But as the Strait of Hormuz is reopened, the Sixth Fleet steams away, the Russians pull their forces back from the Iranian frontier, and the remaining citizens of the tragic cities of Qum and Baghdad begin the appalling task of reshaping their lives, there are perhaps other morals that we should draw from this episode. The first is that we can, happily, have faith in our friends and allies. In the last resort they are both staunch and diplomatic. The second, as Paul Silverlight wrote in the *Sunday Review* only a day before his tragic death, is contained in the pertinent question: would they have dared bomb Iran if they had thought Iran had the bomb? Those who would see us divest ourselves of these weapons without a second thought should perhaps give a moment to asking themselves this question . . .

CHAPTER 12

Herschel Road, quintessentially suburban, shimmered behind a veil of almost-opened buds. As King parked his car
outside the Dawes house, he reflected that there was almost
nobody to be seen in the street. The only figure visible was
a slight, dark man carrying what looked like a shotgun, who
was walking rather furtively along the opposite pavement.
Probably hadn't got a valid licence, King mused. Well,
whether he had or hadn't wasn't Scotland Yard's business.
Your secret is safe with me. Though it was hard to know
what he was planning to shoot. Rabbits on the playing fields
at the end of the road, perhaps. Looked like open fields
beyond there. King turned into the Dawes' front garden.
The man glanced at him and walked on. By the time Esme
Dawes opened the door, he was out of sight.

King had telephoned and was expected. Esme led him
out to where they were sitting on the lawn under a large
beech tree whose buds were just starting to unfurl. The
weather had turned quite summery, as it sometimes does in
April. In the long grass at the end of the garden scarlet
tulips and white narcissi made a *tachiste* effect against the
green. John Dawes lay on a reclining chair in the sun. He
looked very pale. The first sun of the year always makes
even the hale look somewhat unhealthy, overlaid by a layer
of winter white and puffiness. Dawes looked as if he was at
death's door, as indeed he had been but (presumably) was
no longer, or he would not be here but in some intensive
care ward.

From next door came the sounds of tennis. It's a nice life
for some, King thought. While it lasts, but that goes for us
all.

Dawes said, 'We thought of making a tennis court here,
but it would have meant losing the tulips so we didn't in
the end. Anyway, our children were never very sporting.'

'The doctor said you weren't to talk,' said his wife.

'What is life without speech?' said Dawes. 'I'm not dead yet. But the way things are going I may be dead quite soon. I shall therefore go on speaking whatever the doctor says. Was it merely that young man you were interested in, or are you here to discuss my own little affray as well? I don't think they've found out anything about that so far, have they?'

'Do you think they're connected?' King inquired.

'I have no idea. Do you? That's the question.'

'It's an interesting thought. What makes you think there might be a connection?'

Dawes shrugged, as well as he could inside his bandages. 'Our paths had crossed, as you know, or you wouldn't be here now.'

'Inspector King is interviewing us as possible suspects,' remarked Esme.

'But we have unbreakable alibis,' said Dawes. 'I was lying in my hospital bed and you were visiting me.'

'Not all day,' said Esme. 'I believe it happened on Monday, didn't you say, Inspector? I wasn't with you for the whole of Monday. I could have done it. Would quite have liked to, what's more.'

'What exactly did you do on Monday?' asked King.

'Well, I was in London already—I stayed with a friend in Bloomsbury, you know those mansion flats between Gower Street and the Tottenham Court Road. I can give you the address if you like. I went to see John after breakfast and stayed a couple of hours, then I went to the London Library and looked at some magazines, then I had lunch in an Italian café in Jermyn Street, then I went to see John again, then I came back here. I expect I could find people who saw me in most of the places, but I couldn't guarantee it.'

'Perhaps you would have a think and make a list for me.'

Esme said, 'He was such a strange young man. We've known him a very long time of course—I expect you knew that? I'm never sure whether meeting the students is one of the pleasures of this sort of life or one of its penalties. People like Paul Silverlight incline me to think it's a penalty.'

'But did you always think that? Even at the beginning?'

'Even at the beginning.' Esme leaned back in her chair and shut her eyes. Her small, sharp face relaxed and seemed suddenly lined and much older. Her hands trailed on the grass beside her and played with a daisy. 'That's a very long time ago. Can you remember when we first met him, John? Were we living here then?'

'Of course we were. We've been here since the children were little.'

'I suppose we have,' sighed Esme. 'They say that at the moment of truth the whole of your past life unfurls before you like a sort of film strip, but I haven't noticed that happening to me over the last few days. It's all still a blur. Perhaps that means that the moment of truth is not yet. But now you say so, I suppose we were here, because I remember them in the garden here, playing croquet. And in the dining-room, of course. Pretty continuously there. I never ceased to be amazed at the amount Bob Chantrey could eat. Paul was always more delicate in his manners.'

'I was Director of Studies at Princes',' said Dawes. 'They were both pupils of mine.'

'And his sister?'

'Paul's sister? Judith? No, no, that was before all this co-education. She was at Girton, I think. But she was always around with them. I seem to remember that she rather fancied Bob Chantrey.'

'Who had eyes only for Jenny,' said Esme, with perhaps rather more acidity than the occasion demanded.

'And she, of course, only ever wanted Paul,' said Dawes.

King walked back into the centre of town, enjoying the day's unexpected warmth. Full term had not begun, so Sidgwick Avenue was not yet drowned beneath a sea of bicycles. The town, however, was by no means empty of students, hurrying around the libraries, gossiping outside pubs, lolling on the river banks. King looked at them curiously. Were these, then, the influential men and women of the future (always supposing there was to be a future)? He paused by Little St Mary's churchyard, where bluebells and primroses sprouted. A boy and girl, interlaced, passed him, pushing their bicycles while kissing passionately, a feat, thought King, which must have taken some practice. He eyed them curiously. They were quite oblivious of him. They didn't appear to him anything special. His own two, he thought, compared pretty favourably with most of the young people he had seen around here. Would they come here and be the Chantreys, the Silverlights, the Judith Crofts, of their day? Inspector King shook his head. They would not, and he was glad of it.

It was one o'clock. He had declined the Dawes's invitation to lunch, judging that they would feel easier, as he would, eating separately. He found a pub and sat down with a pint of beer and a ham sandwich. The pub was a dingy one, and there was a pool of beer on the table in front of him: an atmosphere which fitted his mood. He stood his own beer neatly in the centre of the pool. While he ate, he studied the list he had made in the train of people he ought to see while he was in Cambridge. Charlotte Dawes, Jenny Chantrey, Peter Conder. He decided he would dispose of the Dawes family before beginning on Silverlight's other friends and acquaintances.

Charlotte was, her parents had told him, working in a bookshop on Trumpington Street, but when King got there he was told she had just gone off to lunch. So rather than waste time he found his car and set off towards Fulbourn and Jenny Chantrey.

Was Jenny, he wondered, the pivot of this sordid little story? If so, he would judge that the stabbing of her father was not connected with the murder of her lover—unless that had been a deed perpetrated by Silverlight himself in some fit of rage against the whole Dawes clan. This, however, seemed unlikely considering that he had been speaking in Trafalgar Square, watched by at least two hundred people, not twenty minutes earlier, and had almost certainly not left this gathering the moment his speech was over. As he drove through the trim villages, thatch and plaster glowing in the spring sunlight, not a lawn unattended, not a cottage unrestored, King wondered what this *femme fatale* was like. The photographs he had seen told him little more than that she had been a pretty girl with a sweet smile. But there were many such—his own wife had been not unlike that, he remembered: and what had time and wear done to her?

He drove into the gates of Fulbourn Hospital, and his heart sank. The modern outbuildings and attachments could not disguise the Victorian asylum beneath. He drove up to the main entrance, explained himself at the reception desk, and asked to speak to Mrs Jennifer Chantrey, whom he understood was a patient here.

He was shown to a small office. Presently the door opened and a young woman in a white coat came in. She introduced herself as Jennifer Chantrey's therapist, and sat down in a chair facing King. 'I don't know if anyone's told you about Jenny. You won't get anything out of her,' she said.

'I'm afraid you must let me be the judge of that.'

'Have you ever dealt with heroin addicts? You do know they're compulsive liars? So even if she does speak, it's very unlikely she'll be of any help to you.'

'Just seeing her,' said King 'will be of help to me.'

The young woman went out and he sat back to wait. He waited for some time. Footsteps came and went in the corridor outside. Finally one set stopped, the door opened, and Jenny Chantrey came in.

What had he expected? He couldn't have said precisely; but he was deeply shocked. One tells oneself that one is prepared for the worst but when the worst arrives, no preparation is adequate. Those photographs, after all, were not so very old, and they had been of a girl, or at any rate of a young woman. The woman who entered the room now looked as if she had never been young. Flat eyes stared like grey pebbles out of a flat grey face. She was plump and rather flabby. Her hair hung in mouse-brown strings around her head. My God, thought King, what are they doing to her? What have they done to her? She wore a chain round her neck with an Egyptian ankh amulet that he recognized from one of the photographs. Otherwise nothing was left:

the laughing girl was totally subsumed in this desperate woman. 'Mrs Chantrey?' he said.

She gave no reaction at all. It was impossible to tell if she had heard him or not. He tried again.

'Mrs Chantrey? Jennifer?'

No reaction. She stood just inside the door, looking past his head towards the window.

'Do sit down.'

She remained standing.

King said, 'I am a policeman. I'm inquiring into the death of Paul Silverlight.'

At first not a flicker crossed her face. Then it suddenly came to life, lit up by a radiant smile. It was as though, for a moment, the girl in the photograph had returned, elbowing her ungainly alter ego out of the way. Jenny said, 'Yes, I killed him.'

'You?'

'Yes.' The girl still wore her rapturous smile, as though she was recalling an episode of the most wonderful happiness.

'How? How did you kill him'

'Well, I've been thinking about this for a long time. Shall I push him under a bus or put ground glass in his food? Or there are all sorts of other ways. Arsenic. Or I could smother him while he was asleep. Or I could shoot him, but that wouldn't be so good because I haven't got a gun and anyway I'd probably miss. That's the way my luck goes. So in the end I settled for poison.'

'What sort of poison?'

'Oh—' but the smile was fading now, and inertia was visibly returning. In the space of less than a minute it had taken over so totally that King could not help wondering whether the confession he thought he had just heard had not been some sort of hallucination. He looked down at his notebook. Well, it was hardly the sort of thing he was liable to make up.

After a while the young woman therapist reappeared. 'How are you getting on?' she said brightly. 'Nearly finished?'

'I get the impression Mrs Chantrey's told me all she's going to,' said King.

'Having one of our mute spells, are we?' said the therapist brightly. 'All right, Jenny, finish your tea and then it's time for your pills.' She stood up to lead her patient from the room. King said, 'Might I have a word?'

'Wait here.'

King waited. The window looked on to lawns and trees. They looked like institutional lawns and trees. King wondered idly how it was that lawns and trees belonging to institutions managed so utterly to assume a non-private character. Was it something in the way they were clipped? In the distance he could hear a lawnmower buzzing. It was a sound he always liked. He sniffed, but no scent of mown grass penetrated into the room. He tried to open the window, but it seemed to be locked. To stop the patients jumping out? he wondered. The door opened, and the white-coated young woman came into the room.

'Sorry to keep you waiting.'

'That's all right, I was thinking.' He looked down at his notebook and said, 'Tell me, was Mrs Chantrey here last Sunday and Monday?'

'No, she was visiting her family. Why?'

'She spent the night with them?'

'Yes.'

'I was wondering if she might have got to London in that time. If she can drive, for instance.'

The young woman suddenly looked up at him, her face a study of shocked comprehension. 'Of course! I should have remembered! She's been fantasizing, hasn't she? It's the one thing that brings her to life, thinking about killing her old boyfriend. Paul. That's the man you were talking about, isn't it? She goes on for hours about it.' She looked at his notebook, which was lying on his lap, then up at him. 'You're not going to tell me you're taking her at her word?'

'Well, the fact remains, he has been killed.'

'But you can't! Mr—'

'King.'

'Mr King, I must insist. Jenny is ill. And I told you, even

when she does talk, you can't believe anything she says. I must warn you, if you persist in this, we shall have to withdraw cooperation. On medical grounds. We simply can't have our patients upset in this way.'

'A man has been killed,' said King. 'My job is to investigate it. And that's what I'm going to do. Thank you very much for your help and cooperation. If I need to get back in touch, then I shall do so.' He stood up, thinking that he sounded like a caricature of a heavy-footed cop. 'Don't worry. I can find my own way out.'

The young woman watched him go in silence. He made his way along the sepulchral corridors to the entrance hall, where the receptionist gave him a bright smile. He got in his car and drove slowly back towards Cambridge. Could it be as easy as this? The words of the young woman doctor echoed in his ears. 'You can't believe anything she says.'

King thought: But I should like to.

'Dead!' said Charlotte. 'I didn't see anything about it in the papers. Well, I can't say I'm sorry, and if you've seen Jenny as you say, you'll know why.'

'Perhaps you'd like to tell me what you were doing Monday. Just for the record.'

'Worked in the bookshop all day. Then I went home and had a bath and met Martin Davies for dinner. He's at Princes'. A research fellow. He will confirm my alibi,' she assured him.

'I'm glad to hear it. It's not worth being sarcastic about these things.' King looked down at his notes. He felt very tired. It had been a long day and there was more of it to come. He still hadn't seen this fellow Conder. 'You imply that it was Silverlight who reduced your sister to the state she's in now?'

'Yes.'

'She started out perfectly happy and normal? And finished like that?'

'I don't know about perfectly happy,' said Charlotte. 'She can't have been, can she, or she wouldn't have left Bob. But she wasn't like she is now. She was pleased and excited, I should say. She was in love with Paul, you see. Always had been.'

'So why did she marry Chantrey?'

'He was there. He was crazy about her. Paul wasn't interested. She wanted to get away from here and she wasn't very adventurous. Why does anyone marry anyone?'

'I often wonder,' said King.

'I'm not inclined to try it myself.' Charlotte paused to shake her head vigorously at an intending customer who was trying the closed door of the bookshop, without success. It was ten to six. King had caught her at the shop, and she had suggested that they talk there. 'Tell me,' she said, 'do you enjoy your work? I've often wondered why people join the police. It seems masochistic, somehow.'

'I'd have expected someone like you to say sadistic.'

'Being universally distrusted.''

'Oh, I wouldn't say universally,' said King mildly. 'I find it fascinating. Never a dull moment. You say she'd always been attracted to Silverlight? But he wasn't interested? So why did he get interested all of a sudden?'

'Search me. If you want my frank opinion, I should say it was sheer spite. A slap in the eye for Bob. They'd been great buddies when they were up here, and then Paul changed sides and couldn't find words bad enough for all his old friends. And a slap in the eye for Daddy, for the same reason. As for liking Jenny, well, clearly he still didn't. It only lasted a few months.'

'Leaving her as she is now?'

'Leaving her ready to become what she is now. I don't think even Paul actually introduced her to the pushers. He wouldn't do anything as direct as that.'

He looked at her sitting relaxed beside the till, small and sharp like her mother, neat, glossy black head of cropped hair, belted blue smock over a scarlet sweater and scarlet stockings. 'You're not very like your sister,' he said.

'No,' she said. 'I'm not. I'm not a sucker. She and my father. Classic Dawes suckers. I'm like my mother. Someone has to have a bit of sense in our family.'

'Would you say your sister and your father were close?'

'Oh, very,' said Charlotte neutrally. 'Still are, as far as anyone's close to Jenny these days. If anyone can get through to her, it's Dad. I expect she should have married him, really, but it was not to be.' She looked him in the eye, eyebrows raised defiantly. But it took more than that to shock King these days. Besides, his mind was on other things, namely, how best to broach the delicate subject of whether or not Jenny had killed her lover. Nothing for it, really, but to go in clodhopping. There is no very tactful way of asking some questions.

'I understand from the hospital that she spent Sunday night at home.'

'That's right, she quite often comes for the night.'

'And goes back in the morning?'

'Yes, I took her back.'

'You have a car?'

'Yes,' said Charlotte, looking puzzled.

'Can your sister drive?'

'Jenny?' Now she looked really surprised. 'I suppose so. I mean, she could. Daddy taught us when we turned seventeen. But I don't suppose she does these days. Why?'

'I was wondering,' said King brutally, 'whether it might have been possible for her to drive to London and back between your going to bed and getting up in the morning.'

Charlotte looked at him, horrorstruck. Small spots of red colour burned on her cheekbones, and her ears turned a hot scarlet. 'Are you trying to suggest that she—that she—'

'I'm not trying to suggest anything, Miss Dawes. But she says she did it. I'm bound to investigate.'

'And you believe her?' Charlotte stood up. 'Goodbye, Mr King. I don't think I've got anything more to say to you.'

'Have a sherry,' said Peter Conder.

'Thanks,' said King. 'I will. It's been a long day.' He sank back gratefully into one of Conder's embracing armchairs and looked appreciatively round the room. 'I didn't realize people still actually lived in rooms like this. Thought they were all in museums.'

'I think I can truthfully say that not many do,' said

Conder with cheerful complacency. 'Unless they're very rich indeed. Which I assure you I'm not.'

They sipped in silence. King looked at nothing in particular: he was trying to place Conder. Where had he seen him recently? This was certainly the first time they had consciously met. Must have passed him on the street sometime today.—Yes, of course, that was it: Conder had been the other man on Herschel Road that morning. King debated whether to make a joke about shooting rabbits, but decided against it. Conder, who must equally have recognized him, could bring the subject up if he wished. However, he did not do so.

The firelight flickered in the last rays of the evening sun. (It was a gas log fire, so much warmer, as Conder liked to point out, than a real log fire.) There are few things more comfortable, King thought enviously, than firelight in a sunny room.

'So you're investigating poor Paul's death,' said Conder.

'You're the first person who's mentioned it with anything approaching regret.'

'I gather from that that you've been talking to the Dawes,' said Conder. 'Well, one could hardly expect much else from them, could one? I expect you'll find that one or other of them did it.'

'If he was murdered.'

'If he was murdered,' Conder agreed equably. 'But I expect you'll find he was. Now that it's happened, I'm really not a bit surprised. It's as if it were almost inevitable, if you know what I mean.'

'Not really.'

'Oh well,' said Conder, 'think why most people get murdered, or at any rate the reasons why people generally wish other people were dead. Paul fulfilled almost all of them, really, didn't he? Sexual jealousy. Hatred because of a supposed injury.'

'If you're talking about Jennifer Chantrey, the injury's real enough.'

'Ah, but did Paul inflict it? That's the question. They all say he did, of course. But things aren't often as simple as that. She was always very unstable, you know. When she couldn't stand Chantrey any more (and one really can't blame her for that, can one? It must have been like being married to Smokey the Bear)—well, she did rather fling herself on Paul. He took her in—probably rather unwise, but what else could he do, in a way? But it was never going to work. So she went to the bad, as they say.'

'You seem to know a great deal about them all.'

'Oh well, Cambridge is a small world, and the college is even smaller. Paul was a supervisee of mine. Besides, I think I may claim the credit for having brought him to see the political light.'

'You mean—'?

'The political Right,' laughed Conder. 'That's another reason they all hate him. A favourite son lost. And such a clever one, too. He makes them all look such fools. They really can't stand it. Couldn't,' he corrected himself. 'And another thing. They all pride themselves on indulging in 'real' politics. All this marching about in the rain—you must have heard about it. But Paul was really involved in politics—where it matters. Where the decisions get made. I expect you know about his friendship with the Prime Minister.'

'Not a lot.'

'Oh well—that's it, really. He—was—a friend of the Prime Minister. More than a friend, a real adviser. She had a great deal of time for what he had to say. And of course what he had to say was anathema to a great many ears. There's another reason, you see.'

'You're most helpful.'

'I do my best.'

'Did this conversion to the Right occur before or after the episode with Mrs Chantrey?'

'Oh, before. A long time before. But old flames run deep, to coin a phrase. Or so it would seem. I wouldn't know, myself.' He paused. 'Of course, the Dawes are a notoriously uncontrolled lot, even in these licentious days. I did hear that the learned professor himself was running after Judith Croft as fast as his legs would carry him. She's Paul's sister

—but of course, you know that. Quite an incestuous little scene, isn't it, really? I'm sure you can find an excellent motive in there somewhere for someone. Poor Paul. One can't help one's family or one's quasi-childhood friends.'

Well, thought King. That explains Mrs Dawes's lack of enthusiasm for Judith Croft, if we are to judge by the tone of voice in which she refers to her.

He declined another sherry. He had to drive back to London that night, and Janine would be annoyed enough at yet another late evening. He remembered that this evening they were supposed to attend a meeting of the PTA at his children's school. Oh well, it would give her the satisfaction of more fuel for her indignant characterization of him as a delinquent husband. He wondered if it would drive her to murder. Conder would undoubtedly think it would.

'One more thing. When did you actually see him last? Was it recently?'

'As a matter of fact, it was. I saw him on Sunday night at a party. Jane Addison's. Perhaps you know her? No? Well, I suppose your paths wouldn't cross—often. She's the literary editor of the *Sunday Review* and her parties are proverbial. Everybody goes to them, and that has to include Paul. Had to,' he corrected himself.

'And she gave a party last Sunday night?'

'I know what you mean,' said Conder. 'It does seem in a bit dubious taste, doesn't it? Poor Jane was in rather a spin about it. But after all, the party was arranged long before all the Arabs started dropping bombs on each other. And people didn't have to come if they didn't want to.' Conder sounded amused. 'Actually, there was a very full turnout, or so I should guess, not having seen the original invitation list. The place was packed. Obviously people didn't feel like interrupting their social schedules too much on account of a bomb being dropped on a faraway town of which they knew little. Even if it was an atom bomb. I should go and see Jane, if I were you. I think you'll find that she was the last person to see poor Paul alive. Anyway, that's the way it looked as if things were going when I left.'

'Thank you very much, sir. You've been most helpful.

And now if you'd just like to give me an account of your own whereabouts after you left the party . . .'

'Of course! You want my alibi.' Conder rolled the word round his tongue in a way that made King feel faintly ridiculous.

'If you please, sir.' And sound ridiculous, too.

'Well, now. After Jane's party I got a taxi back to the friend's where I stay when I'm in London. I did my best not to wake him, so I don't expect he'll remember. Then after breakfast I went to University College where I was supposed to be attending a seminar. It was to have been given by Paul, so you'll appreciate that the occasion was a somewhat abortive one. I seem to remember spending most of the morning making telephone calls to try and find out where he was. Without success, naturally.'

CHAPTER 13

'You look depressed,' said Taggart.

'Nothing but trouble,' said Judith. 'Every time I poke my nose above the horizon the man waiting there with a large wet fish hits me with it, hard.'

'Upset about Paul?'

'Naturally. He was my brother,' she added defensively.

'What else?'

'Nick.'

'What about him?'

'I think he's coming to the end of his patience.' She sighed. 'Or maybe I'm coming to the end of mine. It's the politics. It isn't that he disapproves—well, we'd hardly be together if he did. But he does get left holding the babies rather a lot. More and more.'

'This is the modern world.'

'In that sense, he'd have preferred the old-fashioned one. Most men would, when it comes to it.'

'Don't you have help?'

'Well, yes. But it is rather expensive, and politics doesn't exactly pay. On the contrary. And it isn't the same, Nick doesn't think. Well, it isn't. It's different. We had a terrible row about it last night. A policeman came to ask me questions about Paul, and it was the boys' tea-time, and the help had the afternoon off, so Nick had to come home early from the office and it was the last straw.'

'And what if it was him that was involved in politics?'

'Well, it isn't, it's me, and it's either him or the Peace Movement he says.'

'But you can't help Paul getting killed and the police coming to talk to you about it.'

'Well, Paul's another fly in the ointment. I mean, I would have a brother like Paul.'

'Sounds as if the fundamental mistake was getting married to Nick,' said Taggart, whose opinion this had always been.

'That's what he's beginning to think,' Judith agreed unhappily. 'And here I am abandoning Ben again to come and have lunch here with you.' She looked round her guiltily. Nick was nowhere in sight.

They were sitting in a pub called the Albion, not far from Judith's house. It was filled to bursting with a mixture of traders from Chapel Street market and the middle classes who had taken over the Georgian streets and squares between the Angel and the Caledonian Road. The clientele drank treble whiskies and ate through heaped plates of steak and kidney pie drenched in thick brown gravy. If the events of the past week had shaken them, they did not show it.

'They look like mobsters,' said Taggart. 'Mobsters with a sprinkling of Rudolf Steiner freaks.'

'That's about it. They say that half the crime in London is planned around here.'

'The half that isn't planned in Deptford.'

They sipped their whiskies. Two enormous plates of fish and chips were slammed down on the table between them. Judith picked up a chip and ate it appreciatively. She always enjoyed chips she had not cooked.

'So who do they think did it?' asked Taggart hopefully.

'No idea. He could have done it himself, of course.'

'Do you think that?'

92

Judith shook her head. 'I wish I could. The other's even worse. As for the police, they just ask questions. No knowing what they think at all. It's a man named King. He seems nice enough, but he just asks question after question after question.'

'That's his job,' said Taggart. 'I'm not sure whether it's a sign of deep stupidity or innate civilization, that the police still carry on with all this with the world about to burn up round their ears. Our ears. King, did you say his name was?'

'Yes.'

'That rings a bell.'

'I've got his card.' Judith handed it over. It was not informative. It read "Chief Inspector Brian King, MA, New Scotland Yard".

Taggart studied this for a moment. 'Brian King, MA. Wait a minute. Wait a minute—that's it. Special Branch. I knew I knew the name. I've met him myself. They make periodical little forays into my life from time to time for general intimidation purposes . . . But what the heck's the Special Branch doing investigating a straightforward murder? Was your brother a spy or something?'

'Judging from the questions he asked, I wouldn't have said he thought so. It was all about family affairs. There's enough there, one way and another.'

'I suppose it could just be the people involved,' said Taggart. 'They keep an eye on us all anyway. The Enemy Within. So much more worrying than The Enemy Without. And so much more accessible! So since they're investigating us all all the time, they might as well investigate us for this as anything else.' He sat back and considered this hypothesis. 'Well, I don't know,' he concluded. 'They're all mad. But I shouldn't like to miss an opportunity to embarrass them a bit. Would you mind if I rushed off? I'm doing the diary this week and the deadline's this afternoon. See you soon.' He stood up, smiled, and wriggled out between tweed-suited, beringed cockneys of dubious ancestry and occupation, to where his bicycle was chained firmly to a nearby tree.

Some interesting information has reached the Diary concerning police investigations into the death of right-wing bigot and self-styled thinker Paul Silverlight. These are being conducted not by the CID or the ordinary murder squad but by Chief Inspector Brian King of the Special Branch. What, we wonder, is the Special Branch doing concerning itself with what on the face of it looks like a perfectly unspectacular murder? Was Silverlight a spy with extra-specially good cover? Should this turn out to have been the case, then the mind boggles at the implications— for, as is well-known, Silverlight was a close friend of the Prime Minister herself . . .

CHAPTER 14

'Well,' said the AC, 'I see you've been getting round.'

King said, 'I expect it's that bloody little nuisance Andrew Taggart. I've met him once or twice. All these people know each other, you know. I've given him a bad time once or twice so I expect he's only too glad of an opportunity to get his own back.—But since we're talking about these things, sir,' he added hastily, seeing the AC take a breath as if he was about to speak. 'I still don't understand why it's us that's on this case. It all seems so straightforward. Any number of perfectly good commonplace motives.'

The AC said firmly, 'We have our instructions, and where they came from, we don't argue. So that's that. Maybe it's not so straightforward as you think. What do you think, anyway? Got anywhere yet?'

King shrugged. 'Hard to say. That's to say, someone has confessed to it.'

'Oh? Who?'

'Jennifer Chantrey.'

'The ex-lover?' The Assistant Commissioner sat back in his chair, plainly delighted. 'Well then, there you are.'

'I wish it were as simple as that.'

'My dear fellow, a confession's a confession. It's the best evidence there is.'

King shook his head. 'She's a drug addict. She's an in-patient in a mental hospital. Great big place near Cambridge. That's where I saw her.'

'So could she have done it?'

'She could, as it happens. She was out on a home visit at the relevant time.'

'So?'

'Well, she's a drug addict. They lie all the time. And apparently she's had this fantasy for years. Always talking about killing him.'

'And now she's done it,' said the AC. 'What could be more natural? She's got the motive. She had the opportunity. Might even still have had the key to his flat—did you check that? Poor girl, she probably wouldn't even get sent to prison. Well, she probably wouldn't be fit to plead, would she? Doesn't sound like it. Her life would hardly change. In fact, one shouldn't really say it, but she probably feels a whole lot better for having done it.'

King looked at him unhappily. It was clear what the AC wanted, and obvious how badly he wanted it. Here was the ideal solution he had been praying for. It was equally obvious that here was a chance, not so much for promotion, but one which if he let it slip would ensure his non-promotion. Anyone with the slightest degree of political nous would take the hint and wrap the case up there and then. And goddammit, thought King, it isn't that I can't see that as well as anyone. But somehow I can't do it—at least not yet. 'If you don't mind, sir, I'm still not entirely happy,' he said. 'I'd like to look into things a bit further.'

'Well,' said the AC crossly, 'I suppose I can't stop you if that's what you really think. But I'd be grateful if you'd bear in mind that the taxpayer's money is limited. We shouldn't just throw it away unnecessarily.'

'I'll be as economical as I can, sir,' said King.

MR HUGH MACPHERSON (Lab., Clydebank): Has the Rt Hon. Lady read the latest issue of *New Politics*? And can she confirm that she has not been passing information to and taking advice from a foreign agent?

THE PRIME MINISTER: Mr Speaker, I find the Hon. Gentleman's insinuations quite ridiculous and would suggest that he confines himself to reading matter of a less sensational kind in the future. (Hear, hear!)

MR MACPHERSON: But can the Rt Hon. Lady give any reason why the Special Branch should be involved in an investigation of this kind?

THE PRIME MINISTER: Mr Speaker, I have the greatest confidence in the police, and I feel it is entirely up to them to decide which of their departments should investigate any particular matter.

The Monitor, 19 April

Sources close to the Prime Minister indicate that she is 'incandescent with rage' at the suggestion that one of her close confidants may have been a spy. 'She regards the suggestion as absurd and meaningless,' say the sources, and add that although the Prime Minister takes advice from a great many different people, they are not necessarily recipients of information. These suggestions follow a report in the weekly *New Politics* that the death of Paul Silverlight, one of the leading theorists of the New Right and well-known as a confidant and adviser in Downing Street, is being investigated by the Special Branch. It is the implications of this that are worrying for Downing Street, since the Special Branch is normally confined to investigations of a political nature, while a murder investigation of this sort would normally be the concern of the CID.

'What exactly does that mean?' the chief leader-writer asked the editor.

'What it says.'

'A new Burgess or Maclean?'

'Oh, I shouldn't think so. He didn't have access to anything in particular, for a start. Unless she passed it on for comment or something. For his eyes only. That might be it, of course,' the editor said dreamily. 'Prime Minister implicated in spy ring. Oh boy, wouldn't that be wonderful!'

CHAPTER 15

'Do you mind if I have a drink?' said Jane Addison.

'Go ahead,' said King, politely inviting her to her own whisky. 'No, I won't, thanks.'

'Never drink in the course of duty?'

'That's it.' As she eyed him over the top of the glass he said, 'Look, don't let all this hullabaloo upset you. More than you already are, I mean. It means nothing at all, I assure you. Just journalists after a sensation.'

'I am a journalist.'

'Then you'll know what I mean.'

They were sitting in Jane's living-room. The silvery-green set her off well in the daytime, too. Good-looking woman, thought King. No chicken, but chickenhood was far from being the be-all and end-all in this area. Lucky old Silverlight. On this count he was inclined to believe Conder. Women certainly seemed to have a thing about him.

Jane said, 'I can't tell you how ghastly it feels. To have, well, been in bed with somebody, and then, a few hours later—'

'I can imagine,' said King, trying to do so. This milieu was new to him. He tried to imagine being in bed with Jane. It was not difficult, he found. A fly buzzed on the window-pane. 'Soon be summer,' he said in a Pollyanna tone of voice, then coughed and pulled himself together. 'I'm trying to find anything that may shed some sort of light on his movements the week before. Anything he may have said. People let things drop even if they don't discuss them.'

'Well, he'd been organizing all this Defence Through Strength stuff.'

'We know about that.' He glanced at his watch. His

appointment with Tranter was in two hours' time. Enough for a leisurely interview but not for any hanky-panky, even had such a thought crossed his mind. He was fairly certain, judging from one or two looks she had given him, that it had crossed hers.

'There was one thing,' said Jane. The fly was still buzzing on the window-pane and she glanced at it irritably. 'Must get some fly-spray,' she said. 'Didn't I read somewhere that insects are the only things that would survive a nuclear explosion?'

'One thing's certain, fly-spray won't. There was one thing?'

'I seem to remember he mentioned something about jet-lag, how he was still feeling the tail-end of it. But I don't know where he'd been. Someone came along, you know how it is at parties, and I moved on.' She held out one foot in front of her and critically inspected the varnish on her toe-nails. Today was a day when she worked from home, she had explained, but that was probably better for a chat anyway, wasn't it? She had spectacularly good legs, he agreed. 'I don't know if that's any use to you?'

'Anything may be.' He made a note.

'I can't really think of anything else. Are you sure you won't have a drink?'

'Certain, thanks.' King made his departure. He felt like a fly who has just escaped a rather tempting spider. He was rather glad the fly-spray hadn't been to hand.

Damian Tranter was waiting for him in the Defence Through Strength offices. This time there were no cordon bleu cooks. He was offered a cup of Nescafé, which he declined.

'I'm afraid there's nothing very clandestine about us,' said Tranter heartily. In his navy-blue blazer and old school tie (not being versed in these things, King was unable to say which old school it was) he looked overt enough to pass for the head of MI6 itself.

'I'm not necessarily in search of the clandestine,' said King.

'It's a great loss,' said Tranter gravely. 'A great loss.

What our movement badly needs is people able to articulate a coherent philosophy. For too long—' he studied the row of pens in his blazer pocket while contemplating the beauty of the phrase he was about to bring out—'thinking has been confused with liberal thinking. That's what we need to get across and Silverlight was the man to put it across. I'm not a great brain myself,' he explained. 'I'm more of an organizer. But I can appreciate quality when I see it and Paul had real quality.'

'Why do you think anyone would have wanted to kill him?'

Tranter leaned back expansively. King noticed that the walls of the room were panelled with wood-grain formica. Was it, he wondered, intended to approximate to the real thing, differing only in its increased durability and the uniform nature of its pattern, or was it a positive decorative statement in itself, chosen for its intrinsic appeal? 'That's for you to decide,' Tranter now said, bringing his thoughts sharply back to the matter in hand. King had the distinct impression that he had been about to add 'old man' and had bitten it back only with difficulty. 'But I really can't imagine it had anything to do with his activities here.'

'Had he been travelling anywhere recently that you knew of?'

'Now that you mention it,' said Tranter, 'I believe he did say something about America. As if he'd just been there quite recently. Is that the sort of thing you had in mind?'

'That's the kind of thing,' King agreed. He looked down his list of notes. 'Just one more thing. While I'm here. Did you lot have anything to do with that unfortunate incident at the rally? When Professor Dawes got stabbed?'

Tranter frowned. 'If you knew the number of times I've been asked that. Of course we didn't! So far, this is a war of ideas.' He faced King across his desk, chin up, eyebrows raised. A perfect shave, King noted. Either he shaved several times a day or he had very weak facial hair. Either way, he could advantageously have modelled for a shaver commercial. Perhaps he did: perhaps that was one of the mysterious sources of DTS funding.

'So far?'

'Well, it bloody nearly turned into the other kind last week, didn't it?'

'Ah, I thought you meant something else.' He looked at Tranter, who said, 'Anyway, I don't see any connection.'

'There probably isn't. Just another matter we're investigating.' King rose. 'Thank you very much, Mr Tranter. I won't take up any more of your time.'

CHAPTER 16

Andrew Taggart cycled thoughtfully along the streets leading to Primrose Hill. A light rain was falling. March winds, April showers, thought Taggart. Huh. The mythical April shower, as depicted by poets through the centuries, was a pleasure to be caught in. He had never encountered one such. Bloody cold and penetrating they usually were, especially to the cyclist. Today's was carried on a strong westerly breeze that, on a cycle, felt like storm Force 10. Nevertheless, Taggart was not tempted to abandon his bike —not even by mad motorists like the one who had all but knocked him over as he negotiated Adelaide Road, pulling out without looking, stupid bastard. Probably wrote letters every week to the *Hampstead and Highgate Express* about how dangerous cyclists were to pedestrians when they used the pavement instead of the road. However, unlike a taxi, the bicycle was always there when he needed it; unlike a car, it did not get stuck in traffic jams; and unlike a motorbike, it was not an instrument of suicide and it could travel free on a train.

Having reached his destination, which was Jane Addison's house, he dismounted and chained his steed to the railings. Taggart was on his information-gathering rounds again. From the panniers slung on either side of his saddle he produced a notebook and a pair of trousers, neatly folded. He slipped these on over his shorts and felt ready for any social encounter the next hour might have to offer.

Trouserless encounters were not what he had in mind. He was on the scent of something much more interesting, a story.

He rang Jane's bell. It was a Monday, so she was at home. He had told her nothing except that he wanted to see her. She opened the door, and he stepped in with the familiarity of ancient friendship. At the beginning of his working life Taggart had joined a training scheme run by the BBC, and there he had met Jane, who was at the time a television researcher. This, as everyone had told her, was a dead-end job. If you were no good, you remained a researcher since nobody would promote you. If you were good, nobody wanted to lose you so they did not promote you. Either way you were a loser. Jane, being intelligent, capitalized on the one great asset the job provided—contacts. One thing you did have was an opportunity to get to know everybody. One of the people she had got to know in this way was the then editor of the *Sunday Review*. Things had gone on from there. He was no longer the editor but she no longer needed his patronage. Life worked like that. Taggart, too, had failed to make his mark in television. He was too bad at politics, for one thing. He was not interested in being polite to the right people, or in keeping an eye out for the right opportunities, or in making ruthlessly for them when they presented themselves. He preferred life as a magazine journalist, where there was little need to bother with the politics which pervade all large organizations and which are the price to be paid for the security of a seat in Aunty's lap.

When Jane opened the door, therefore, he saw not the powerful lady whose patronage could help a career and whose lack of interest could destroy one, but old Jane whom he had known twenty years ago and in whose basement flat he had shared many a take-away Chinese dinner. As for him, he had changed hardly at all, either in manner or appearance, since those days. The same rather scrofulous black beard, which made one itch to squeeze the blackheads beneath; the same propensity to spit out unwanted morsels, such as bacon rinds, regardless of company or location, which made some people rather chary of being seen with him in places considered smart. Others of his friends, Jane included, always enjoyed his company, finding it made them feel younger: twenty years younger, to be precise.

'Well,' she said, 'this is an unusual pleasure. You usually do this sort of thing by phone, don't you? Or are you unusually flush for time?'

'My dear Jane, the pleasure of meeting you face to face ... any excuse ...' he murmured. 'No, as a matter of fact I may be on to something rather big and in those circumstances I don't trust phones. You never know who's listening. I know, I know, everybody likes to think their phone is tapped, but mine definitely is and for all I know so is yours. And phone-boxes are so awkward. And smelly. And it's a lovely day, or it might have been. And so on.'

'So what can I tell you? I lead a very boring life, from your point of view.'

Taggart said, 'You knew Paul Silverlight.'

'Not well,' said Jane.

'Well, shmell, what do I care? You spent the night with him, didn't you? The night before he was murdered?'

Jane slammed down the kettle she was filling. 'Look, what is this?' she snapped. 'First I get a damned policeman and now you. Presumably the whole of London's talking about it. I suppose people have to have something to gossip about. I shall just have to stop having parties.'

'Oh, don't do that. Who knows how much longer there'll be a world to have parties in, anyway? Only needs another wobble like last week. That was nearly it, I can tell you. Maximum alert at all USAF bases. Gulf crawling with nuclear subs. And the Russians knowing that the Pentagon was promising itself a first strike in those very circumstances ... Actually, the joker that released that bit of paper probably did us all a service, coming when it did. It was probably the one thing that stopped them actually doing it.'

'But how does everybody know?' wailed Jane. 'The slightest move one makes.' She pushed her hair back with a characteristic gesture, so that Taggart was reminded once again of the plump, rosy-cheeked girl he had known. The roses had gone at about the same time as the Size 14 hips, if he remembered right.

'They don't. They surmise, like me. Well, now I do know, of course. Not that it matters, as you say. The only point of interest is that the fellow was killed not very long afterwards. Don't flatter yourself—I'm not even criticizing your taste. He did have lovely blond hair. You've always gone for that, haven't you? Lucky you don't live in California or you'd never get any work done at all!'

'I was thinking that myself the other day, funnily enough.'

There was a moment's silence while they both thought about Californian blondes.

'Anyway, you mentioned a policeman. That was really why I came to see you. Was his name King?'

'That's right.'

'Ah! And what sort of thing did he seem to want to know? Anything in particular?'

'The only thing that really interested him,' said Jane, sounding rather hurt—as she was—'was when I told him that he'd been talking about feeling jet-lagged. But I'm afraid I've no idea where he'd been or if he'd been anywhere. Sorry. Is that the extent of your interest too?'

'That's it,' said Taggart. 'Thanks for the tea. I'm in an awful rush. Mind if I go now? You know how things are.' He took off his trousers, folded them neatly into the pannier and remounted his trusty steed.

In excellent mood, he cycled back to his house and made for his study. The Special Branch—indeed, King himself —had searched this room more than once in quest of illegal papers and other treasures. What they were always hoping to find was Taggart's 'contacts book—' a volume in which he would have listed for their convenience, in alphabetical order, all the people he called on for information at different times. As though, thought Taggart scornfully, anyone in his position would keep such a document!

Taggart's house was a nightmare location for any tidy-minded officer to search. It was a small terrace cottage near the New North Road, and the only parts of it not strewn with papers were the kitchen and the bathroom. Many of the papers were toffee papers, but many of the others looked very like working notes. No one was ever allowed to touch any of these papers for fear of losing them. Over-zealous girlfriends were dismissed or confined to the kitchen (which was the only place they could sit down anyway). It was Taggart's boast that he could always go straight to any piece of information he wanted, and judging by his working output, he did so with great efficiency and speed. Police officers and girlfriends alike, facing the accumulated bits of paper of years, could only admire this ability.

Its secret, had anyone been there to see, was now revealed. Looming above the sea of papers like some half-submerged rock in one of the upstairs rooms was a micro-computer. Next to it, almost invisible, stood a telephone on a table. Taggart waded towards this bank of modernity and dislodged a pile of files to reveal that the computer was standing on a desk. Extracting a disk from one of the desk drawers he inserted it in the computer, typed in a long and complex code, and a list of names and telephone numbers appeared on the monitor screen. This, had the Special Branch but known it, was Andrew Taggart's contacts book. He selected a number in Washington, DC, checked that he was in American office hours, and dialled. After a brief and non-committal conversation (you never knew who might be listening) which seemed to satisfy him, he said, 'Right, I'll see you in a couple of days,' and hung up. Then he cleared the number from the screen, switched off the computer, and walked down the road to a travel agent.

CHAPTER 17

The AC said, 'Off to America?'

'Yes, sir.'

The AC leant back in his chair. King reflected on the unchanging nature of certain situations. Even the passage of all those years had not wholly dispelled the similarity between his feelings as he faced the Assistant Commissioner and those which he recalled experiencing when summoned before the headmaster. The technique he had employed then for preserving calm in the face of impending (though unspecified) doom was the same as one he had seen recommended for delaying orgasm: he thought hard about something quite unconnected with be topic immediately in hand (so to speak). He concentrated now upon his plans for a new, improved herbaceous border in the summer (should the summer ever come). He was considering the relative merits of *gypsophila paniculata* and achillea for the space in front of the delphiniums when he heard the AC saying, 'Why America?'

'He'd just come back from there. I've got a feeling that the death may be tied up with his visit in some way.'

'Oh dear.' The AC looked and sounded pained and disapproving.

'You'd like it to be Jenny Chantrey, sir, wouldn't you? Trouble is, I'm not at all sure that it was her.' King felt rather like a man who finds himself voluntarily signing his own death-warrant.

'I get the strong feeling that people would prefer the solution to be kept in the family,' said the AC. 'And it would be so easy to keep it there.'

'People?'

'I don't really want to specify who.'

'But in that case, sir, why bring us into it in the first place? If it's all straightforward, it's all straightforward.

The AC looked faintly uncomfortable. 'That's not quite what I'm saying. If it were straightforward, then as you say, it wouldn't have been handed to us. People obviously thought it might not be. It might just be his connections— you know about that, of course—'

'Yes.' Gypsophila won on the whole, King decided. That light, airy look was what he needed there. Perhaps some red roses in front.

'So if you could bear that in mind—'

'Do they want us to find out what happened?'

'I think we'd better do that anyway. Yes,' said the AC, studying his fingernails, 'I suppose we'd better do that.'

CHAPTER 18

Taggart stood by the Pan-Am desk at Heathrow. It was
7.30 a.m. The usual mob of frustrated travellers milled
around, but the desk Taggart stood by was deserted, which
was not surprising, since the flight was not due to leave
until noon. Presently one or two other people turned up,
presumably also intending passengers. They all looked
somewhat furtive. Nobody spoke and nobody moved away.

Ten minutes passed. Taggart could stand it no longer.
'Excuse me,' he said to a middle-aged woman standing
nearby and feigning a look of nonchalance while failing to
read the morning paper, 'You don't happen to be waiting
for a Mr Honig, do you?'

The words galvanized the desultory group which had by
now assembled. The woman said eagerly, 'You aren't Mr
Honig, are you?'

Taggart had to admit that he was not. He added that,
from internal evidence—viz., that he was not available on
Friday afternoons or Saturdays—he deduced that Mr Honig
must be an Orthodox Jew, and he plainly was not that,
either. At that moment a party of Hasidim wandered by.
One passed near the waiting group. The woman said, 'Excuse me, but are you Mr Honig?' The Hasid, terrified,
scuttled away. 'Lucky next time,' said Taggart.

Just then a bearded, hatted figure swept into their midst.
A rusty black coat covered his ample paunch. 'I am Honig!'
he cried, sweeping the coat open with an expansive gesture,
and produced a handful of airline tickets from an inside
pocket. 'Who wants?' and, having distributed his largesse
to the waiting applicants, he made off in cheerful conversation with two Pan-Am officials.

Well, thought Taggart in some surprise. It works. Only
the staff of a journal as bankrupt as *New Politics* would have
to descend to such ploys in order to fly to America in the
course of business. Mr Honig, the editor assured him, was

regularly used by New Politicians on transatlantic matters. You paid an office in Piccadilly and telephoned Mr Honig in Stoke Newington the day before you needed the ticket. He provided an always available source of tickets on scheduled flights to wherever you wanted to go at stand-by rates, no notice required, no uncertainty involved. It was hard to know why everybody in the world didn't use Mr Honig.

Just over twelve hours later, Taggart knew.

The pilot was just droning that they were now commencing their descent towards New York. The flight was three hours late (well, a mere three hours, thought Taggart, a bagatelle, really. One couldn't reasonably start grumbling until the delay was six or seven hours.) The jumbo was jammed full. That, of course, was Mr Honig's job. His bargain-basement tickets made sure that no expensive space was wasted on empty seats. Any tickets unsold from his quota went straight to the stand-by desk. Ergo, all Mr Honig's flights would be full. Since most of the extra three hours had been spent waiting in the plane for takeoff clearance, this meant that three hundred-odd people had now been cooped up in it for almost ten hours. It was, naturally, now a slum. Passengers who had entered the plane looking spruce and transatlantic, with capacious bags, smartly-tailored suits and large dark glasses, now queued dejectedly for the increasingly disgusting toilets, trousers creased, shirts sweaty, hair awry. The party of Hasidim was seated just in front of Taggart. They looked very unhappy, their pasty faces and luxuriant beards, incongruous anywhere in the twentieth century, totally unreal in a jet plane. They kept saying '*Oy gevolt!*' to each other in tragic tones. Taggart wondered if they, too, had been supplied by Mr Honig at discount rates. It seemed somehow fitting that they should get their tickets back to Brownsville from Stoke Newington.

The plane landed at Kennedy after yet more delay, due this time to failure to get landing clearance. The Hasidic moans increased in volume with every ten minutes that passed. Taggart debated whether to have yet another double vodka: his mind was made up for him when the stewardess firmly told the man across the aisle (who had been drinking triple scotches all the way over and was by now barely able to speak) that the bar was closed. At this point the captain announced that they had permission to land, and the ear-splitting descent began, accompanied by howls from the Hasidim, many of whom had colds and presumably suffered earache accordingly.

They touched down. An hour and a half later, having retrieved his case and waited in the usual interminable queues in the customs and immigration hall, Taggart emerged and found the bus for La Guardia Airport, en route for the Washington shuttle.

Taggart and King only narrowly missed each other in New York Immigration. King, travelling on time with British Airways, found that the flight before his into the customs hall had come from Naples or Palermo or some such place, and was filled with small, panic-stricken Italians all unable to speak English and all having enormous amounts of baggage. The one in front of King had a large tin trunk. The customs man insisted on opening this. Inside among other things, was a plastic bag containing a live eel. The Italian looked despairing. He explained, in Neapolitan dialect, that the eel was a special delicacy, a present for his relatives, all of whom were waiting for him in the next room. The customs man, understanding not a word of this, looked nonplussed. No Italian-speaking customs man was to be found. Should he confiscate the eel? And if so, what in hell was he to do with it? The argument sounded as if it could go on for a long time. King despaired and found another queue.

He finally left the immigration hall just before Taggart entered it. How, he wondered, was he to get to Princeton? King had never been to the United States before, and the shrieking mob in the arrivals area inclined him to turn around and go straight back to Europe again. Diffidently, he mentioned the name to one or two taxi captains. They in turn mentioned it to drivers. 'Where is it?' a driver asked. 'If you know where it is, I'll take you there.' But King did not know where it was. He thought that was the kind of thing taxi-drivers knew. Not, apparently, in New York.

He looked around him. So this was New York. It was certainly loud. He could see no likely source of information as to what he should do next. In England he would have taken a train, if he did not have a car, but he felt unwilling to launch himself into the unknown perils of the American road system immediately after a tiring journey, and he had heard somewhere that there were no trains in America any more. He could, of course, ask a policeman. If he showed his card he had no doubt that, however fierce the normal inclinations of the New York cop, he would be helped. But he did not somehow like the idea of his first contact with his brother officers in the New World being in the role of supplicant.

At that moment someone tapped him on the shoulder. It was a correct-looking middle-aged man. 'Excuse me,' he said, 'but did I hear you say you wanted to go to Princeton? Would that be Princeton, New Jersey? Because if so, what you want is a limousine. Come with me. I'm going there myself.'

By the time they left Kennedy, although it was still only 7.15 p.m. New York time, King was beginning to flag. It was gone midnight for him, and it had been a long day. The limousine turned out to be a sort of minibus, shabby but not too uncomfortable. He stared out of the window at New York, which turned out to be endless lines of small brick houses lining the Long Island Expressway. Where were the skyscrapers? He craned for a sight of them. They loomed up, pale grey against the deep blue evening sky, and were quickly gone as the limo turned on to the New Jersey Turnpike. Here, where the marshes outline the toilet-roll pastel silhouettes of the oil refinery storage tanks, King dropped off, and by the time they arrived in Princeton it was dark.

Next morning Taggart knocked on a smartly-painted door on one of those streets near the Capitol where the town-houses are being reclaimed for the middle classes. Where in London the signs of gentrification are shiny kitchens visible through area windows and elegant plantings of senecio and artemisia in the just opened-up coalhole, in Washington the telltale is the number of barriers and alarms fortifying the newly resplendent residences. All the lower windows of this house were covered on the outside by wrought-iron grilles and on the inside by sliding metal shutters. The front door had several keyholes and a spyhole, and probably a small cannon mounted just inside. Some time after the knock a voice boomed out of the loudspeaker grille asking him who he was. He gave his name. There was a further wait, presumably while the occupant surveyed the outdoor scene through the spyhole. Then, cautiously, the door opened. Taggart slipped in and his host shut the door quickly behind him, in the manner of one raising the drawbridge and letting down the portcullis as expediently as possible. 'What's the rush?' asked Taggart. 'Where's the fire?'

'You live in this area a while, you'd know that's no figurative question,' replied the house's occupant reprovingly. 'There's an apartment building in the next block, some guys came in while they were having a dinner-party, raped all the women, set fire to the place and left, they still didn't catch them. It's happening every day.'

'Were you expecting to be raped?'

'I suppose not.' His host, a tall man with curly brown hair and a pleasant, epicene face, sighed regretfully. 'Still, there's a whole lot of money invested in this place and I'd hate to see it all burn up unnecessarily, know what I mean? Coffee?' He gestured towards a kitchen just visible through a small forest of housetrees.

Over the coffee Taggart said, 'Did you manage to find anything?'

'About your friend? Oh, sure, they all knew him. He was with a friend in Princeton. Name of Art Brownson. Works at the IDA. That's the Institute for Defense Analyses,' he explained. 'War games place. Very high-powered. Princeton's a great place for that sort of thing, of course. Ever been there? Oh, you'll love it. Last bastion of the old south this far north, know what I mean?'

The difficulty with his Washington friend, Taggart always

felt, was that you could never be sure whether he was being serious or not.

'Do you know Brownson?'

'Not personally. I know of him, of course.'

'Of course.'

The secret of a journalist's success is the same as that of a spy's: knowing people, and knowing people who know people. In his mind (though not on disk: not even there— who knew when one might encounter a computer-literate policeman, or rival?) Taggart had his acquaintance cross-filed. This particular friend, called on a hunch, was the key to an extensive East Coast gay network.

'And Silverlight?'

'That had been going on a while. So they say. It was the real thing. They say. A real beautiful friendship. He'll sure be sore when he hears what you've got to say.'

'H'm.' Taggart sipped his coffee and thought about this a while. Nice to score on a hunch, of course, but he couldn't see quite how it advanced his story. All the motives remained on the other side of the Atlantic.

'Anything else?'

'There was something. Only a rumour.'

'Rumour is what I'm after.'

'Rumour is that he has connections with the Company.'

'Who? Brownson?'

'Yup.'

'But surely,' said Taggart slowly, not sure how to put this tactfully, 'surely—being gay—wouldn't that—?'

'The strangest types slip in,' said his host, clearly nettled. 'Hadn't you heard about Watergate? Maybe he goes for red wigs. Anyway, it's just a rumour.'

Once again, Taggart wished he could tell when his friend was being serious.

CHAPTER 19

Contrary to King's belief, America did have trains. Andrew Taggart arrived at Princeton in one, taking the metroliner from Washington to Trenton and then changing on to the local. It would have been quicker to rent a car and drive, but he was in no particular hurry and this way was cheaper.

Arriving in Princeton by train, he was able to savour part of what his Washington friend had meant by the Old South. The approach was through thick woods. In these woods, now brilliant green in the warmth of late spring, stood shacks, and in these shacks, black people lived. White people in Princeton, however, did not live in shacks. Taggart's friend had told him, among other useful items, that Princeton contained the largest percentage of millionaires per thousand of population of any town in the States. On the main street, dominated as it was by the university campus, it was impossible to see any particular sign of this. There was, however, a definitely peculiar quality about the place. Taggart tried to analyse what it was. After consideration, he decided that it arose from the odd nature of the finish of the university buildings, or at least the older ones. These were all solid stone edifices, some with ivy and stained glass windows. Yet despite their solidity they looked like nothing so much as Hollywood flats, a film set for some Ivy League comedy, which would fall over if someone forgot himself and hit them too hard. It was the opposite of the stage illusion of cardboard made to look like solid stone. Here, the buildings were of stone to look like cardboard.

The air of unreality was further enhanced by the immaculate state of everything. This was, after all, New Jersey, home of pollution. Yet here, smooth green lawns stretched apparently to infinity, dogwoods were coming into bloom, fine trees dotted the parkland, thick woods housed not only shacks but science parks and the Institute for Advanced

Study . . . One had the distinct impression of New Jersey being kept at bay only by constant vigilance and the application of enormous numbers of dollar bills wherever necessary.

Taggart looked at his watch. Four o'clock. He felt very tired: jet-lag always caught one at this time of day. Better find somewhere to stay. The most apparent place was the Nassau Inn, set tastefully back in its square. It would cost a lot, no doubt, but it would do for a night until he had time to find somewhere more suitable. Anyway, it was where King would probably be staying, if he was here, as he might well be. Ought to be, anyhow. Taggart had rung his office just before leaving and had been told that Inspector King was away and no one could say when he would be back. Did he want to leave a message? He did not.

Taggart entered the Nassau Inn, first making sure that King was not leaving it. He would prefer not to meet him. But no King was in sight. At the reception desk a highly-finished middle-aged blonde looked at him coolly. He had the impression that he was not the class of customer the Nassau Inn preferred, though how they could tell merely at a glance it was impossible to say. They had no divine insight into his credit card holder. He inquired if they had a room? The woman was not sure. She consulted her oracle and spoke to someone on the phone. Yes, but only for one night. One night, Taggart assured her, was all he wanted. When he had his key he inquired casually if another Englishman, a Mr King, happened to be staying here. The woman consulted her oracle again. Yes, he was. 'Is he a friend of yours?' she asked. 'If so, you'll be pleased to know that he's in the very next room to yours.'

Savouring this intelligence with mixed feelings, Taggart mounted to his room, cautiously surveyed the corridor, let himself quickly in, lay down on the bed and fell deeply asleep.

CHAPTER 20

King at this moment was actually sitting in the adjoining room, wondering what to do next.

He, too, would have liked to go to sleep. But he did not feel he ought to do so. King was a conscientious man. The social conscience which had been awakened in his student days, and which had led him into the police force because he thought he might be able to do some good there, had not been stifled even by several years in the Special Branch. He was not stupid nor unambitious, and so not inclined to disregard promotion when opportunities beckoned; and community policing was not the way to the top ranks of the force. Nor was he corrupt, which was why he was not really interested in CID work. That was too like belonging to a club in which there was very little difference between hunters and hunted. When new acquaintances, on finding out what he did for a living, expressed their surprise, he pointed out that a man has to do something, and this was more interesting than most jobs: as witness, here he was sitting in the Nassau Inn at the taxpayers' expense. The job took him away from home a lot, of course, but he found he regretted that less and less—and so, he suspected, did Janine. Why, then, did they not divorce? Well, why should they? They had arrived at this more or less satisfactory arrangement, and in fact got on quite well provided they did not see too much of each other. Which they did not. He would have liked to see more of the children—of course: though, as they got older, there was less and less of the 'of course' about it. He had loved them when they were small, but the bigger they got, the less attractive he found them. As with his wife, he was glad to have them—at a distance. So here he was. And since this was costing the taxpayer a bomb, which might or might not be justified in these dark days and which he could not help feeling the curious figure of Paul Silverlight scarcely merited, then the taxpayer ought to get value for money. But in what, exactly, did that presently consist?

His position here was distinctly anomalous. If he did find something out, then it had been made pretty clear that nobody would want to know, unless it fitted certain patterns which suited them. And what were those? He did not know exactly: and did not want to know, since his job was to find out the truth. What other people then did with it was up to them—he had managed to acquire that much cynicism, at least. But he would prefer not to know for certain that his work was going to be discarded, before it was even complete. There was also, as he was aware, a more worrying aspect to this. If people really didn't want something found out, and if they were the people he was beginning to think they might be, then his own position was none too clear and possibly none too safe. He ought to look out. Quite what for, he couldn't say—that was just the trouble.

At least it was quite clear what he ought to do first. He was here to see the person who had written to Silverlight signing himself 'Art', and whose address had turned out to be that of one Arthur Brownson, who worked at the Institute for Defense Analyses. That much had been easy enough to find out, and a quick glance through the Princeton telephone directory had given him both Brownson's home telephone number and that of the IDA. He would certainly prefer to call him first of all at home. One didn't want to embarrass or antagonize people needlessly, and an unknown foreign policeman ringing the IDA would hardly be exercising the height of discretion. But Brownson was not yet home. So what now? He felt tired, but did not want to go to sleep yet. He guessed this must be jet-lag, and determined not to let it affect him. That much at least he could do for the taxpayer. He would take a shower and go out for a stroll round the town. Maybe he would even find the street where Brownson lived.

Of course King quickly found Brownson's house. Princeton is a small place, and that was why he had gone for a walk —to find it, by chance. It turned out to be a two-storey, wood-framed place, nineteenth or early twentieth century, graceful enough, as such houses are, and despite the simplicity of its white-painted exterior probably extremely expensive to rent or buy. There was a light in the front window, and as King watched, a figure moved across it—doubtless Brownson himself.

This put him in a quandary. It was not part of the plan. He was tired, and, not having contacted his quarry at home, had not expected to be faced with him in the flesh this evening. Of course he could perfectly well have returned in the interval between King's telephone call and now—had evidently done so, indeed.

Well, at least he was in town. That was something. But what now? The answer to this question was of course obvious. King had come here in order to interview Brownson. He should now do so. But he did not feel like it. He was tired. Duty, however, called. If he went back to the hotel now he would be plagued by conscience, and by worries that, although he was in town today, there was no guarantee that Brownson would be here tomorrow. He might be going on holiday, or on a business trip. No time like the present. King's better self won. He found himself ringing the front door bell.

The door was opened by a youngish man, slight, with dark hair just beginning to recede. He might have been Italian. He had a small moustache. For some reason King was taken aback. This was not what he had been expecting, though what he had been expecting he would have found it hard to say. What he in fact said was, 'Mr Brownson?'

'That's right,' the young man said. 'Who are you?'

King showed his identification and said, 'I'm over here in connection with an inquiry I'm conducting into the death of Paul Silverlight. I believe he was a friend of yours.'

'Paul!' the young man said. 'Dead?' He seemed stunned. 'You'd better come in.' He held the door open and King went inside.

It was his first sight of an American domestic interior, and he was struck by the enormous amount of greenery it contained. Every corner, every surface, seemed to be occupied by a plant, so that the effect was of living in a sort of

116

jungle. Between the plants, items of expensive equipment could be made out—a bank of hi-fi, a word-processor, a large painting. Brownson said, 'You'd better sit down,' and King looked round for a chair. All he could see were two enormous sofas covered in pale leather. These seemed somehow unsuitable for the business in hand, but there was nowhere else to sit. He sat on one, Brownson faced him on the other. 'Now,' said Brownson, 'you'd better tell me what this is about.'

King explained what had happened.

'But why are you here?' Brownson demanded. 'He died over there, the reason's over there. Wouldn't you say?'

King said that no satisfactory explanation had yet presented itself "over there". Somewhere in the house a wind-chime sounded, a tone reminiscent of San Francisco in the late 'sixties. Evidently Brownson was not as young as he looked. Someone had once remarked to King that you could date the adolescence of any woman by the style of her make-up. A new theory: date the adolescence of a university professor by his knick-knacks . . .

'But what do you want me to tell you?' Brownson demanded. 'I don't see what I can tell you.'

'I want to know if you'd seen him recently. I have reason to think that you had, or obviously I wouldn't be here. And if you did meet I'd be grateful if you'd describe the meeting in detail,' King said. He had the uncomfortable feeling that he had lost the initiative in this interview—that somehow it was he who was being questioned.

'I'm sorry,' Brownson said. 'I don't have to talk to you, and I really don't think I will. For one thing I'm sure it's irrelevant and for another I'm not feeling very pro-British just now. You guys just seem to fuck us up any way you can. Don't you realize how dangerous things are just now? In fact the whole idea of conducting a homicide investigation at this moment seems totally bizarre. Jesus, what does one guy matter, even if it is Paul, when the whole human race is being juggled by a load of stupid Arabs and Commies?'

'I thought that was all over,' said King uncomfortably. He had lost the initiative again.

'Take it from me, it isn't,' Brownson said. 'And I'm in a position to know. It would have been all over if your intelligence services weren't as leaky as sieves.'

'Speaking as a part of those services,' said King, 'we might be more efficient if we received help from those quarters where we might expect it.'

'I don't see what call your intelligence services have to be investigating anything to do with Paul,' Brownson said. 'He's one of the few Brits I've met who was politically sound. You guys just don't realize what's happening in the world. I suppose he was killed by some Commie. Europe's just full of Commies. Haven't you got your hands full over there?'

'I'm not here to take part in a political discussion, Mr Brownson. I'm asking for your help in an investigation.'

Brownson said, 'I told you, I'm not interested in discussing anything. Do you have an official authorization for all this?'

King said, 'Well, I—'

'OK, you don't,' said Brownson. 'You can't make me talk and I'm not interested in talking. Sorry.' He got up and walked towards the door, opened it politely and held it for King. 'I'd like to help you but I really don't think I can. Enjoy your stay.'

King remained sitting. 'If you won't talk to me, then I shall have to call on my colleagues over here. You won't be able to ignore them quite so easily, Mr Brownson.'

'Do what you like. If I haven't anything to tell, then they can't very well make me tell it, can they? And now if you don't mind—' he consulted King's card—'Mr King, I have work to do. Have a nice day.'

King walked thoughtfully back to the hotel. He would have put a lot of money on the proposition that Brownson was feeling worried, even guilty about something— and something not unconnected with Paul Silverlight. But what?

CHAPTER 21

Taggart woke early the next morning. Looking at his watch, he saw to his horror that it was half past five. He was wide awake: no use staying in bed. He got up and had a leisurely bath. That took him to six o'clock. Well, lots of Americans got up at six o'clock. It was one of the many deeply uncivil-ized aspects of American society, but it did at least mean that he ought to be able to pick up breakfast somewhere.

Sure enough, a restaurant along the street was just open-ing up. The burly proprietor, white, with a wide Slavic face, was yawning and pouring himself a cup of coffee. The cook, black, was heating his griddle. This division of labour was very noticeable in Princeton. It embarrassed Taggart some-what, and had presumably been part of what his Washington friend had meant by that cryptic remark. Everyone here seemed to accept it as normal.

Taggart ordered eggs, bacon and hash browns and ate them slowly while he thought what he would do next. That took him up to a quarter to seven. It was a lovely day. The sun was well up in a clear blue sky, the dogwoods looked freshly washed (they probably were freshly washed, by diligent blacks wielding enormous hoses), the wooden fronts of the houses were fresh with white paint. He decided to walk around to see if he could find another hotel and/or the Institute for Defense Analyses.

He found the IDA first. It was situated some way from the rest of the campus, in a field surrounded by a high wire fence. Taggart vaguely remembered reading about it in connection with the student anti-Vietnam war protests in the early 'seventies. Nothing much had happened — nothing much in the radical line ever did happen at Princeton, perhaps the most reactionary of the Ivy League universities — but the authorities had been sufficiently outraged by the mild sit-down around this establishment and the campus police had waded in. Taggart at that time had been a student

119

reporter spending the summer covering the American protests: he had been assured that it was not worth coming to Princeton. Since those days the IDA had faded back into the obscurity it preferred. It was a nondescript-looking place —as why should it not be? They weren't likely to decorate it with a mural of missiles. At this hour there were only one or two cars there, no doubt belonging to cleaners.

He was standing peacefully contemplating this scene when he felt a tap on his shoulder and, turning, found himself facing a very wide policeman with a flash on his shoulder reading CAMPUS POLICE. No doubt one of the very ones who had helped clear away the demonstrators all those years before. He looked like a man whose heart was in his job. 'This is private property, mister,' he said.

'Really?'

'Really.'

'I would have thought that began inside the fence.'

'You would of thought wrong.'

'I was just looking,' said Taggart, feeling like an injured innocent. He hadn't even been thinking of taking photographs—the place was too boring for that.

'Then just look somewhere else. You don't work here, do you? I thought not. Sorry, mister, it's just a rule. Nothing to do with me. Why, you might be a Soviet spy, mightn't you?' His hand was on his holster as he spoke. Taggart shrugged: there was no point arguing and no reason to bother. Issues of principle (this is a free country, isn't it? I thought that's what this place was all about, defending freedom . . .) were not going to weigh highly with the wide officer. So he smiled sweetly, said, 'Have a nice day,' and strolled off in the direction of the town. When he looked back, the policeman was still staring after him. He waved and continued on his way. So much for the IDA.

One of the town's many coffee-shops had now opened up, so he took the opportunity of going in to have a coffee and ask if they knew a hotel that was not the Nassau Inn. Even if he had been able to stay longer he would have felt disinclined to do so, not only because of the proximity of King but because last night the place had echoed into the small hours with the hoots of carousing Princetonians, evidently the place's hallowed customers (unlike him). He saw no reason why tonight should be different. What he wanted was somewhere smaller and shabbier. The coffee-shop knew of somewhere a little way out of town. He went back to the Inn, called it up and booked a room for the night. Sometime today he would rent a car. But that could wait. First, he would try and see Brownson. He glanced at his watch. Still only eight o'clock. He looked up Brownson in the book and dialled his number.

A voice said, 'Hello.'

'Mr Brownson?'

'Who is this?' said the voice testily.

'My name's Andrew Taggart,' said Taggart in his most smoothly ingratiating tones—those which every journalist adopts instinctively when trying to persuade a reluctant interviewee. ('The thing is, this will all be most tremendously beneficial . . .') 'I'm a journalist and I'm over here on a story and I'd be most awfully grateful if you could spare me a moment or two to come and see you.' He noticed himself becoming excessively British, another uncontrollable reaction when in the United States.

'I don't think I have a moment today.'

'Tomorrow, then.'

'Or tomorrow.' The voice sounded curt. At any moment he would hang up. Taggart cursed. Undoubtedly King had been round there already, stamping all over the pitch with his great copper's clodhoppers. Quickly he said, 'I've got an urgent message for you from the Company.'

There was a pause while Brownson considered the import of this cryptic sentence. Then he said 'All right, come round now. But be quick. I'm a very busy person. I take it you're in Princeton?'

'At the Nassau Inn.'

'And no doubt you know where I live. I'm surprised you're not calling from across the street. That's what most journalists do, isn't it?' And he hung up.

Taggart checked with the desk the whereabouts of Brownson's street. During the short walk he pondered his best line of approach. Whatever it was, he hoped it wouldn't be King's. That, clearly, had induced no spirit of friendly cooperation. Having got this far, he found that he had arrived.

It was some time before the door opened in response to his ring. Either Brownson had been in the lavatory (nerves?) or he wanted to induce nerves in his interlocutor, for example by making him wonder if he had used the lapse between phone call and now to make his escape to the IDA, where experience had already shown that he was likely to be unapproachable, should that be his wish.

'Mr Taggart?'

'That's me.'

Brownson motioned him inside, then sat down and picked up a cup of coffee. He did not offer Taggart any, an omission which Taggart, who felt awash with coffee, did not regret. He sat down himself, brought out a notebook and pen from his pocket, and smiled at Brownson. He had found that people for some reason felt reassured by the production of these antediluvian tools of the journalist's trade. Brownson, however, was different. 'If you're planning to interview me, I'd prefer a tape-recorder,' he snapped.

'Sure.' Taggart rummaged in his briefcase and found his recorder and a new tape. He loaded and tested it: all in order. He set it running. 'OK?'

'We'll see.' Brownson indicated the machine. 'I'd rather you didn't have it running just yet.'

Taggart pretended to switch it off.

'I really don't know why you're so worried by me, Mr Brownson,' he began. 'I don't think we've ever met, have we? I mean, I don't think you have any occasion for personal resentment, surely?'

'Nope.'

'I suppose Inspector King's been here,' said Taggart resignedly. 'He really isn't very subtle.'

Brownson looked black. 'Look, you told me you were a journalist. I agreed to see you. But now it seems you're a policeman. Well, you can just get the hell out of here. I'm not interested.'

122

Taggart held up his hands in horror. 'Me a policeman! Perish the thought! Mr Brownson, I assure you King's an old enemy of mine. He's in the Special Branch. A poor thing, but our own. He's utterly honest, which you'll agree is a drawback in any policeman, and quite stupid. I don't expect he asked you anything very pertinent at all, and if he was impertinent, well, it was quite without meaning to be. I've often wondered how he got so far in the force, and I've come to the conclusion that it's because there are so few honest coppers that some of them have to get promoted just to show that it isn't an actual disqualification.' He took a deep breath and went on quickly, 'I know he's here because he has the room next door to me at the hotel. He doesn't know I'm here because the idea hasn't crossed his mind. I will admit that we're both interested in the same story.'

'And that is?'

'Paul Silverlight's death, of course!' Taggart sounded surprised. 'Surely he told you that?'

'We told each other very little.'

'Ah, so he was here!' One thing established, at least. 'Well, Paul Silverlight, who I believe was a friend of yours, is dead. Murdered. Did he tell you that?'

Brownson nodded. Through the closed demeanour it seemed to Taggart that he was very upset, a curious reaction, Taggart thought, to the death of Silverlight. Taggart said, 'I'm a friend of his sister. She told me about it.'

'I didn't even know he had a sister.'

'They hadn't seen a lot of each other recently. They— diverged politically. Silverlight was considered quite an extremist in Britain, you know.'

'A kind of William F. Buckley, huh? Well, you guys can just do with some people like that, it sometimes seems to me. Thing about Buckley, he's a whole lot cleverer than most other people.'

'And so was Paul, is that what you're saying? You're probably right. Anyway, he got killed, and when people came to think about it, they weren't so very surprised.'

'Why? That's a terrible thing to say about anybody.'

'Because,' said Taggart patiently, 'there were really a large number of people with very good reasons for hating him. I won't go into them here, but take my word for it. I shouldn't think he told you much about certain aspects of his life.'

'All I know is, he was a real sweet guy. And here you are saying these terrible things. I don't know why I don't just pick you up and throw you out.'

'Because you're too interested in what I have to say!'

'I can tell you one thing I have to say. It's what I said to King. If there are so many good reasons for Paul to have been murdered back there, then why are you guys over here? Why don't you just get back home and get on with the job like good little sleuths?'

'Because none of them did it!'

'Do you think I did? Because let me tell you, brother—'

'I don't. Of course I can only speak for myself, but I doubt whether King does, either. As I say, I'm not in his confidence. For all I know, he was at a dead end with the obvious things, found that Silverlight had recently been over here, and came over on the offchance to have a look.'

'But you didn't.'

'Not quite.' Taggart considered. What exactly had it been? 'Well, the other things were all personal. Personal matters, mostly to do with an old love-affair where he'd behaved quite stunningly badly. I'm not even sure he realized quite how badly he did behave. He was such a theoretical sort of fellow, wasn't he? Theories about everything. It wouldn't surprise me if he even had theories about sex, the lower role of women, something like that.'

'Very likely. He didn't like women a whole lot,' said Brownson drily.

'Just so. But as things turned out, it seemed less and less probable that it was anything to do with that. So what would it have been?'

'You're asking me?'

'Not really. It must have been to do with his politics. After all, that was the only other contentious thing about him. He wasn't involved in any crime, so far as I know.'

'You'd better ask your policeman.'

'That's another point. The fact that it's him. Normally you'd just use an ordinary cop to look into something like this. But King's in the Special Branch. I know, because I've met him myself sometimes in the way of business, as you might say. That's the political side, and it means that there's some political angle to all this, though I've no idea what it might be.'

Taggart looked over towards Brownson. The other man's hands were clenched and his knuckles were white, though his face was relaxed and quite without expression. Clearly for him this was one of those occasions when it would have been useful to be a smoker, thus providing not only a screen behind which to hide but a meaningless occupation for hands and features. However, it was out of the question that Brownson would smoke. Every detail in his house proclaimed a wholefood-eating, bicycling, jogging, anti-smoking health freak—not least the total absence of ash-trays. Such silent statements take on in America a positive force that they have never acquired in Europe, which is altogether more easy-going about the physical self.

Brownson said 'So? How does all this involve me?'

'Let's look,' Taggart said expansively, leaning back on to the padded blond leather, 'at recent political activities which may have got someone worked up. Silverlight's and others. You've got to admit there's been plenty going on.'

'I'll admit that freely. But what's been going on, as you put it, has been rather larger than Paul, wouldn't you say?'

'No doubt about it,' said Taggart cheerfully. 'Still may be, wouldn't you say? All those peacekeeping chaps knocking around there with—battlefield nuclear weapons, isn't that the technical term? And the Russians really wishing like hell that the Iranians would go ahead and block the strait, or that Iran and Iraq would bomb hell out of each other's oilfields. Seems to me that if I were Russian that would suit me down to the ground. But,' he said, wagging a finger, 'but, but, but. First things first. It may have been a coincidence or it may not, but there was a sort of forerunner to the events in the Gulf, and that was the disclosure of US policy with

125

regard to pre-emptive strikes. Remember? Well, my impression is that that has affected the course of events recently quite substantially—though you would know far more about that than I do. And it's going to have made a lot of people very cross indeed. Wouldn't you say?'

Making a visible effort, Brownson stood up. He crossed to the window and stood looking at the activity in the street, which was increasing as the morning wore on. Stationwagons full of children and dogs were being driven up it by housewives bound for the nearby school; after a detour to the supermarket they would return laden with oreo cookies and Pampers and the checkout booklets on how to eat more and stay slim. It could be said that they typified what pre-emptive strikes were being planned to save. A few students wandered up and down, but this was not really their territory: the fraternity houses were not in this street, it had no shops and was not very near the campus. Music boomed from some open windows. The toilet-roll oil refineries might have been a million miles away; the shacks in the woods, in another world.

Brownson said, with his back to the room, 'That really is ridiculous. You can't seriously think Paul had anything to do with that? Quite apart from anything else, just look at his politics, man!'

Taggart said, 'I'm not thinking anything. I'm just surmising about the possible.' He looked inoffensive and insignificant, sitting quietly on the sofa scratching his rather ragged little beard. He appeared quite at home, which might have seemed curious considering his unkempt and even grubby appearance. This was a place inhabited by people who cared about appearances. But (one could imagine the censorious *New Politics* leader) did they ever give a thought to anything else? Taggart, however, did not seem even mildly censorious, only interested. He was actually at this moment dreaming of digestive biscuits, a staple food of his and one which he found stimulated the brain better than anything else. When he wanted to think quickly Andrew Taggart always made a beeline for the biscuit packet. He had not so far found any acceptable American substitute, no cookies on this side of the Atlantic achieving the necessary combination of mealiness and subtle lack of sweetness. He did not anyway feel that he could ask Brownson for a cookie, of whatever sort.

'And what makes you think that was possible?' inquired Brownson, still staring out of the window. There were no curtains, just bamboo blinds, now rolled up. It really was a 'sixties sort of decor.

'It's not so much a question of politics as of access,' Taggart said mildly, watching his interlocutor's back stiffen.

'And what do you mean by that, exactly?'

'Oh, you know what I mean. Coming here. Knowing you.'

'I'd be very careful what you say if I were you, Mr Taggart,' said Brownson. 'This may be getting actionable.'

'Don't be silly,' said Taggart reasonably, using a tone of voice and a phrase guaranteed to induce near hysteria in any interviewee, most of all this one. Curiously enough, this was not the intended effect. Some people found this ineptness endearing. 'Let's consider a scenario,' he went on. 'It's just a possibility. There must be thousands, but let's try this one. Silverlight comes over for a holiday—combined business and pleasure, perhaps. He comes to stay with you. Off you go to work one day and Paul's left here by himself to root around.'

'He would never have done a thing like that.'

'Why not? Was he devoid of normal curiosity, d'you think? It's the first thing I'd do, and I bet you would too. Or perhaps it's only decadent Europeans that do these things. Anyway, he finds this piece of paper and maybe he's genuinely horrified or maybe he thinks he'll help you with your war games and fly a genuine kite and see what happens or maybe he's just feeling in a mischief-making mood. I don't know. I don't know if the piece of paper was genuine, either, but it must have looked pretty genuine to take everyone in, even if it wasn't. So he helps himself, or maybe he just takes it down the road and photocopies it. Actually, come to think of it, I suppose it wasn't genuine, because even if you had access to that sort of thing, you wouldn't just leave it lying around where anyone could find it, would you? Unless it was partly your idea of course. Motivation the same, but you actually hand it over to him. In fact that seems almost more probable, don't you think? At any rate, he takes it home and sends it off, with the result we've all seen. Wow! So either someone who has some idea of what may have been going on gets very angry and bumps him off, or else he never realized it would be so awful, honestly, Mum, and can't bear another moment of it. How about that?'

'Tell me more. You're a talented storyteller, Mr Taggart.'

'Thanks. Actually, there's something I would rather like to know and I wondered if you might be able to help me. You see, I don't know how it looks to you, but it does rather seem to me that an awful lot of people miscalculated in this affair.Thought people hadn't got bombs when they had, that sort of thing. I mean, most people didn't think Iraq had it, because the Israelis were supposed to have dealt with that. And obviously nobody thought Iran had it. Well, what could be more satanic than the bomb? I just wondered if anybody really did know. I mean, you'd know that sort of thing, in your set-up, wouldn't you?'

After a moment—considering whether to answer? what to answer?—Brownson said, 'We'd have a good idea.'

'So did people know?'

'About the Iraquis?' Brownson shrugged. He seemed more relaxed now, back in the familiar framework of his job, perhaps. 'Yeah, we guessed they had something. Probably still have. That wasn't very large, the device they exploded over Qum. If they had enough stuff to make that, they had enough to make more than that. Iran, that's another matter. The Shah wanted bombs, of course. Ordered a whole bunch of nuclear power stations to get the plutonium. His Energy Minister, guy named Fesharaki, was horrified. Explained to His Imperial Majesty that Iran was flaring enough natural gas each day to give the country all the power it needed. The Shah told him to mind his own business and said that what he really wanted was bombs. So Fesharaki and some other guys wrote him a letter explaining that if you wanted bombs, there were a whole lot more efficient ways to get them. Then the revolution came and Fesharaki kept pretty quiet. Then one day the phone rings and it's some guy saying the Ayatollah wants to see him. So he says his prayers and sets out, thinking, This is it. But it turns out that the Ayatollahs have found his letter to the Shah, and what they want is a holy Islamic bomb, and Fesharaki is the guy to get it for them. So he says all right, but he'll have to find all his colleagues, and most of them are either dead or out of the country. So they give him an exit visa to Sweden, and off he goes and never comes back. He's in the States now, which is how we know all about it. When he left, they weren't nearly there. Didn't have the plutonium, for one thing. They must have been working on it since.'

'Well, it's not that hard to get plutonium, is it?' said Taggart. 'I was reading something the other day about all the plutonium that's officially missing from nuclear installations. It's enough to make a person's hair stand on end. A few grammes here, a kilo there. You only need a little patience and a lot of boodle.'

'Sure,' said Brownson, getting up. 'However. All this is nothing but speculation, right? And you can speculate till you're blue in the face, but you can't prove a thing.'

'Not a thing,' Taggart agreed cheerfully. 'That isn't my job. I'm not a policeman, you see.'

'No, you're just a two-bit gossipping snooper,' Brownson said. 'And if you publish a word of this I'll have you in court so fast you won't know what hit you and you won't have a cent left afterwards. That, I promise you.'

'The thing is,' said Taggart, 'I haven't a cent anyway. And you'd have to prove it wasn't the truth, wouldn't you, anyway?' He began packing up his things. 'That's what you do all day, isn't it?' he asked. 'Fly kites?'

CHAPTER 22

Taggart wandered away towards the Nassau Inn. It was now mid-morning, ten o'clock, and the streets were full of people, purposefully on their business or just strolling in the strong spring sunlight. The day seemed as if it might become almost hot. On the campus magnolias shone expensively. Boys in thick-soled shoes and checked trousers called to immaculately-laundered girls.

Taggart noticed none of these things. His mind was intent on his tape-recorder, lurking in his briefcase, the battery still running. He hadn't liked to touch it before leaving Brownson's. The defence analyst was angry and worried enough already without putting the wind up him still further and possibly inciting him to violence. Taggart hoped that the machine had caught enough of the conversation. He had left the case a little open and placed it a little in front of him, in as advantageous a position as he could, but he had had of course to be careful there, too.

He was just crossing the street which led to the square on which the hotel fronted when a car seemed to swerve towards him, nearly knocking him over. It happened too suddenly for him to jump clear, but the car just missed him, as if the driver had lost his nerve at the last moment in some homicidal game of chicken. Taggart was too surprised to catch more than a glimpse of the driver, who was nothing more than a dark head—but then, in some lights, fair heads may look dark when glimpsed in the driver's seat of a car. As for the car, it was medium-sized and, he thought, red—probably. It might have been a genuine piece of bad driving. It might have been a mistake, and the driver so rattled that he obeyed his first instinct, to drive off as fast as he possibly could. Or it might not, in which case the sooner he put distance between himself and Brownson the better.

Hadn't he realized, Taggart wondered, that (tape-recorder or no tape-recorder, and of course as far as Brownson was concerned there was no record, either aural or written, of their conversation)—nothing could ever be proved? No one, except possibly Brownson, had actually seen Silverlight take the paper, had ever talked to him about such a paper—maybe connived with him? Who could tell? Only Brownson, and one of the few certainties of this matter was that he was never going to tell anything.

Not, one might reasonably suppose, that anyone actually needed to prove anything for Brownson to feel worried. The mere suggestion, if well-founded, might well be enough to lose him his job. He had certainly seemed rattled enough. At the end, just before Taggart left, when he was standing up ready to go, Brownson suddenly lost his cool, up till then so ostentatiously preserved. He said, 'I must be mad. Here you are standing in my house making preposterous suggestions, and here I actually talk to you as if you had the slightest right to be here. Hell, I don't even know how you got here. Unless you're some sort of undercover agent, but you don't act professional enough for that. Can't a person come over and visit with a friend any more without everyone in the world knowing all about it? You weren't a friend of Paul's. I don't have to be any kind of detective to figure that out. So how did you even know he was here? I don't believe he ever told anybody he was coming to see me.'

'I have my sources,' Taggart said. 'You know journalists never reveal their sources. It's a cliché. Let's just say, someone like Silverlight, someone always notices him.' He finished shutting his briefcase, straightened up and said, 'Thanks for your help, Mr Brownson. If I can ever help you in any way, feel free to call me.'

'The one way you can help me is by keeping quiet.'

'Ah well, that's the one thing I can't promise.'

After his near encounter with the car, Taggart felt quite shaky. There was nothing he would have liked more than to sit down in the Nassau Inn's pleasant coffee-shop for a quiet cup of tea. But that would probably be unwise. He went to his room, put his things together, came down and paid his bill. He remembered to look carefully both ways every time he entered a new space, but luck was with him and he did not see King: nor, as far as he could ascertain, did King see him. Then he found the nearest car rental company, rented himself the smallest car he could and drove, not towards the hotel where he had booked in for the coming night, but towards Washington.

He found his friend in. When he knocked on the door and, after the usual rigmarole, it opened, he was greeted with a dismayed cry. 'Andrew! Did something go wrong? I didn't expect to see you again so soon! What happened? Are you going to tell me?'

Taggart shut the door carefully behind him, put down his briefcase and got out the recorder. Then he led the way into the kitchen and they both sat down while he played his tape. The briefcase had muffled the sound scarcely at all.

The machine fell silent. Taggart said, 'And then I think he tried to kill me. At least someone tried to run me down in the street, and I can't think of anyone else in Princeton who would want to do that. So I thought I'd better hop it, fast.'

'Are you sure you weren't followed?' asked his friend anxiously.

'Quite sure.'

The tall man was walking up and down thoughtfully. He had picked up a watering-can and was watering the potted greenery as he passed, automatically stopping to pick off a dead leaf here, cluck over a trace of greenfly there. He said, 'I wouldn't be too sure that it's necessarily just Brownson gunning for you.'

'Why, who else? Nobody else even knows I'm here.'

'Maybe.' The tall man did some more walking, some more watering. 'What strikes me is that you probably got why Silverlight was killed. What you didn't get is who killed him.'

'So who did? Since you sound as if you're so sure.'

'Well,' said his friend, 'I should imagine it was the CIA, wouldn't you?' He put down the watering-can, which was now empty, and sat down. 'Look at it this way. Someone like Brownson gets watched, right? All those guys that have

132

access to stuff like that get watched, and since he came out of that closet, you can be real sure they watch him real hard. So they know as well as I do that Silverlight was there. Hell, if I know it, they know it. So when the leak happens, they have a pretty good idea where it might have come from. Right?'

'Sounds plausible.'

'It is plausible. So what do they do next? Well, it's too late to stop the leak. Too bad. But it's not too late to make an example of someone. Right? So that's what they do. And when you and this policeman come along with this story, why, I imagine our friend Brownson catches on real fast. He can guess what happened. Don't flatter yourself, friend. Brownson's just as shit-scared as you thought he was, but it isn't just all on account of you. But you are right about one thing,' he went on thoughtfully. 'You sure are right to feel scared yourself.'

CHAPTER 23

By the time Taggart returned from Brownson's house to the Nassau Inn, King had left for his own morning's investigations. He, too, had awoken early on account of the jet-lag, but, unlike Taggart, had rather enjoyed the sensation of lying lazily in bed conscious of the fact that nobody knew where he was. When he could lie no longer he got up and took a leisurely bath. Then he glanced at his watch and was horrified to see that it was still only seven-thirty. He dressed, and went down to breakfast.

King did not think much of the Nassau Inn. He had never much gone for the olde, but at least in England it was generally old as well. Not that there was any intrinsic virtue in that, but it did give a certain underpinning of authenticity. King had not known what to expect of America, but (he now realized) he had not expected the olde, with which Princeton was encrusted—being, of course, by American standards, thoroughly old as well.

Over his hot cakes and maple syrup he pondered his situation.

Pointless returning to Brownson without something solid to confront him with. But what? There was something, he was sure, but he didn't yet know what it was. Well, there was a short cut to that: he could call his opposite number in the CIA and see if they knew anything. There was a man he knew, Kowalsky, whom he had helped out more than once in a similar situation. He got out his Filofax diary and looked in the address section at the back. Yes, he had a number for Kowalsky. Well, that was one thing to do. He glanced at his watch. Eight-thirty. Just about the time to call. Kowalsky was the kind of person who gets to the office on time—always supposing he was at the office.

He was in luck: Kowalsky was at Langley and happy to talk to him. They exchanged greetings, compared notes on their wives and families, and finally got down to business. 'Well, Brian,' said Kowalsky. 'So what can I do for you? I take it this isn't just a social call or a vacation trip.'

King could picture him sitting there at the other end of the phone, the wide, pock-marked face set in an expression of earnest endeavour. Kowalsky was very serious about his work. He explained briefly why he was in Princeton.

'I get it. You want to know if there's anything on Silverlight or this guy Brownson, right?'

'What I need is something to back up this feeling I've got,' King said. 'You know what I mean.'

'Leave it with me,' Kowalsky said. He would get the files, if there were any, and call right back.

King sat back and waited. He had bought a *New York Times*, and now he would have time to read it. There was certainly a lot of it to read.

Time passed slowly, as it does under such circumstances. King glanced at his watch. Ten minutes. Well, it shouldn't take more than half an hour to find out if there was anything there or not. He turned to Section 2 and read that for ten minutes. Still nothing. He looked out of the window. It was a lovely day. He would have liked to go for a stroll, but felt he shouldn't leave the room in case the phone rang. He had brought a book with him, Neville Cardus on cricket, one of his favourites, but it all seemed so far away from here that he found himself quite unable to take it in. He looked at his watch again. Three-quarters of an hour. What on earth was Kowalsky doing? He picked up the telephone and called Langley again.

'Hello, Dick? Brian here again. Look, I'm going to have to go out soon. I wondered how you were doing.'

Kowalsky was embarrassed. 'Brian, I'm sorry, but there seems to be a stopper on this one.'

'What d'you mean, a stopper?' But he knew, before Kowalsky told him.

'Well, you know, Brian, a stopper. There may be files, but they've been lost and somebody just doesn't want them found. I'm sorry. I'm surprised it didn't get through to your end before you came here. You must have had authorization, right?'

'Sort of.' King recalled his conversation with the AC.

'Well, that's that. Better luck next time. I suppose you'll be going back to England now?'

'I suppose so.'

'Well, just in case you were thinking different—I can tell you one thing. They aren't just not helping. They're hindering, Brian. They're hindering, and that means, keep right off if you know what's good for you.'

'Thanks anyway. Look, Dick, just one thing. Do you know what's behind this?'

'I don't,' Kowalsky said, 'and I didn't ask. Just the sort of attitude I guess you should take. Good luck, anyway. Have a nice day.'

Well, that was that. King felt annoyed as he put down the receiver. It was not just that he was wasting his time but that, if he hadn't made that call, his chances of finding anything out would actually have been better. Now they knew where he was and what he was doing, the shutters would be up. And if they wanted to hinder, as Kowalsky put it, they knew how to do it—none better. He felt like kicking every piece of furniture in the room, but decided to go out for a walk instead. He would visit the Institute for Defense Analyses, where Brownson worked.

When he arrived there he found much the same uninstructive scene as had confronted Taggart earlier in the morning, though at this time of day (it was by now nearing ten o'clock) there was of course much more activity. He, too, was approached by the wide officer.

'Can I help you, sir?'

'No, thanks, I was just looking around.'

The campus policeman squinted at him, screwing up his eyes in the morning sun. In the distance some loud machine could be heard at work keeping New Jersey at bay. 'You British?'

'Well, yes.' King decided against showing his identification. There was not much to be gained from that now.

'Funny thing, all you British getting interested in this place all of a sudden.'

'What do you mean?' King felt suddenly excited. Was he going to find out something about the Silverlight business from this unlikely source?

'Nothin',' said the man. 'Just that you're the second limey today I've met nosing round here. What's going on? They doing a job for you or somethin'? You worried about security or somethin'? Because if so, believe me—' he tapped his massive chest—'security here's just fine.'

'There was another Englishman here this morning?' King said incredulously. Then he told himself not to be silly. Princeton must have any number of Englishmen—or Scots or Irish, this fellow almost certainly couldn't tell them apart—on the faculty. All universities were full of visiting foreigners.

'Yeah. Little, dirty-looking guy with a little beard. I told him to push off, and he did.'

'Why, what was he doing?'

'Just looking around. Just like you. Mind, I'm not telling you nothin'. You're a nicer class of person, know what I mean? You want to look at this place, you look.'

'Thank you, officer.'

And a fat lot of good it will do me, King thought. He wondered who this mysterious other Englishman could be and whether he was anything to do with the Silverlight business. But that seemed unlikely to the point of impossibility. Nevertheless, the thought nagged him and would not go away. He found himself glancing behind him as he walked, as if he might be followed and—what? Conked on the head? Held up at pistol-point? The only people he could think of who might be inclined to do that were Brownson and Kowalsky's lot, and the one thing that could definitely be said about them was that they were not British. Besides, they might move fast, but not that fast—Kowalsky's lot, that was; as for Brownson, the policeman would presumably have recognized him anyway.

These thoughts carried King a fair distance. He found himself crossing a stream into some thick woods, carpeted with skunk cabbage and littered with fallen trunks. Obviously the manicuring accorded to all trees within Princeton city limits did not extend here. Overhead, new leaves shone against a clear blue sky. He came out of the woods and into what must have been an abandoned orchard. The trees here were dead or dying: he was over the frontier and back in New Jersey. His eye was caught by a splash of bright orange-yellow. He bent to see what it was. Between the dead trunks looped weedy vine-like stems, bearing poisonous-looking orange-yellow fruits. There was something singularly repulsive about them. King plunged back into the woods. Suddenly he could not wait to get out, out of Princeton, out of America. If 'they' didn't want Silverlight's death looked into too closely, who was he to stand out? It wasn't as if it concerned him personally. He would spend a day in New York—now that he was here, after all!—get some presents for Janine and the children, and take the first convenient plane back to London.

New Politics, Friday, 28 April
NEXT WEEK: Who Killed Paul Silverlight?—an exclusive investigation by Andrew Taggart reveals an extraordinary story of political intrigue and gangsterism. We predict an

exceptionally heavy demand for this issue. To be sure of getting your copy, order *New Politics* today at your newsagent . . .

CHAPTER 24

The Assistant Commissioner, standing on the steps of No. 10 Downing Street, felt nervous. It was, as it happened, the first time he had visited the place in his official capacity, though he had of course passed it countless times. The message had been waiting for him when he arrived at the office this morning. The Prime Minister would like to see him at 10 Downing Street at eleven o'clock, if that was convenient. As it happened, it was not at all convenient. It meant cancelling several appointments, including an urgent meeting which had been particularly difficult to set up and would be even more difficult to move. But one does not get to be Assistant Commissioner without knowing when a phrase is a mere form of words.

The Prime Minister received him in a comfortable, rather chintzy sitting-room. She was sitting in an armchair going through some papers. She put these aside when the Assistant Commissioner entered, rose and held out her hand with a charming smile. 'So good of you to come at such short notice, Assistant Commissioner,' she said. 'I'm sure you can imagine what it's about.' She tapped a copy of *New Politics* open beside her on a small side-table. 'This.'

The AC nodded gloomily. 'I thought it might be that,' he said.

Like everyone in Central London, Scotland Yard got its copies of weeklies like *New Politics* on the evening before the official copy date, since they had to be available then in order to reach all parts of the country by the following morning. The trail had assaulted his eye almost physically, and he had immediately summoned King, on whom the effect had been (if one were to judge by his reaction) like a

138

blow on the solar plexus. The AC had thrust the opened page under his nose; he had read it, taken it in, and collapsed into a chair looking pale.

'Well, King? Can you tell me anything about this?'

'Nothing at all, sir.' King seemed breathless, possibly the result of shock. The AC was pitiless, however.

'You must have encountered him along the trail, surely? Two people investigating something like this at the same time generally tend to bump into each other.'

'I'm afraid not, sir.' King's mind went back to Princeton. That was the other Englishman at the IDA, of course. Taggart. He'd even had his description. 'I think he was in America at the same time I was, but we didn't meet. He must have kept out of my way.'

'Evidently.' The AC was tapping his copy of the magazine with the tips of his fingers, a habit King found intensely irritating. 'I suppose you wouldn't have any idea of what he's proposing to say in this great revelation?'

'I have a vague idea, sir. But I don't know about the detail. I drew rather a lot of blanks as to detail, if you remember, sir. In fact, not to put too fine a point on it, I was warned off. By our friends. I may have mentioned it. So what with that and what with what you said before I went—'

'I don't recall saying anything much before you went.'

'As far as I'm concerned, the investigation is still pending, sir. No definite conclusions. Yet,' said King unhappily.

The Prime Minister said, 'This is one of those unfortunate affairs.'

'I understand he was a personal friend of yours.'

'In these matters one puts one's personal feelings to one side,' said the Prime Minister firmly. 'My concern at the moment is for the political situation. Which, as I'm sure you're aware, could not be more delicate. The world literally stands on a knife-edge.' She paused while this sank in. The Assistant Commissioner found himself wondering if politicians habitually thought in clichés, as well as speechifying in them. When he was younger he had assumed that public and private selves were two quite separate entities. Since he had grown older and more senior, however, and had consequently met more politicians and others in public life, he had been forced to the conclusion that this was not the case as often as the more pompous and idiotic brand of public pronouncements might lead one to wish. If people said things often enough they came to believe them.

'The important thing is that the Alliance is seen to stand firm,' said the Prime Minister. 'It would really be most dangerous if the anti-Americanism fostered by CND and organizations of that sort were to get any encouragement. One doesn't want to give them anything to seize upon. That's why that Pentagon so-called leak was so unfortunate. Of course one doesn't want any repetition of a story like that.'

'Of course not.'

'You get my drift? I'm sure I don't have to spell things out in words of one syllable to you, Assistant Commissioner.'

'Of course, Prime Minister. That was our view of the case also.'

The AC sighed. Life is very unfair. Here he was with the Prime Minister in Downing Street and receiving, not compliments on a delicate case delicately handled, but a reproach, however oblique. Yet in point of delicacy it was hard to see how he could have done better. Of all the officers at his disposal, King was the least interested in political flourishes, the least likely to see the Silverlight case as one where he might make his indelible mark. He was not a man with a mission, which made things easier if it got to the point where he had to be warned off. It seemed, according to a telex recently arrived on his desk, that this point had indeed been reached—directly, and over there, as well as indirectly and over here. And he appeared to have accepted it. Of course he had been, and perhaps remained, obdurate on one rather important point. He seemed inexplicably determined not to believe Jennifer Chantrey's confession— in every way the ideal solution to this affair. After all, why shouldn't she have done it? The AC sighed. He was caught between scandals. It was a choice between the politically disastrous (as the triumphant tone of Taggart's trail left him in no doubt that any revelations from that quarter would be) and the possibility of a civil liberties outcry about railroading a defenceless victim. If Jennifer Chantrey had been accused, then the tabloids would undoubtedly have had a field-day in any case. He could see the headlines now: COLUMNIST KILLED BY JILTED LOVER. SILVER-LIGHT KILLED BY PROFESSOR'S DAUGHTER. Well, that wouldn't have worried him. In fact, it hovered before his eyes like the mirage of an oasis before the proverbial desert traveller. For of course, once Taggart published his piece, that option was almost certainly closed. It should all have been a matter for discreet congratulation. As it was—

'One can't be too vigilant where these wretched journalists are concerned,' the Prime Minister was saying. 'No sense of public spirit there at all. All that concerns them is their little sensation of the moment. The question is, what to do next,' she ended in a spurt of directness. 'Do you know what's in this story?'

'No, we haven't been able to obtain it. They're keeping it very much under wraps.'

'We could try a D-notice.'

'We could, but I'm afraid they'd just ignore it. Taggart isn't very open to suggestion, and neither is his editor.'

'Or the Official Secrets Act.'

'Until we know what's in it we don't know if it comes under that.'

'Well, then, there we are. You'd better find out what's in it, hadn't you? Thank you so much, Assistant Commissioner. I know you're a very busy man.' The Prime Minister smiled again, this time a trifle frostily, and held out her hand. The interview was at an end.

Back at the office the AC summoned King. 'You may like to know that the Prime Minister is personally very concerned about this case,' he said.

'That still doesn't make it any easier to know what to do about it.'

'Perhaps not, but it means that something has to be done. She's particularly concerned that this Taggart piece should not appear.'

'Ah.'

The two men looked at each other.

'Well,' said the AC. 'So go and see that it doesn't.'

CHAPTER 25

Thursday was always a busy day for Jane. It was the day the review pages were put together, and there were always panics because something had not arrived, or was too long, or too short, or for some other reason unusable. On Thursdays she got to the office early and left it late. Everyone knew that Thursday was a bad day to ask Jane for anything.

It was therefore not merely with irritation but with surprise that she took a call from Reception that Thursday saying that Andrew Taggart was there and asking to see her.

'Can't it wait till tomorrow? You know I'm always terribly busy on Thursdays.'

'He says not, miss.'

'Well, you'd better send him up.'

Taggart arrived to find her crossly sub-editing a particularly verbose piece which had arrived late and typed in single spacing. A picture researcher who arrived with him slapped down a folder of engravings on her desk and stood waiting. The phone rang, and then rang again. Jane looked through the pictures and said, 'None of these will do.' She read through the review again, struck out two paragraphs, called her secretary and told her to retype the piece, and finally turned to Taggart. 'Sorry. You know how things are on Thursdays.'

He said diffidently, 'I've come to ask a favour.'

'Ask.'

The telephone rang again, and while she answered it Taggart tried to decide how best to put his request. He was still engaged in this task when the conversation finished.

She put down the receiver and said, 'It's not like you to be at a loss for words.'

'The thing is, what I'm worried about hasn't actually happened yet.'

'That is the position of most of the world,' she returned drily.

'I think it may have something to do with that, too. That's why I'm so worried. Look,' he said, producing a proof copy of *New Politics*, 'This is going to appear in tonight's edition.'

Jane read the trail and looked back at him with raised eyebrows.

'I've got to get away,' he explained. 'Till next week's edition is out. They're going to bust a gut to stop it.'

'Why?'

'Because it's a story that a lot of very important people particularly don't want to come out.'

'Have you written it?'

'Not yet. If it isn't written they haven't got anything to work on and they can't get David.' David Cooper was his editor at *New Politics*. 'And I'm waiting for the final piece of information.'

'Which is?'

Taggart glanced round. Jane's office was a glassed-off partition in the corner of a huge room full of journalists and telephones. Everyone was preoccupied with his or her particular story. There can be few places safer in which to have a private conversation than the corner of a large newspaper office. 'First, the favour. Can I come and stay with you this week? I've got to get out of my house. They're sure to do it over and try and take me in on some charge.'

'How could they do that?'

'They'll think of something.'

'Don't you think you're being rather melodramatic?' Jane asked.

'No. Can I?'

She sighed. 'I suppose there's no reason why not. The children have gone away with their father for Easter. You can stay up there.'

'I wouldn't be—disturbing anything?'

She gestured to the trail. 'As you know only too well. Love's young dream nipped in the bud. I hate to say it,' she sighed, 'but darling Paul is turning out infinitely more interesting dead than alive. Now it's your turn. What's this needle information you're waiting for?'

'It was a CIA job,' Taggart said, 'and I'm waiting for the name of the person who did it.'

CHAPTER 26

Thus it was that Detective-Inspector King's efforts to prevent Andrew Taggart revealing all about the death of Paul Silverlight were as fruitless as his attempt to probe that mystery himself had been.

King was chagrined (to say the least) at the new twist the affair had taken. He had felt foolish and annoyed on his empty-handed return from America. He was convinced that Brownson knew what had happened, or at least part of it, and quite at a loss to see how he would ever come into possession of this information. With no cooperation there and a pointed lack of enthusiasm for the case here, there seemed to be very little he could do. Quite apart from anything else, he felt that his own position was very anomalous. It was hardly a compliment to have been picked for this particular case, in which the more he found out, the more he realized that no one wanted him to find out anything. Had they then thought him so incompetent as to be a safe bet? Had they—or at any rate the AC—known all along what the real story was, more or less?—more than he knew now, after all his efforts? And if they were so keen not to find out, or at any rate not to reveal, what had happened, why waste his time? Why mount an investigation at all? Why not just let the affair die a natural death?—easy enough, that: the inquest had merely to record a verdict of death by misadventure, and sleeping dogs would lie happily enough. Perhaps they thought Paul Silverlight knew too many influential people for that. But certainly he, King, hadn't met anybody who struck him as likely to make a great issue out of Silverlight's death. Only two people had seemed genuinely upset: Brownson and Judith Croft. But Brownson only wished to hush the whole thing up—or so it seemed—and Judith's grief had been more related to the past than the present.

Well, it had been an insult, and a waste of time. Now the only thing to do was put it behind him and get on with other things, of which plenty presented themselves. When, on his return from America, Janine and the children had asked him about his trip, it had been easy enough to head them off. They weren't really interested, anyway. The presents he had brought them back interested them far more— Princeton University T-shirts, a bottle of bourbon, and some other small items. His children hoped he would go again. If he did, they would provide him with a list of things to bring back.

And now this! He had little hope of being able to do much. Taggart and *New Politics* must have anticipated the effect of their trailer. He said as much to the AC, who was unsympathetic. 'I don't care what you do,' he said, 'but do something.'

That was all very well, but it is not easy to catch an eel bare-handed.

David Cooper was brisk and unhelpful. 'What exactly did you want?' he inquired coldly across his desk. A faint aura of gin wafted on his words, the remains of a liquid lunch, no doubt. Lucky blighter, thought King. He could have used a large gin and tonic himself.

'We should like to have a look at this piece by Taggart which I see you mention this week, if you don't mind, sir.'

Cooper looked pleased and King's heart sank. There must be some reason why he looked pleased. 'I'm afraid I can't help you there.'

'I think you might be well-advised to help us, sir. I don't anticipate much difficulty in obtaining a search warrant under the Official Secrets Act, if I have to.'

'Search away, officer, but you won't find anything. As far as I'm aware, the piece isn't written yet.'

'Do you make a practice of advertising stuff that doesn't exist?' King inquired sarcastically.

'Doesn't yet exist,' Cooper corrected him gently. 'It will, I've no doubt. Andrew Taggart has never let us down yet. I've the greatest faith in him.'

King stared at him. Was he telling the truth? Probably: they had doubtless worked out this strategy in advance precisely because they anticipated some sort of reaction from the authorities. 'Would it be asking too much to let me see the piece when it is written, just so that we can make sure there's nothing actionable in it?'

'Much too much, Inspector.'

'I can only say, sir, that you will have only yourself to blame for any trouble which may ensue.' With this unsatisfactory parting shot King left the office. At least his next move was obvious. He would have to find Taggart.

He was not in the office; it was reasonable, therefore, to assume he might be at home. To Hoxton, therefore, King now made his way. What a place to live, he reflected. Not so long ago, no respectable person would have dreamed of living in Hoxton, not by choice. Wouldn't even have much liked walking around there. Now, however, it was 'coming up', to coin an estate agent's phrase. King, in a pub in Islington recently, had overheard some of the local trendies discussing the locality. It was getting altogether too middle-class for them, it seemed. 'Nothing for it,' one of them sighed. 'We shall have to move east.'

Well, Hoxton was east all right, but if it was coming up it still had a long way to travel before it arrived, King considered, viewing with some distaste the scrofulous terrace inhabited by Taggart. His own parents had spent the earlier part of their married life in Dalston, which was where you moved to from Hoxton when you became respectable, and had got out even of there as soon as they could. To choose to live in this part of London seemed to indicate a positive perversity, which did not surprise King in a person like Andrew Taggart whose whole life, after all, was spent in a series of attempts to disrupt the workings of authority. King might have studied sociology, but that had not turned him into an anarchist. People sometimes forgot that it was possible to be a sociologist and have a social conscience without necessarily being a socialist (let alone an anarchist). That was part of the trouble with Janine, he sometimes felt. She felt let down in some way. She had thought the person she was marrying (him), given his interests and his career, would turn out to be some kind of mould-breaker. But King was not interested in breaking moulds. He was interested in the most efficient ways of keeping them intact. That was why he had become a policeman.

He stopped his car in front of Taggart's house, indistinguishable in point of peeling paint from its neighbours. They, however, were not yet gentrified, to judge from the crone who, in answer (it seemed) to his knock, opened the next-door front door and stuck her head out. The head was swathed in a headscarf tied turban-style, and was furnished with flashing dentures. ''E's not 'ere,' she told King. 'Asn't been 'ere for days. It was Mr Taggart you was looking for, wasn't it? I fought so. Seen you 'ere before,'aven't I? You the police or somefin?'

'Why would you expect the police to be visiting Mr Taggart?' asked King in a spirit of genuine inquiry.

'People come knocking on doors round 'ere it's the rent or the busies,' explained the crone. 'Mr Taggart don't pay no rent. 'E bought it, didn't 'e? So vere you are.'

'When d'you expect him back?'

'I don't expect nuffin, mate. I was just askin'.' The head disappeared and the door slammed.

Never one to take information on trust, King knocked again. There was still no reply. Acutely aware of being observed from behind next-door's grubby net curtains, he peered through the letter-box on to a motionless, soundless vista of lino and stairs. The place certainly seemed deserted. He craned to see if he could make out any mail piled up inside the door, but the angle of vision was too narrow. No milk or newspapers, but Taggart was not a man to drink much milk and he might not take a paper. Or might have cancelled it. Like Cooper, he had evidently taken his precautions. King went into the next street to see if he could get a glimpse of the back of the house. It was just visible. All the windows were shut, although the spring day was fine and warm. He watched for a while, but there was no sign of movement. The crone was probably right: Taggart was not at home.

CHAPTER 27

At that moment Taggart was, in fact, standing in a small post-office in Clapham waiting to see if anything was waiting for him *poste restante*. Like almost everyone he knew, Taggart was convinced that his telephone was tapped and his mail intercepted. Unlike most of his acquaintances, he was correct on the first count and even, spasmodically, on the second. The present occasion was a case in point, when his invariable habit of acting on these assumptions was proving a serious inconvenience to King, who considered that such paranoia was in itself evidence of guilt.

'Name?' said the sad-looking Indian behind the counter.

'Maclaren.'

'Nothing for Maclaren.'

Taggart walked out into the spring sunshine, whose effect was only to make Clapham High Street look uglier and more tawdry than ever. He felt extremely light-hearted. Until the letter he was waiting for arrived, or until delivery could be postponed no longer, he did not have to worry about writing. If copydate turned out to predate the arrival of the letter, then things might turn out more difficult—not because there was any difficulty in writing a perfectly good piece and promising the final crumb for the following week: that was normal serializing practice. Simply, all sorts of people would then be looking for him and it might be hard to stay out of their way. He could hardly ask for police protection, after all.

But for the moment all he had to do was enjoy the lovely weather and make his way back gently to Primrose Hill. His evasive measures ought to be enough to keep the cops off his back for a week, and he doubted if anyone else would try anything until they could see how much he knew. Or guessed. Meanwhile, what a scoop! And how furious they must all be! He did not pause to characterize 'they' in detail. As with every good journalist, 'they' were whoever would have liked to stop him publishing the story of the moment. Given his interests, and given the government's predilection for secrecy at whatever cost and no matter how irrelevant, 'they' were often the government of the day. He wondered what they would have done if King had found out the truth first—which Taggart was tolerably sure he had not done and would not do. Hushed it up, probably. They always preferred to hush things up, and Washington would no doubt be pretty cross if this came out. Which, of course, it was about to do.

He amused himself meanwhile by trying to spot likely places for an ambush, should anyone be contemplating such a thing. He ought to keep clear of Clapham North tube station if his information had not arrived by next week. He always felt insecure on this platform, a narrow strip of asphalt between two busy lines: what could be easier than to trip in front of one or another train? One was more secure with a good wall behind one, no doubt about it. Memo: next week, he would use Clapham Common. He didn't much fancy Chalk Farm, either. No escalator, and the lifts out of order more often than not. A man could so easily slip and break his neck on those endless spiralling stairs . . . No, clearly the tube was out. He would have to take buses or taxis. He certainly wasn't going to risk himself on a cycle —that was the way to offer oneself up to all comers, though of course it did offer a certain versatility if one's pursuer was caught in a traffic jam. Logically a motorbike would be the best thing to get around on, but Taggart was terrified of motorbikes. To commit suicide was merely to make his putative pursuer's job easier, after all. Meanwhile, on foot, he kept a careful eye on dark alleys and concealing garden walls. Either no one was lying in wait, or his precautions defeated them. He made it safely to Jane's house.

He let himself in and was surprised at the relief he felt on shutting the door behind him. He didn't think anyone had noticed him coming in. The square was full of children playing in the sunshine. Rows of mothers sat on the benches and indulged the luxurious sins of adult life. They smoked and talked about lovers and money, books and clothes. One of them had brought out a bottle of wine and some plastic glasses. They drank with the deep appreciation of those who spend their waking hours dispensing milk and Marmite. They were not interested in an unglamorous and unobtrusive stranger letting himself quietly into Jane Addison's house.

He had the afternoon to himself. Jane would not be home till late. Happily he wandered round the house investigating her private life. Not that a great deal of it was on show. There were no letters lying about on desks or tables, and most of the desk drawers were locked, the unlocked ones containing nothing more interesting than stationery. He had not yet got to the point where he would pick the locks of friends' drawers, and anyway, he hadn't the tools to hand. Jane probably had something that would do, but he dismissed that thought almost before he consciously experienced it. For one thing, suppose she came home . . . ? Books —well, naturally there were plenty of those, mostly still wrapped in their bright dustjackets as supplied direct from the publishers. It was lucky for authors, Taggart reflected, that most people were not literary editors or their friends, or nobody would ever buy a single book. It was remarkable, he had noticed it often, to what lengths such people would go to avoid buying a book which they wanted to read and could perfectly well afford. He had done it himself more than once— telephoned publishers requesting review copies, or asking a literary editor friend to get him a book in return for a hundred-word notice. Jane seemed to prefer novels about intelligent women experiencing the mid-life crisis in London or New York. As most of the novels published seemed to be about this topic a wide choice was available. She also liked biography, especially of successful women, and Bloomsburiana, much of which was the work of friends and acquaintances. There was a wide range of detective stories but no science fiction. Little on politics, nothing on the bomb. For the first time it occurred to Taggart to wonder whether Jane was quite trustworthy. Not that he thought she was in any way politically active, but she had some strange people at her parties—Paul Silverlight, for example. Perhaps he shouldn't have told her anything? Well—perhaps not, but if he hadn't, she wouldn't have agreed to put him up. Every favour demands a quid pro quo. And her political, or apolitical stance, had certain advantages from his point of view. The police, or whoever, would not think of looking for him here. If he had gone to Judith Croft, for example, he could have expected a very short delay before being tracked down.

He would have been highly gratified, therefore, had he been a fly on the wall of King's office just then. For at that very moment Inspector King was sitting with Andrew Taggart's file open on his desk making a list of likely friends and acquaintances with whom he might be passing a few days.

King had of course tried ringing the office, on the off-chance that he might find a secretary who was unaware of the situation and who might know of a telephone number where Taggart could be contacted. But if such a young woman existed, he had not spoken to her. Not that he expected any joy by phone—simply, all telephone numbers have an address attached. It did seem absurd that with all the resources of the Metropolitan Police at his disposal he should be unable to track down such a relatively well-known figure as Taggart. It made him feel foolish—a feeling he had experienced more often than he liked since he took on this case—and he had little doubt that it made him look foolish. Still, he was doing his best, and his worst enemy would have to admit that Taggart had an exceptionally large number of acquaintances with whom he might choose to hole up—always supposing that he was staying with friends, and in London, and not, for example, in a small hotel in Clacton-on-Sea. A man was watching Taggart's house, to make sure they didn't miss him slipping in and out. Meanwhile King perused his list.

At the top of it was Judith Croft. She was known to be an informant of Taggart's, and they had been seeing a lot of each other recently.

A short time later, then, there was a knock on the Crofts' door. A man in a vaguely postal-looking uniform stood there bearing a package in his hand and asking if he might leave it for Mr Taggart.

Ben Croft, who had opened the door, looked blank. 'Who?' he said.

'It's for Mr Andrew Taggart. I believe he's staying here.'

'No,' said the little boy. 'I'm Ben, and there's my mummy and daddy and Jonathan. Do you want to see my mummy?'

The man had little choice, since at that moment Ben's mummy arrived at the door. 'Taggart?' she said. 'There's no one of that name here. You must have made a mistake.'

The man agreed that he must indeed have made a mistake, apologized, and left. He drove away in an unmarked van. When he had gone, Judith stood staring thoughtfully after him. Then she rang Taggart's number. Of course, there was no reply.

While King was thus drawing his first blank, Taggart was relaxing with a cup of Jane's tea and a selection of recent novels. He was unable, however, to get absorbed in any of them. Did Margaret Drabble and Fay Weldon write for an exclusively female audience, he wondered, or was it simply that he was out of practice with fiction? Five o'clock: time for the news. Tension was mounting again in the Middle East, it seemed. A member of the international peace-keeping force had been shot on the Iran-Iraq frontier. Each side accused the other of the outrage, and both leaders were making hysterical speeches. The airwaves were filled with politicians and pundits assuring the public that, this time, there was nothing to worry about. Things must be getting bad for them to be trying that hard. He turned the radio off and began to wander around the house. It was a comfortable place: Jane was good at comfort. It grew naturally around her, just as junkheaps grew naturally around him. The grey-green sitting-room was situated somewhere in the

1930s or 40s, with those big, boxy armchairs which are to be found in any provincial auction-room. He picked his way round the potted plants (was this passion for outsize indoor greenery part of some collective guilt on the part of the over-civilized about the death of the forests?) and wandered into Jane's bedroom. A large bed was covered with an enormous quilt. There was a sofa, a desk, a bulky Edwardian wardrobe filled with rather showy clothes in bright colours with feathers and threads of Lurex interwoven here and there. Most of these needed pressing. Taggart burrowed behind the crumpled plumage to find the guilty secrets which might be hidden at the back of the wardrobe. What was he looking for? A secret panel? A bugging device? Caches of old love-letters? There was a litter of long-abandoned shoes and once-used handbags, beads and stockings and old blouses which had slipped down behind the racks and been forgotten. But the wardrobe back seemed solid and there were no visible bugs, though of course any one of the innumerable buttons contained in the wardrobe could have contained a device. Though, come to that, why should it? Jane, he reminded himself, did not lead that kind of life.

Taggart shut the doors of the wardrobe and wandered over to the window, which overlooked a vista of messy London back gardens. Some even had plants: as he watched, a keen gardener, with a quick glance round, tweaked a clematis flower so that it bloomed to his, the owner's, side of its trellis and did not lavish itself on an undeserving neighbour. Truly capitalist behaviour, thought Taggart, worthy of a Silverlight himself.

He glanced at his watch again. Curious how often he was doing that this afternoon: must be that housebound feeling. How was he going to get through a whole week of this, for God's sake? Now if Jane were here ... He hallucinated happily while staring at the huge bed with the dream-pink quilt, which now began to vibrate with hypnotic rhythm while she moaned 'Oh! Don't stop! Go on! Go on ... !' Hallucination, however, is both more and less satisfactory than real life: more, because it outdoes life; less, because it can't last. It didn't. Six-fifteen. Time for a drink. The phone rang. It was a real effort not to answer it, but the effort had to be made; if it was for him, then it was a call he didn't want, and if it were neutral—i.e. for Jane, which seemed probable, seeing that this was her house and no one knew he was here—then it wasn't his business.

At eight o'clock he heard a key in the door. He felt a curious mixture of relief and guilt, the usual lot of the self-invited guest awaiting the occupant of the house. It was Jane, closely followed by Peter Conder. 'Andrew!' she called. 'Are you here?' Taggart appeared in the door of the drawing-room.

'You look awfully guilty,' said Jane. 'I can't imagine what you've been doing, to look like that. Where've you been? I tried to phone you, but there was no reply.'

'Sorry. I'm not answering the phone.'

'Oh, it doesn't matter, really. Simply, Peter dropped by and suggested dinner, so I said, why not come round here. I just thought I'd let you know.'

Taggart said, 'Please don't let me intrude. I'll make myself scarce.' He could think of nothing he wanted less than an evening spent in the company of Conder. But they would have none of it. Jane was sure she had something in the freezer; Conder was positively cordial, his long, thin face falling uneasily into lines of sociability. 'Jane has told me you're on the run,' he said with a queer eagerness, savouring the tang of colloquialism on his tongue.

It was Jane's turn to look guilty. She flashed an appalled look at Conder, who was, or seemed to be, blithely unaware of the enormity of his indiscretion (in betraying the enormity of hers)—or who might simply have been amusing himself at the expense of both his companions. Scarlet-faced, their hostess busied herself with the freezer, burrowing into its depths for something suitable for dinner. Taggart said, as lightly as he could, 'Oh, it's nothing, probably the merest paranoia.'

'Do tell me more,' said Conder. 'It's not often, you know, that one finds oneself in the middle of a detective story.'

'I can see Jane's been exaggerating as usual,' said Tag-

154

gart, and Jane, simultaneously, said 'How about bœuf Stroganoff? There seems to be quite a nice lot of it here.'

'Bœuf Stroganoff on the run,' said Conder. 'I'm sure it'll be delightfully spicy.'

'Look, I'm not even sure I am on the run. One merely likes to take precautions,' Taggart said. 'Obviously I should have taken even more.'

'Oh, don't worry. I'm the soul of discretion.' Conder produced a bottle of wine from a bag, and Jane said, 'Perhaps we should open it now.'

The wine was a 1976 Beaujolais, soft and delicious. Taggart said, 'The way things are going now, we ought to drink as much of this sort of thing as we can get as quickly as we can.'

'Oh, not again!' Conder cried. 'But do tell us more. You're so well-informed.'

'I merely repeat what I hear on the news.'

'Oh God,' said Jane. 'The children'll be on at me about whitewashing the windows again.'

'Building igloos is more the kind of thing you'll need to know about, if the scientists are right. And if we aren't all pulverized first,' Taggart said, stirring the Stroganoff.

'I have little faith in scientists,' declared Conder. He poured himself another glass of wine. 'They aren't even very good at telling us what the weather's going to be like tomorrow. As for the long-term forecasting, it's abominable. To my certain knowledge there's a man who writes in *New Scientist* every week, and one week he tells us that the greenhouse effect is going to have us all frying in deserts in twenty years, and the next week he says that sunspot cycles mean that the new Ice Age is on the way. Alternately, year in, year out, and they still take him seriously. So who are we to believe, poor anumerate humanists that we are? One must simply have faith.'

'Do you have faith?' Taggart asked.

Jane said, 'Oh, he's always going on about faith. When I get a book in about faith, I send it to Peter for review. He is my faith correspondent.' She took the Stroganoff off the stove, and they sat around the circular table by the kitchen window. The light was fading towards dusk. Jane lit a couple of candles and put them on the table; Conder opened another bottle of wine; Taggart apologized for not having provided any himself. 'But I wasn't expecting to be dined, let alone wined.'

'But, my dear fellow, with your line in dinner-table conversation, why should you worry about mere wine?' said Conder, in that way he had of saying something that might be intensely polite or abominably rude. 'You were telling us about being on the run.'

'Sorry. I'd rather not talk about it. Why are you so interested, anyway?' Taggart wanted to know. He picked up his glass and then put it down again. It is hard to drink a man's wine while you are being rude to him.

'Paul Silverlight was a friend of mine,' Conder said simply, making Taggart feel worse than ever. He looked furiously at Jane. He hadn't come here to be put into this kind of situation. But she was concentrating on her meal and would not meet his eye. 'I'm dying to know who did it. And why. Won't you tell us?'

Taggart shook his head. 'Sorry.' He did not enlarge on what he did or did not know and Jane, making up for recent indiscretions, did not press him.

The meal proceeded in awkward silence, since none of the participants could say anything they really wanted to in the presence of both the others. Conder left early, saying he had to get a train back to Cambridge. When he had gone Jane leant back against the hall table and said, 'I'm most awfully sorry. He was in the office—leaving a review—and he said why didn't we have some dinner and I said why not come back here—and then I remembered—but he seemed so keen to meet you.'

'I can't imagine why.'

'I think he's just very upset about Paul and wanted to talk about it.'

'Sorry I couldn't oblige. But you see how it is. Quite apart from anything else, the last thing I want to do is let things out in dribs and drabs.' While she was fervently agreeing he glanced at his watch. It was time for the late news. They

156

turned on the television, but there seemed to be no new developments in the Middle East, or none that had reached the newsdesks. Then they went to their separate beds, and while Jane tossed and turned, thinking of Silverlight, whitewash and sandbags, Taggart fell into a dreamless sleep.

CHAPTER 28

Next day Taggart rose early and took the train back to Clapham. This time there was a letter for Maclaren. As he took it he felt his mouth dry and his knees give slightly. He left the post office and looked round for somewhere he could sit down and digest its contents in peace. There was nowhere very apparent in Clapham High Street, so he walked down towards the Common.

It was a beautiful day, warm and windless—a promise of summer, should the world chance to reach summer this year. He sat down on an empty bench, brought the letter out of his pocket and looked at it. It was postmarked Washington DC.

The letter itself was very short, amounting to no more than a few sentences. They seemed to leap off the page and jump up and down beneath his dazed eyes. They read: 'The word here is that the guy who did the job is a university professor who also holds rank of major in the Company. He was an old friend of Silverlight's and would have had easy access. His name is Peter Conder. Does that mean anything to you?'

For a while Taggart did not move. He felt as if some sort of superglue was riveting him to the bench, as if indeed he never would move again. Now, he thought, I must think very carefully what to do. This sentence occupied his mind for some time to the exclusion of all else. Then, slowly, life began to return to his numbed brain. Well, he thought. Two places I mustn't go to. My place and Jane's. Can go anywhere else. If he didn't follow me. He looked round, but

157

there was no obvious sign of Conder anywhere. Though presumably CIA majors, if following a target, did not make themselves apparent. All he could see, rather to his surprise, was life going on as usual. A dog peed against a nearby tree, watched with enormous interest by a small child. A man emerged from a grocery shop across the road carrying a shopping-bag full of food. Judging by the bulges in the bag, most of this was canned: perhaps he was stocking up his shelter. Taggart felt infinitely far from these ordinary activities. The letter had moved him instantaneously from their world.

There was a phone booth not far away. He went to it and dialled Jane's number. She was still at home, thank God. (Funny how one kept thanking personages in whom one did not believe for favours they had not done one.) He said, 'It's Andrew. Look, I won't be coming back. Don't ask why. Anyone been asking for me?'

'Only Peter. He rang and said he had some information that might be useful to you. Seemed very disappointed that you weren't here. I said you'd probably be back later.'

'Well, I won't. Don't think I'm being ungrateful. It's just that something came up. I'll be in touch. Thanks anyway for all your help.'

'All right.' She sounded puzzled. 'This is all too cloak and dagger for me. I'll look out for your piece.'

That was something else, of course. He had to write the piece, and soon. Get out of London, that would be best. But where to? Let fate decide. He would go to Clapham Junction, since that was nearby, and take the first suitable train he saw.

The streets were busy now, full of shoppers and strollers. They moved slowly, the prevalent pace being that of people whose main concern is to pass the time: mothers with young children, waiting for bedtime, or the unemployed, mooching about in the sunshine and hoping that they would not be driven back to their dingy rooms by a change in the weather. The pavements were narrow, and more than once Taggart was nearly pushed into the road by aggressive prams, two abreast. He swore under his breath, glad that none of his feminist friends was present to take the brunt of unreconstructed chauvinism. Granted that babies must be transported somehow, was it necessary to fill the pavement with pantechnicons for their convenience?

While he was thinking these vengeful thoughts, a fat girl, running hard, very nearly succeeded where the prams had failed. Intent upon her business, whatever that was, she ploughed past him with such force that he stumbled off the kerb and would have fallen into the path of a passing bus had not a wiry old man caught his arm and pulled him back on to the pavement. The bus pulled up with a screech of brakes. The old man shook his head. 'You want to look where you're going, mate.' The bus-driver swore. 'I don't need no one committin suicide under my bus, friend,' he yelled.

Taggart, shaken, tried to recall what had happened. He looked round for the girl, but she was nowhere to be seen. Her face seemed faintly familiar. He tried to remember where he might have seen her before, but could not do so. Could have been anywhere or nowhere. Hers had not been a face one would remember. It was probably his imagination, anyway. He wondered what to do next. Well, nothing much to be done. His original plan was as good as any. He continued towards Clapham Junction.

By the time he got there it was almost midday. He bought himself a beer and a sandwich, which made him feel better, both because he had been hungry and because for a while he could pretend this was just a normal day. Then he bought a paper and studied it for imminent signs of the end of the world. Soviet troops were massing on the Iran border, but so far this was only second headline stuff. Still worth trying to preserve himself, then. He went and studied the timetable. In ten minutes there would be a train for Brighton via Gatwick airport. He would take that.

The train was full, as usual, of people lugging enormous suitcases and rucksacks to remote corners of the planet. They sat quietly in that resigned way people have when they know they are only at the beginning of what will be a long journey. In a corner a young man was reading *New*

159

Politics. Taggart craned to see what he was reading. It was the page trailing the article he was about to write. As usual, it was only with the utmost difficulty that he restrained himself from tapping the man on the shoulder and saying, That's me, you know. Misplaced narcissism: the unfailing surprise and pleasure at seeing oneself read and (presumably) taken seriously. And what effect would that have, anyway? Probably the fellow would never believe a word he read in the magazine again. It's remarkable what an effect on the disbelief threshold the fact of actually knowing the author of a piece can have.

He sat back and watched the south London suburbs streak by. He had meant to think, during this journey, about his next moves, but for the moment he was incapable of thought. There was room in his mind only for consciousness of being alive, and of the fact that someone had tried to kill him. Except that that seemed hard to credit. Why on earth should a totally unknown girl try to push him under a bus? There were circumstances he could think of . . . but this, or she, was not one of them. It must have been a mistake. She simply hadn't realized what she had done. He tried to put the incident out of his mind.

That organ, however, still refused to function as a mechanism for thought. The proximity of the window did not help, either. He was as usual hypnotized by the sight of so many unguarded, undisguised lives. The front of a house is the façade it presents to the world; but the back, seen only from the railway line, is the reality. Lines of underpants, whitish nappies and enormous brassieres blew in the light wind, weedy patches of garden were flanked by anally neat squares of perfectly-clipped lawn. Kitchens, living-rooms, bedrooms, were open to the public. A cat dug in a newly-raked vegetable plot; a child carefully tore a tulip to bits. East Croydon. Next stop Gatwick.

He wondered for a moment whether to get out there and take a plane to—anywhere. But what would be the point of that? The Company was not confined to England. He would be as likely, or unlikely, to be safe anywhere else as here, and basic arrangements—money, getting the piece to the magazine on time—would be that much more difficult. Gatwick came and went, and Taggart was still on the train.

He got off at Brighton, a small, grubby figure under the green iron curlicues. Where now? The Metropole? He was tempted. If one must skulk, why not skulk in comfort? On the other hand he would be noticeable at the Metropole, whereas he would blend effortlessly into something seedier.

It was not hard to find something seedier. He settled for a place just behind the promenade. It was called Johnson's. A voluminous blonde, presumably Mrs Johnson, bustled out to the reception desk. The place did not smell too damp, and it was neither quite empty nor (at this season) full. Taggart signed in, using his real name. To use another would require altogether too many subterfuges, too much concentration. Why should anyone come looking for him here? And why draw unnecessary attention to himself? 'That will be fifteen pounds, thank you, dear,' Mrs Johnson said. Taggart nearly drew unnecessary attention to himself on the spot. 'But I haven't had anything yet,' he protested. But Mrs Johnson was having none of this. 'It saves trouble if you want to leave first thing in the morning,' she explained. Taggart did not. But neither, having settled on Johnson's, did he want to bother to find anywhere else—and anyway, everywhere else probably practised the same iniquitous system. He paid, took his key, and went up to Room 15.

The room was the usual cheap hotel room. A bed, an uncomfortable armchair, a chair and table in 1950s modern style with spindly tubular legs. The wallpaper was an overpowering red tartan, the carpet brown with red flowers. Taggart, however, was less distressed by the décor than many others might have been. He liked somewhere nice but (as his own house showed) could get along well enough anywhere. He was preparing to dispose his effects about the room when he realized he had no effects to dispose. Perhaps that had something to do with Mrs Johnson's insistence on his paying the first night's rental at once. What was more, he had no typewriter, either. He would have to buy or rent one.

Outside, Brighton was buzzing in the sun. Innumerable antique-dealers inspected each others' wares. Taggart realized that he had better not ask for an old typewriter—in this town, to use the word 'old' was to invite an immediate price hike. It was an enduring mystery how the age before mass production had nevertheless produced such masses of stuff to feed the insatiable maw of the antiques market. Wandering through the Lanes, he found a second-hand typewriter shop and bought a battered portable. It worked, and that was all he asked. It would not have to last long. Some pyjamas, a toothbrush, typing paper, obliterator, envelopes; a wholefood snack at one of the innumerable health emporia, and he was complete. Within an hour and a half he was back at Johnson's Hotel, contemplating the tartan wallpaper.

CHAPTER 29

Taggart set the typewriter upon the rickety table. He hoped the tubular legs would stand the strain. It wasn't a heavy machine, but the table did not look as if it had been designed to be used. He inserted the paper and two carbons. The paper was thin, but even so the typewriter didn't like it. Taggart told it it could lump it. This was a piece which needed carbons.

Then he sat back and made some notes on the back of an envelope. Although he knew exactly what he wanted to say, there must be no danger of forgetting some vital detail. After a while, however, there was no putting off the evil moment any longer. He set his notes to one side where he could see them, and began to type.

WHO KILLED PAUL SILVERLIGHT? he tapped out, and sat back to consider the possible answers to this pertinent question.

There can have been few recent deaths more greatly relished by a large number of people, for a variety of different reasons, than that of Paul Silverlight, leading light of the radical Right.

162

Well, the dead can't sue for libel, and anyway, libel only exists where there is no basis of truth. 'Although still only in his thirties, he had managed to collect more real enemies than most of us manage given twice that long. The question is, why was he killed (assuming that he was killed, and did not commit suicide)?

Was this what Freudians might like to call 'a family affair'? On the face of it, this seems the likeliest possibility. It is a commonplace that most murders are committed by a relative or close acquaintance of the victim, and Silverlight's personal behaviour was as unpleasant as his political opinions. He had fairly recently run off with the wife of an old friend, and then abandoned her. The girl has since taken to drugs and had a nervous collapse. There were therefore a number of people with good reasons to hate him.

All the likeliest suspects, however, have unshakable alibis for the time in question, not least the father of the girl, Professor John Dawes, who was in hospital recovering from a stab wound at the time Silverlight died. (This, too, is a crime that seems to have gone singularly uninvestigated, but that is another story.) And, as readers may remember, the affair is not in the hands of the CID, but is being handled by the Special Branch, in the person of Inspector Brian King. We may take it, then, that the authorities do not think this was a family affair after all.

So was it political? One of the curious things about Silverlight's life was that his personal enemies might have been expected to be among his bitterest political enemies, too. So the most obvious suspects in both departments seem to be ruled out.

However, an item of interesting information which may be relevant to this case has come the way of *New Politics* recently. We have discovered that Silverlight was in the habit of paying frequent visits to Princeton, where he stayed with a close friend, Arthur ('call me Art') Brownson. Brownson works at the Institute for Defense Analyses, a war games set-up connected with the University.

If we now approach the case from another angle, it becomes very interesting. What is the single occurrence which has most infuriated the Establishment on both sides of the Atlantic recently? It could be argued that it was the leak of the Pentagon paper setting out the conditions under which America would launch a 'first strike' nuclear attack on Russia and/or other suspected nuclear powers. Although it has been denied that this was genuine, there are very good reasons to believe that it was. At any rate, whether or not it emanated from the Pentagon, it was probably instrumental in precipitating the recent terrifying outbreak of nuclear war in the Middle East, where Saddam Hussein was concerned to use his bomb before it could be destroyed by the Americans. (The irony is that the Americans were as uncertain as everyone else whether or not Iraq really did have the bomb. And no one, least of all the Iraquis, thought Iran had one.)

Arguably, the leak prevented the Americans from actually putting this policy into effect, although there is no guarantee that this has made the world a safer place, since the Russians are almost certainly now so frightened that they have put themselves on a 'launch on warning' footing. Anyone who has had anything to do with computers will be suitably terrified at the thought that only an unverified computer warning stands between us and the outbreak of nuclear hostilities on a world scale.

Although great efforts have been made to identify the source of this leak (Scotland Yard is of course called in these days as a matter of routine, the Prime Minister being, it is said, particularly paranoid about leaks), no progress has been made.

Could there be any connection between the death of Paul Silverlight and the undiscovered source of the leak? It is of course the sort of thing which might be available at a high-level war-games institute. Dr Brownson, questioned by *New Politics* on the subject, noticeably failed to deny this. And it may be coincidence, but the present writer was very nearly knocked down by a car just a few minutes after interviewing Brownson on this very topic.

At this point Taggart sat back and thought again. Once might be coincidence, but twice . . . ? Cars, buses—modern life was fraught with hazards. So convenient, so easy to arrange an accident. What had people done in the old days, before the invention of the internal combustion engine? Pushed people under the nearest cart-horse? With an effort, he wrenched his concentration back to the matter in hand. Time enough for speculation later.

It turns out that Inspector King was also in Princeton interviewing Dr Brownson, although he did not get very far in his quest. Little birds pass on the curious information that this was not entirely his fault. The CIA has instructions not to cooperate in this case.

Why should this be? There seem to be two possible reasons. One is that Silverlight was a CIA operative who got bumped off in the course of his work. The other is that he got seriously up someone's nose—possibly by leaking the contentious document—and was bumped off by the CIA.

If we now choose to investigate the second of these scenarios, two interesting questions arise. Who did it, and how far—by which I mean how far up—does the cover-up extend?

Naturally the CIA wants to protect its operatives. But why should Scotland Yard abet it in this? Could it be that certain persons (though not, it seems, poor Inspector King) knew all along the real reason for Silverlight's death, and hoped for a token investigation to legitimize a cover-up? It seems that either murders committed by our Allies' secret services are not really murders at all, or else some extremely exalted personages must be considered accessories to homicide.

So who actually did the dreadful deed? At least one of the names mentioned as a possibility would come as quite a shock to Silverlight's friends and acquaintances. It is naturally impossible to print speculation on such a topic, but our readers will be pleased to know that we have passed all relevant information on to Scotland Yard.

Taggart read this through, raised his eyebrows, folded the top copy and put it in an envelope. Then he scribbled a quick note to David Cooper, including the information Mr Maclaren had received at Clapham. This envelope he sealed and addressed to the editor at *New Politics*. He took the second copy, with a similar note, and addressed it to Cooper at home. One way or another he should get the information. The third copy he put in his inside pocket, to photocopy as soon as he could. Then he went out and posted his letters.

Having done this, he felt as if a great weight had been lifted from his stomach. It was always the same—he always felt it in the stomach. The cat was now well and truly among the pigeons, a state of affairs which always called for celebration. So he went to Wheeler's and celebrated in oysters and a half-bottle of champagne. He had two dozen oysters and enjoyed every one of them. He looked round the restaurant carefully before committing himself to it, but no one he knew was among the diners. The piece would be published Thursday evening, and all he had to do now was keep safe until then.

After his exertions, Taggart felt suddenly tired and depressed. There was always, he found, a terrible sense of anticlimax at such moments. He went back to Johnson's and would have liked to take a bath. However, there was no bathroom attached to his bedroom, and the door down the corridor marked BATH was locked. He went down to the reception desk where a tired young man was on duty. This young man had the deepest, blackest bags under his eyes that Taggart, an old Fleet Street habitué, accustomed to night editors in the early hours, had ever seen. Did he never sleep? What had he on his conscience? At other moments Taggart would have given rein to his natural curiosity and tried to find out; but just now, he felt very much as the young man looked. So he merely said, 'I'd like to have a bath, but the bathroom seems to be locked.'

'Doesn't just seem. It is,' said the tired man laconically.

'Oh. Well, can you unlock it for me, then? Or give me a key?'

'Sorry. No baths after ten o'clock.'

'But that's ridiculous.' Taggart had a feeble resurgence of crusading spirit. 'Anyway, what if I had a room with a bath? How would you stop me having one whenever I wanted?'

'No hot water.'

Taggart gave up and went to bed. The tired man looked after him enviously.

Next day was Sunday. That meant that Cooper would not get the piece until Tuesday morning. These bad new days no post was collected between Saturday lunch-time and Monday morning. Still, the deed was done, and the envelopes as safe inside a postbox as anywhere else. Taggart woke at ten. Noises of footsteps on the stairs and above his head hinted at the presence of other guests, though so far he had seen none. He stretched and thought about breakfast. Undoubtedly he had missed the breakfast for which he had paid yesterday; would there, he wondered, be hot water on Sundays at Johnson's? Cautiously, tying the cord of his pyjamas tightly, he ventured into the corridor and scuttled along to the bathroom. The door was open, the atmosphere steamy. He returned to his room at speed, collected the sponge-bag he had bought yesterday, and rushed back to the bathroom. He was not going to be forestalled this time.

Bathed and refreshed, he sauntered out in search of newspapers. It was another beautiful day, a day, he told himself, to be in Brighton, not London. The newspapers were full of crisis and despondency, so he rolled them up tight, put them in his pocket and tried to put the world out of his mind. It looked as if the rest of the population of Brighton was doing the same thing. Assertive French teenagers had taken possession of the beach and promenade; between them threaded solid middle-class Brightonians, darting mildly xenophobic glances at the continental exuberance surrounding them. The antique shops, of course, were open, and doing great trade: most of the buyers were other antique-dealers. They seemed to have a real aversion to letting an object fall out of the hands of the trade and into the possession of the lumpen public. Nobody was behaving as though World War Three was imminent. Of course, Taggart reflected, maybe it wasn't. One must always allow for that possibility. Simply, Silverlight's little excursion had brought it all that much nearer. Or postponed it, of course. There was no knowing. Not for the first time, Taggart wondered why he had done it. What had happened was clear enough; why, not clear at all. He entered the Lanes. A café was open: he went in and had some breakfast. Next door was a bookshop. Full of coffee and doughnut, he wandered in to pass the time. On the shelves was a copy of Silverlight's last book. Taggart bought it. The girl behind the cash desk looked as if she had something to say about the book, but if so she remembered in time that the customer is always right, even if Right.

Just after he had left the shop, Taggart had an unpleasant shock. He was walking along when he noticed a man just in front of him, thin, long-headed, neat, dark hair—reminded him of someone: who?

Conder!

Why was he so surprised? Conder must be searching for him high and low, as the saying goes. Must want to find him quickly, too, before it was too late. Well, it was too late: but Conder was not to know that. How on earth had they managed to trace him to Brighton? As usual when panic-stricken, Taggart was sweating, and his knees seemed to be giving way slightly, which was worrying—suppose he needed to run? He crossed the street. The man did not seem to be looking anywhere in particular, but that was probably part of the CIA training. The essence of shadowing is not to look like a shadow. He caught a glimpse of the man's face in a shop window.

It was not Conder.

It was not Conder; but Taggart was no less scared. The incident had reminded him that he was almost certainly on somebody's hit-list. If he knew what was good for him he would get into hiding and stay there. He bought some more papers and returned to Johnson's, there to turn his back on the tartan wallpaper, try to ignore the inviting sunshine, and bury himself in his reading-matter.

He stayed there, with brief excursions into the exterior, until Tuesday lunch-time, living on hotel breakfasts, bought sandwiches, and chocolate-covered peanuts, of which he was especially fond. But at about eleven o'clock on Tuesday, he knew he could stand it no longer. Who would be looking for him here, now? Cooper would have received his copies of the piece. It was out of his hands and he could stand that tartan wallpaper not a minute longer. He descended the stairs. Behind the reception desk Mrs Johnson loomed. 'Going out at last? Haven't been taking advantage of the lovely weather, have you? I've noticed. Well, you do notice these things. Been poorly, have you?'

Taggart agreed he had been poorly, paid his bill and left. As he stepped into the street, he felt as if a weight had been lifted off him. Such was the wonderful feeling of lightness, he could barely restrain himself from leaping into the air. He did restrain himself, however. Now was no time to attract unnecessary attention. He studied the menu-boards posted outside the pubs. Shepherd's pie, soup of the day—wonderful words. He settled on an inviting-looking place near the Lanes, ordered a pint and a heaped plateful, and settled down happily at a table near the window. It was still early, and there was plenty of room.

He was concentrating on his plate when a voice said, 'Mind if I share your table?' It was a voice he recognized, though he could not immediately place it. Conder!

He looked up. It was not Conder. It was King.

CHAPTER 30

That Tuesday, King was feeling as gloomy as he had ever felt. Anomie had struck again. There seemed to be absolutely nothing he could do. If Taggart had had a car, for instance, he could have put out a search request for it. But he did not, so that avenue was not open to him. Nobody of Taggart's name or description had rented a car recently. He had not, so far as it was possible to ascertain, left the country. And a fat lot of help that was. The whole of the British Isles remained. Naturally a description had been circulated, but policemen have plenty on their minds and it seemed unlikely that anyone would go far out of their way to locate a person who, after all, had not even committed a crime. Something might come up, of course, but King rather doubted it. Meanwhile, there was nothing to do but wait.

It was a lovely day again. What he would really have liked to do was dig his garden. It could do with a good day's work and so could he. However, this course of action was out of the question. Quite apart from anything else, Janine was having a coffee-morning about something or the other, and he would be an object of curiosity and polite inquiry.

What, then, was he to do with himself? Well, he could go to the office and sit at his desk staring at the telephone, aware every moment that nothing was happening and that people wanted to know why not. He could imagine no prospect more distasteful, but there seemed nothing for it. With a regretful glance at the waiting garden (he ought to spray for black spot, and the lawn needed mowing, and he really ought to mulch the raspberries), he got into his car and set out for the hateful place.

As he entered his office, the phone was ringing. Listlessly, he picked it up. 'This is Brighton here,' said a voice filled with youthful keenness. King took an instant dislike to that voice.

'Mm?'

'Is that Inspector King?'

'Mm.'

'Look, I think I may have spotted your chap.' The voice sounded beside itself with doggy eagerness.

'Oh yes? What did he look like?'

'Well, like the description. You know. Little straggly beard, about five-nine, bit shabby.'

'I know. So what's he doing?'

'Well, that's the thing. I just happened to be on the train

from London. It was my day off. This chap walked into the compartment. Actually I don't know if I would have remembered but I happened to be reading *New Politics* at the time. I like to keep up with things.'

'Uh.'

'Well, I was reading this thing by Andrew Taggart, and that brought it to mind that we were looking out for him, and then, well, there he was.'

'Wonderful. So where is he now?'

'Well, I didn't know quite what to do. So I tried to follow him when he got out—'

'Got out where?'

'At Brighton. But the trouble was, I wasn't carrying my warrant card and I couldn't just find my ticket and by the time I got through—'

'He'd disappeared.'

'Well—I'm afraid so.'

'When was this?'

'Saturday.'

'Why the hell didn't you tell me earlier, then?'

The voice sounded only very faintly abashed. 'Sorry, sir, we've had a bit of a panic on here and it slipped my mind till now. I did try on Saturday but I couldn't find you anywhere.' Saturday, what had he been doing Saturday? With difficulty he remembered. After a fruitless morning sitting at his desk he had given up in disgust and taken his son to a football match, something he was always promising to do. The rarity with which such promises were kept was one of the main bones of domestic contention.

'You could have left a message.'

'I did,' said the voice, sounding injured. 'I was ringing to see whether you'd got it.'

He flipped through the pile of papers on his desk. Underneath one of them was a page from a memo pad with a name and a Brighton number. He should have noticed it. 'Must have got mislaid,' he said smoothly. 'You've no idea where he is now?'

'Sorry, sir.'

'Well, thanks anyway.'

After he had hung up, he spent five minutes cursing keen young constables who forget to carry their warrant cards. Still, he might as well go to Brighton and have a look. Nothing else offered, and he liked Brighton. He felt a lot more cheerful as he stepped into his car, although he did not expect to find Taggart awaiting him at the other end of his journey. The sun was shining as he sped down the M23 towards the Sussex downs.

When he got there, it was as he had hoped. The sea sparkled, the shingle crunched under his feet. He felt braced, though he could still think of no conceivable course of action. Still, away from London and the unsympathetic ægis of the AC he felt lighter, more cheerful, altogether better. He would change jobs, he promised himself, if he could only think of another job that would suit him. Or have him. He didn't much fancy going into security work.

Time for lunch. He knew of rather a pleasant pub, not far from the Lanes. He would have something to eat and consider what to do next. He found the place, bought a large crab salad and a pint, and looked round for somewhere to sit. And could not believe his eyes.

'God!' said Taggart in disgust. 'What on earth are you doing here?'

'Looking for you, of course,' King said jovially.

'Why? I haven't done anything illegal.'

'I wanted to talk to you about Paul Silverlight. Perhaps I ought to remind you,' said King sternly, 'that it is illegal to withhold information from the police in a case of this kind.'

'I'm not withholding anything. I only got the information myself a couple of days ago, and I was going to pass the whole lot on to you as soon as the piece was safely in the can. So don't panic.'

'I'm not panicking,' King assured him. 'And what precisely was this mysterious information you were going to pass on?'

'Who did it, of course. Isn't that what you want to know?'

172

'There are lots of things I want to know. So, who did do it?'

'Peter Conder.'

'And exactly what evidence have you got to support this extraordinary theory?'

'Oh, nothing you could base a court case on,' Taggart assured him. 'But he doesn't know that. Actually, now that I think about it, I'm rather glad to see you. It's Conder I've been afraid of running into. You'd constitute what's technically known as police protection, in an emergency.'

'And just why did Peter Conder kill his good friend? We'll leave aside the how for the moment.'

'It was a CIA job. Silverlight leaked that paper. Conder works for the CIA and I imagine he was detailed to do it. Ask your friends. You ought to have better contacts there than I have, surely?'

King thought bitterly about Kowalsky. He said, 'What an extraordinary story. Do you actually propose to print stuff like that?'

Taggart shrugged. 'Carefully phrased, of course.' He turned back to his plate. His lunch was getting cold. Damn King. He began to eat again. King, too, turned his attention to lunch. After a while Taggart said, 'There's something I've been meaning to ask you.'

'Oh?'

'Yes. Do you enjoy your job?'

King leaned back to consider this. At the moment, he could think of no satisfactory reply. 'It's a job.'

'True, but why that particular job?'

'I could ask you the same.'

'Oh, I enjoy mine,' Taggart assured him. 'Simply, it struck me that they were rather similar. Only I have the satisfaction of doing something that goes with my principles. I mean, my job is to undermine people like you. The defence of democracy and civil liberties and all that kind of thing. But all you do is try to undermine people like me. I mean, does that really give you any pleasure? You seem a sensible sort of chap on the whole, but rather glum. I thought it might be the uncongenial nature of your work.'

'Thanks,' said King. 'What are you trying to do? Disaffect me? Turn me into a double agent?'

'No, I just wondered what it was about people like me that worries you so much.'

King considered. It was not a question he had confronted before, though it must have had something to do with his joining the police in the first place. After all, that was not what most sociology graduates did, not even if they thought they would spend the rest of their working lives as community liaison officers. And if he was honest King had to admit that he had never envisaged spending the whole of his working life in that particular slot. He said, 'You want to upset things.'

'Things upset themselves. I just describe them. What I want to know,' said Taggart, 'is why, for example, you think that hushing up the facts about Silverlight and Conder is intrinsically more desirable than letting it all come out.'

King shrugged miserably. He hated Taggart. The AC, in this situation, would have had no doubts. Anything that Taggart wanted uncovered must, *ipso facto*, be better hushed up. But in this particular case he was the fall-guy. He said, 'I didn't say we were hushing anything up. I merely wondered whether you could prove your extraordinary suggestion.'

'Not hushing things up? Don't be silly. I can smell a hush-up at a hundred yards and this one smells to high heaven. Well, I'll tell you,' said Taggart. 'It's because the CIA doesn't want any embarrassment and they're leaning on you, so you're leaning on me. They made sure you didn't find anything out in the first place and now they're dancing with rage. Isn't that it? Poor old King. Caught in the middle. Well, it's too late. It's all written and printed now, and there's no earthly way you can stop it except by creating an even bigger scandal.'

'We don't yet have trial by newspaper in this country, I'm glad to say.'

'And I haven't been so damned stupid as to name names, I'm glad to say.'

They glared at each other across the table. Taggart said,

'Well, I'm off. No point staying in Brighton any longer. Feel like giving me a lift back to London?'

'Not in the least,' said King, and strode out of the pub.

'I'll send you the piece,' Taggart called after him. 'Hope you enjoy it.'

CHAPTER 31

The nearer Taggart got to London, however, the more nervous he felt. The pit of his stomach was heavy, and by the time he reached the corner of his street he could scarcely breathe. It came almost as a shock to see how peaceful everything was. The place was empty, silent, exactly as usual. Cats peered down from walls, a milk float chugged slowly by. The pavement was littered with sweet-wrappers and dog-turds. He approached his front door. Locked, as he had left it. He was just putting his key into the lock when the front door of the next house opened and the crone's head appeared.

'Oh, hallo, Mrs Venables.'

'Mr Taggart, thank goodness you're back. Whatever've you bin doing? The people that's bin lookin fer you!'

'Oh? Who?' Taggart felt his mouth dry out. It was imperative that Mrs Venables should not realize he was nervous or she would create and spread unending baroque theories as to why this should be so. 'I was only in Brighton,' he added.

'Well, I don't know, do I? I can't ask everybody oo knocks on your door oo they are, can I? Busies, I think they was.'

'More than one?'

'Ooh, I couldn't say.' And Mrs Venables disappeared.

Probably King, thought Taggart. Well, there's no one here now, at any rate. He glanced quickly up and down the street. Still nothing but cats. Even the milk float had disappeared. He unlocked his door and went in. A mound of post impeded the door: everything else was as he had left it. No one had broken in, then, or not through the front door. The familiar quiet reassured him. Perhaps he had been having unnecessary paranoid fantasies. He put a kettle on, sat down at the kitchen table and began to go through his mail. When he had had a cup of tea and felt calmer, he rang the office. Yes, the piece had arrived safely. He said he would look in later and rang off.

What now? He glanced at his watch. Five o'clock. It was good to be home. Perhaps he would have a bath. Wash the remnants of that tartan wallpaper forever from his recollection. He looked happily out of the window. A man was coming down the street. The figure seemed vaguely familiar. Wasn't it—? Now calm down, Andrew: last time, it wasn't.

This time, however, it was. Peter Conder—purely by chance? Tipped the wink by King? Or had he been watching all the time from somewhere nearby?—Peter Conder was purposefully approaching his front door.

Taggart was not conscious of even thinking what he should do next. Of their own accord his feet carried him quietly downstairs, out the back door, down his five-yard patch of garden and over the back wall. All the back gardens of his terrace adjoined not only each other but the back gardens of the parallel terrace of houses fronting the next street. From time to time Taggart, idling in his study (which overlooked the garden) had fantasized about the escape-route he would use *in extremis*. Over the back wall, turn left, through that gap in the fence which was screened by the elder, behind the sycamore, over into the yard filled with old mattresses, and he knew that the back door of that house was never locked, because streams of children were constantly in and out of it. Slip in there, quickly out through the front, and there he was in Matilda Terrace. Nip quickly into the Kingsland Road and there you are.

And here he was. No taxis in the Kingsland Road, that went without saying. Not exactly taxi country, here. He leapt on to a passing bus, regardless of the fact that it was going in precisely the opposite direction to what he wanted, and made his way tortuously towards the *New Politics* office.

176

'You look terrible,' said Cooper. 'Where've you been?'

'Brighton.'

'Brighton! All that sea air. I'd have thought you'd look better than that.'

'I didn't get any sea air. I stayed in my hotel room. You got the piece.'

'Yes.'

'OK?'

'Yes.'

'Then you understand why I stayed in my room.'

'It seems a little paranoid,' said Cooper mildly. 'Why on earth should anyone think you were in Brighton? You could have been anywhere.'

'You'll never guess what happened as soon as I left my room.'

'No.'

'I ran into King.'

'Oh my God.'

'Well, there was nothing much he could do by then. We had a long discussion. I told him about Conder. He didn't know anything about it, or else he's a very good actor. I don't think he's a good actor, though. He was really shocked.'

'But surely they must know . . . ?'

'I expect somebody does. They haven't told poor old King, though. I'm sending him a copy of my tape. And the piece, of course. That should embarrass a few people. I'm more worried about Conder. He must be feeling a bit desperate.' Taggart did not mention his recent ignominious exit from his own house. Somehow that lacked a certain bravado. 'Has anyone been asking for me?'

'Jane Addison rang a couple of times. Seemed outraged when I said I didn't know where you were. I spoke to her. I expect there've been others. You'll have to ask Sarah.'

Sarah was the irreproachably upper-class girl who was the general *New Politics* secretary.

'Andrew,' she greeted him rapturously. 'I don't know what you've been doing but your phone's been buzzing non-stop. I've a list of messages as long as my arm.' She produced them. They were mostly from other journalists. Some were from King. All of them asked him to ring them back. 'Then there was someone else,' Sarah went on mysteriously. 'Wouldn't leave a message. Just kept wanting to know where you were. Sounded extremely correct and extremely fed-up. Where were you?'

'Brighton. Did this person leave a name?'

'No.'

'Well, I won't bother with any of that lot,' said Taggart, and took himself off for a long, luxurious, above-board walk in what remained of the sunshine. The weather seemed to be breaking. Just his luck.

The phone was ringing when he got back. Sarah said, 'It hasn't stopped. They've just seen the early copies.'

'What do they want?'

Sarah shrugged. 'How would I know? The name of your mysterious murderer, I expect.' She held out a list of those who had phoned. Every national newspaper and most of the weeklies, plus radio and television current affairs departments. Some were friends, all were acquaintances. Taggart handed back the list. 'I'm off,' he said. 'Tell them I've gone to Brighton.'

Up and down Fleet Street editorial conferences focused on the same thing. Scandals such as this were after all what the place was built upon, and what was more, they offered a welcome respite from the uniformly gloomy news on the international political front. The *Sun* put three men onto the story with instructions to find the mysterious CIA major, no expense spared, no questions asked as to how. Down the road at the *Mirror*, the same question was under discussion.

'I hear they're putting their royal team on to it,' a Mirror-man remarked gloomily. 'I expect they'll kidnap Taggart and wire him up to the ring main till he talks.'

'Then kidnap him first,' said his editor unsympathetically.

'I've been on to Cooper,' said the *Monitor*'s investigative reporter. 'Taggart's gone into hiding.'

178

'Does he know?'

'I think he does, but he's not saying.'

'Perhaps someone'll leak it to us,' said his editor hopefully. 'Don't you know the secretary there—Sarah Somebody-Somebody? Why don't you ask her out to dinner? We'll pay.'

Television News that night ran pictures of Silverlight superimposed on film of the *New Politics* offices (a nondescript building near Covent Garden) and Taggart's house. The cats were still there.

Taggart, walking from Dalston station on the North London Line, approached his house with caution. There seemed to be an unusual amount of activity around the place. As he walked quietly down an adjacent street, he noticed two taxis turn into his terrace—an unusual, almost a unique sight. He turned away from his house and made a roundabout approach which would enable him to view the place from a corner some distance away. As he watched, a large van drew up and disgorged a television film crew. Taggart turned quietly round and returned to the North London Line whence he had come. From there, he took the next train to Broad Street.

'What a mess,' the AC said. 'Do we at least have the name of this mysterious personage? Or are we to learn that from the front pages of the Sunday papers?'

'I have the name of the person Taggart has in mind,' said King.

'And who is it? Or are you keeping it a deathly secret as well?'

'It's a man named Conder. Peter Conder. He's a don at Cambridge. I interviewed him after the death,' King said heavily.

King watched the AC closely to see what effect, if any, this information would produce. The thought had crossed his mind, too, that they might have been making even more of a fool of him than he had thought. After all, if there was a list of acceptable culprits, there must be a list of unacceptables as well. There was, however, no telling.

'And did he have an alibi?'

'Seemed to. I have to admit,' said King heavily 'that I didn't pursue it as hard as I might have. The very idea seemed so unlikely, somehow. He was a colleague—'

'I know Conder,' the AC cut in. 'As you say, hardly the obvious suspect. What motive do our friends on *New Politics* assign, precisely?'

'They say he's employed by the CIA.'

The AC sighed. 'You were supposed to be stopping all this,' he said. 'Not one of your most successful efforts. As it is, I see no way out of it. We'll have to send the file to the DPP. God knows what she'll have to say about all this.'

Having failed to find Taggart, the journalists moved across to the fashionable side of Islington.

'Paul Silverlight was your brother, is that correct, Mrs Croft?'

'Do you have any photographs of yourselves as children together, Mrs Croft? Of course we'll pay . . .'

'Your politics are very different from your brother's, aren't they, Mrs Croft? How do you explain that? Do you think perhaps this means he really agreed with you underneath?'

'Have you any idea who did it, Mrs Croft?'

Judith, standing at her front door wiping floury hands on her apron (she had been in the middle of baking Ben's birthday cake in a fit of remorseful domesticity) was bewildered. She had not yet read that week's *New Politics*. 'I don't know what you're all talking about,' she said, as cameras clicked ('Mrs Judith Croft, CND organizer and sister of the late Paul Silverlight, stands at her front door in fashionable Islington . . .')

'Haven't you read this, Mrs Croft?'

The *Sun* man shouldered his way to the front of the milling mob. 'Mrs Croft, don't take any notice of all these people, I am authorized to offer you five thousand pounds for your story.'

'Go away!' she cried. 'Just go away, all of you!' She turned her back on them and slammed her front door. Pictures the next day bore the caption 'Judith Croft, sister of the murdered man, was upset at the new allegations about him. Here she turns a distraught back on photographers . . .'

'Well,' said the news editor resignedly, 'at least you've got a picture.'

CHAPTER 32

Broad Street station was a place of which Taggart was particularly fond. It was run-down and shabby and he felt an affinity with it. Willow-herb grew in the cracks of its concrete platforms, and the rusting lace of its Victorian iron train-sheds recalled a less utilitarian age. It was with some reluctance that he abandoned it and set off down the rickety wooden steps which led to the roaring madhouse that was the forecourt of Liverpool Street, the station serving the east of England.

It was four o'clock. The next train to Cambridge left at four thirty-six. Taggart suddenly felt rather nervous. How had he got into this, anyway? He sat in the corner of a second-class carriage and pondered. The familiar train smell of dust and old farts was reassuring. He remembered why he was doing this. Of course—it was a continuation of his personal battle with the government in general and the Special Branch in particular. Well, he had won that one. He had found out what they had not wished to be found and he had published his information, or most of it, to their undoubted fury. He ought to be feeling pleased. But pleased was somehow not relevant to the way he felt at the moment. Which was scared. But that was ridiculous. Britain was not some banana republic. People still had to have a reason for killing or maiming someone here—which was presumably what he was scared of? Well, no mere presumption. He had always been a physical coward. Sticks and stones may break my bones but words will never hurt me.

The train made its unhurried way through the Essex countryside. Cottages expensively renovated for commuters could be seen through the windows. Old men were weeding their allotments, or just staring at their plants growing. It was not the world inhabited by politicians or, Taggart thought, by me.

Through this alien stage-set the train rattled. Cambridge at last: mean streets round the railway sidings. When Taggart went to get off, he found the doors blocked by a crowd of football fans fighting to get on. He gave up and went up to another door. He did not feel strong enough to tackle gratuitous fights.

He walked slowly up Station Road, past the language schools, right at the Hills Road roundabout. He had been here a few times, not often, and was always surprised and rather appalled by the contrast between the scrimped feel of the fen town and the sumptuous buildings of the university. There were hardly any fine or even decent houses here to ease the transition: yellow brick cottages, two up, two down, suddenly gave way to lacy stonework and Wren chapels. Princes' was off Trumpington Street. A woman wheeling a howling infant in a pushchair directed him down Downing Street, and suddenly he was in the university, stepping across Princes' Gothic threshold and inquiring at the porter's lodge if Dr Conder was there. If not he would wait: but they thought he was, which meant that he must have returned to Cambridge immediately after failing to corner him at home. He was directed to Conder's rooms. He crossed a wide court and entered a doorway with stairs leading up. On the wall a list of names was painted. Dr Conder lived on the ground floor. Taggart glanced up: there was his name over the door. The big outer door was not shut, which presumably meant he was in. Taggart knocked on the white-painted inner door, and was greeted by an urbane voice. 'My dear Andrew, I'd been hoping to see you. Do come in.'

Taking a deep breath, in he went, hoping that beating heart and weak knees were not outwardly visible. There was no reason why they should be, of course.

'It isn't second sight,' said Conder amiably. 'I was watching you crossing the court.' He was seated in an armchair by the window, a book on his knee, a writing-pad on the arm of the chair. 'Would you like some tea?'

'No, thanks,' said Taggart. He did not trust tea made by Peter Conder. Look what had happened to Silverlight when he drank a cup of coffee in the same company.

'No? Well, I hope you won't mind if I have some. I was just about to.' Conder crossed the room to the door leading to his kitchen. 'Do sit down,' he called, but Taggart wandered around, admiring the carving around the fireplace, the linenfold panelling, the book-laden shelves.

'Nice place you have here.'

'Isn't it? If you work very hard you may approximate to something like it yourself one day.' Conder had returned and was sitting watching his visitor, sipping his tea.

'I don't expect so.'

'Nor do I.'

There was a pause. Then Conder said, 'To what do I owe the pleasure of this visit?'

'I understood that you were looking for me.' Taggart looked him in the eye and found his stare calmly returned.

'So I was. I rather expected to find you at home. In fact I could have sworn you were there. The lady next door said you were.' Conder took another sip of tea. A clump of students, boys and girls, wearing rainbow hair-dos and absurd clothes, burst across the court laughing and shouting. Conder frowned. 'Exams in two weeks,' he remarked, Cassandra-like. Taggart wished he was with the students.

'I enjoyed your piece,' said Conder. 'Managed to get an early copy in London. Have you ever thought of taking up writing thrillers?'

'No, real life's good enough for me.'

'Lucky you,' sighed his host. 'And who is the mysterious killer, might one inquire? I notice you don't mention names.'

'I wouldn't like to make myself or the paper liable for libel proceedings.'

'Ah, then, you don't have proof.'

'Is that my job? I've passed my information on to the police.'

'Such as it is.'

'Such as it is.'

183

Another pause.

Conder said, 'I think you'll find that poor Paul committed suicide. Of course I wouldn't presume to denigrate the quality of your information, but I understand from some quite unimpeachable sources that that is actually what happened. Quite understandable, of course, poor fellow. He probably thought he'd set World War Three off by mistake.'

'Perhaps he had. Though I'm not so sure about the mistake.'

'Oh, I believe everything's under control now,' Conder said comfortably.

'I wish I could feel so sanguine.'

'Of course you don't. You professional doom-peddlers would be out of a job the minute you felt sanguine.' Conder paused to let this piece of patronage sink in and added, 'So you see, it all makes perfect sense.'

'Except that his fingerprints weren't on the plastic bag.'

Conder was unperturbed. 'Oh, Inspector King's been letting you in on the technical details, has he? Well, I expect they got a bit blurred. Things do.'

'According to my information, he was killed by the CIA.'

'So you said. So interesting. What makes you think that?'

'A quite unimpeachable source.'

'Talking of sources,' remarked Conder, as he might draw attention to a particularly interesting passage, 'did you know that poor Art Brownson died? Quite suddenly, I believe.'

'Another notch in your gun?' inquired Taggart.

'Oh, really,' said Conder crossly. 'What do you take me for? Al Capone? That's what I've been wanting to talk to you about. Perhaps someone's told you that I've been trying to get in touch? While you've been staked out somewhere writing your filthy little innuendoes or skulking in your back bedroom not answering the door. Though I can't quite see why you prefer to talk to me here than there.'

'People know I'm here. I asked for you at the porter's lodge.'

Conder gave an exasperated sigh. 'Well, I assure you your next-door neighbour knew I was there, just as she knew you were. You certainly don't need any watchdogs with a

184

neighbour like that. Anyway, that's not the point. I understand you're insinuating that I did it.'

'You've read the piece. Do I mention your name anywhere?'

There was a silence. Conder glanced at the book he had been reading and made a note on his pad. 'Do excuse me,' he said, looking up. 'Otherwise I'm sure to forget. You know how it is.'

'I know how it is,' said Taggart. 'It was you, wasn't it?'

'Is that what you've told the police?'

'Among other things, yes.'

'And quite what did you hope to achieve by that?'

Taggart thought about this. It was not, in the heat of the moment, a point he had considered: he had simply taken it for granted. 'The apprehension of the villain, I suppose,' he said, feeling foolish and rather primitive. Conder had that effect on one.

'Really,' remarked the villain (if it was he) in a tone of voice that indicated this was an entirely new concept for him. 'And what good do you suppose that would do?'

'Old-fashioned notions of retribution, I suppose.'

'Well, it's your adjective.' Conder leaned back in his chair. The pad fell off the arm on to the floor: he retrieved it and set it neatly on the window-sill, adjusting the pen so that it lay parallel to the lines of writing. 'I can't myself quite see the point, even if it were to happen.'

'Don't you think it will?'

'No,' said Conder. 'It won't. The inquest will bring in a verdict of suicide and that will be that.'

'You seem very well-informed.'

'You have your sources. I have mine. And you've got to admit that my version seems altogether less unlikely than yours.' Conder made another note. 'Just because you write a letter to the police telling them you think I did it doesn't mean they automatically come and arrest me. This isn't the Doge's Venice, or the Shah's Iran, or somewhere like that. We don't just pay off grudges with anonymous tip-offs, I'm glad to say.'

'I haven't any particular grudge against you.'

'No, it's me that has one against you, really, isn't it?'

'I'd better look out, then.'

'Mm,' agreed Conder. 'Oh yes, there was something else I wanted to ask you. One thing you left out of your extremely interesting account of all this. Why did he do it? Why did my old friend Paul incur the wrath of the CIA, supposing that was what he did, by leaking this document? It's something which seems a little hard to credit, don't you think? Did you know him at all? Have you read anything he wrote?'

'I've met him once or twice. And I've even read his latest book.'

'Well then! You must admit it's a puzzle. The whole of your story seems rather weak, but I'm not sure that isn't the weakest part of all. And now,' said Conder briskly, 'if you'll excuse me, I've rather a lot of work to do. It seems to me we've said all we're usefully going to, don't you agree?'

CHAPTER 33

'Look, I don't know what's going on over there,' quacked the voice over the Ambassador's telephone. 'But one thing I can tell you, they're going to be pretty sore over at Langley if this thing goes into much more detail. One thing we just do not need at this point is another Philip Magee. I'm getting a whole lot of flak here. People are worried about our guys' safety. And right now we need these guys. Suspicions are one thing but names are quite another. Know what I mean? And they aren't going to be the only ones that are sore.'

'I'm doing what I can, Mr President.'

'You know how it is,' quacked the voice. 'At this moment we need to be absolutely sure of our position. We've enough delicate moments without it being delicate with our Allies, goddammit. I've been on to the Prime Minister but I wanted to confirm this with you. That story needs to be killed, and fast.'

'Just the story, huh?' joked the Ambassador feebly. But his interlocutor did not see the joke.

'Keep me informed,' he said, and rang off.

'It isn't a demotion, King,' said the AC. 'Don't think that, for goodness' sake. It's simply that it was felt in some quarters that your special talents were being wasted in this department. After all, we don't have that many senior policemen with degrees in sociology, do we? And with this new Community Liaison Unit starting up—'

'All right, sir,' said King. He was sitting opposite the AC, who was doing his level best to avoid meeting King's eye. 'Not demotion. Just kicked sideways.'

'This damned awkward case,' the AC mumbled. 'Our friends across the water . . .'

'Got to show that someone's been kicked somewhere.'

'Not quite like that . . .'

'They should just keep their dirty tricks to their own country. It's big enough.'

'You'll find all the details here,' said the AC, briskly handing over a file. He had had enough of being made to feel in the wrong. In my position, he thought, you get it from all sides. Nothing but bloody flak. If a crime occurs then there is, *ipso facto*, a guilty party, and it was time, in this case, that the guilt started to settle in the correct places. One was not sure, or not officially sure, of the culprit in the case of the death of Paul Silverlight. (It was now being suggested by the most authoritative sources that the culprit was in fact already dead, being Silverlight himself who had unaccountably committed suicide, perhaps, although this was equally uncertain, in connection with the leaked Pentagon document.) But there was only one person who could have bungled the investigation in the myriad different ways in which it had unarguably been bungled.

'I hope you enjoy your new posting,' said the AC. 'You won't find it quite so sensitive, which might be something of a relief to you. You must let me know some time how you get on. Goodbye now.'

*

'What I still don't understand,' said Andrew Taggart, 'is why he did it.'

'Why who did what?' said Nick Croft. He was lying back with a glass of wine in his hand. It was after dinner. The night was hot and the window was open on to the Crofts' back yard, a small space fragrant now with honeysuckle, so that it was almost possible to forget that one was in London. The children were in bed and Judith and Nick seemed unusually peaceful. Whether this would survive the next telephone call summoning Judith to the political flag it was impossible to say. For the moment, things were as Nick would have wanted them to be: domestically ordered and relaxed.

'Silverlight. Why he leaked that paper.'

'No idea. He did and someone did him in for it. What more do we need to know?'

'It isn't the need to know so much as the deep unsatisfactoriness of not knowing. I read his last book,' said Taggart to Judith. 'Have you read it? It's barmy, well, I think it's barmy, and deeply unpleasant—all those very good reasons why we should send the blacks packing—but it isn't inconsistent. It's all of a piece and that wasn't. Was it?'

Judith was sitting in a rocking-chair by the window. She rocked back and forth, not very evidently listening to the conversation. Her eyes were half shut, her dark hair shadowing her face. Taggart could never make out what her feelings were or had been about her brother. Did Nick know, he wondered. Did he want to know? Probably this, too, was one of the topics which he preferred to avoid. Too much unpleasantness altogether.

Judith said, 'I've been wondering about that. I've been thinking about it a lot.' She went on rocking, back and forth, not looking at them. She had a glass of wine in her hand, which occasionally caught the light as she rocked. Taggart found himself fascinated by it, wondering if it would spill. It did not, as if it were balanced on some sort of ball-bearing which kept it steady. 'Actually, I think it was in character,' Judith said.

'Really?' Taggart was astonished. Even Nick showed

some surprise. He said, 'Tell us more. On my small acquaintance with your brother, that's not what I should have thought.'

'That's the point. Small acquaintance,' said Judith. 'That's what people had with Paul. I can't think of anyone who had much more. The ones who bothered to try didn't get much encouragement. Ask Jenny Dawes.'

'I got the impression he had quite a relationship with Brownson in Princeton,' said Taggart.

'And look what he did to him,' said Judith dreamily. 'I doubt whether Mr Brownson's career has been much enhanced by all this.'

'Brownson is dead,' said Taggart. 'I heard the other day.'

There was silence while they took this in.

'Well, there you are,' said Judith. 'I should look out if I were you. You lived to tell the tale this time but who knows how far you can push your luck?'

'Are you saying it was just spite?' Nick asked, returning to the earlier topic. He sounded rather shocked. 'I hope my sister has better things to say of me when I'm not there.'

'No,' said Judith dreamily. 'I don't think that was it. I think it was more—gratuitous. An *acte gratuit*. A desire to see what would happen if he did—whatever it was. Took on Jenny. Leaked the paper. I can imagine it quite easily, myself.' Nick looked alarmed, but said nothing. What was he imagining might happen? wondered Taggart. 'I wouldn't do it,' said Judith. Nick looked relieved. 'But I can see how one might. Can't you?'

Taggart thought of Jenny, destroyed, and of Silverlight himself, destroyed. He said, 'If I were ever tempted, all I'd have to do is think of your brother.'

Nick said lazily, 'You still haven't told us who did it. Do you really know, or was that just a spicy hint to make a good story?'

'I really know. At least, I'm pretty sure. But I don't have proof and libel suits come expensive.'

Judith said, 'Well, at least it doesn't sound as if it was Jenny.'

'Jenny?' Taggart was thunderstruck.

'You know Jenny confessed? John Dawes told me. Inspector King told Charlotte when he was questioning her. He'd just been to see Jenny in Fulbourn. Still, obviously she isn't the person you had in mind.'

Taggart was silent for a moment. Then he said, 'Do you happen to have a photograph of her?'

Judith looked surprised. 'I expect so. But it'd be rather old.' She went to a bureau in the corner of the room and rummaged about, emerging with a bulging box full of photographs. After a few minutes riffling through this, she emerged with a couple of pictures. 'These are from Cambridge,' Judith said. 'But they'll give you some idea.'

The pictures showed groups of laughing young people in the sun, including a much younger Judith. Leaning over his shoulder, she pointed out the rest of the crowd: Silverlight, Bob Chantrey, and a slender girl with long hair. In one of the pictures, Chantrey had his arm around her shoulders; but her gaze was fixed on Silverlight, who was staring at the camera.

'Does she still look like this?'

'No, she's utterly changed, poor thing. Got much fatter and coarser, and—sort of—lost expression.'

Taggart squinted at the photograph, trying to superimpose this description on to the girl in the photograph. Plus —how many years?

'When was this taken? How long ago?'

Judith reckoned back, gazing at the photo. 'Must be— oh, fourteen, fifteen years. It's hard to believe.'

'Well, it could be,' said Taggart. 'It could just be.'

'Could be what?' they wanted to know.

Taggart described the episode in Clapham, when the fat woman had almost succeeded in pushing him under a bus. He kept staring at the photograph. It could be. It could just be.

'But why should she want to . . . ?'

'We'll come to that,' said Taggart. 'Maybe. First things first. Could she have done it? You said she was in Fulbourn, didn't you? Is she there all the time or does she come home?'

'Oh yes,' said Judith. 'She was on a home visit that night,

the night Paul was killed, and I got the definite feeling that the Dawes were worried that it really might have been her. Apparently she's been fantasizing about doing it for years. It was the only thing she'd talk about. Literally. Otherwise she was just silent. I understand that she's a lot better now. They're hoping she'll be able to come out quite soon. I imagine they were terrified she'd be tried—the strain would just about have finished her off, wouldn't it? No matter what the outcome was.'

'Genuine catharsis,' observed Nick.

Poor old King, thought Taggart. How he must have been tempted, poor sod. But why hadn't he just taken the easy way out and believed her?

'I saw your brother that night, you know,' he said to Judith. 'We were both at a party at Jane Addison's. So was Peter Conder. And—wait a minute!' He frowned, trying to pin down a face imprinted fleetingly on his mind— just before he left—talking to that art critic, that fat ass Tobit—

'It was her!'

That was where he had seen her before, of course. The girl in Clapham. That had been the girl talking to Tobit. Taggart had noticed them talking, or rather had noticed them stop: the classic end to a conversation at that sort of party, he remembered thinking, as fat Tobit hurried off to speak to the gallery director, leaving the earnest girl to fend for herself. So it hadn't been an accident that time in Clapham—that would have been just too much of a coincidence. But how on earth . . . ? And why him . . . ? He would have to think about it. Meanwhile, events marched on.

'I take it that wasn't who you had in mind, then?' said Nick.

'No,' said Taggart. 'That isn't who I had in mind.'

'So who was it?'

'Peter Conder,' said Taggart: and the Crofts chorused in unison, 'I don't believe it!'

CHAPTER 34

Private Eye, 28 May
Who killed Paul Silverlight? That's the question half London
has been racking its brains to answer ever since the bright
young man of the Right was found dead in his flat last
month. Many possible candidates suggested themselves,
including Professor John Dawes, veteran lefty idiot, whose
daughter Jenny has been left a gibbering wreck by the
appalling Silverlight. Dawes was ruled out because he was
himself in hospital at the time recovering from a murder
attempt. (Obviously politics is becoming an increasingly
dangerous game.) Now journalist Andrew Taggart hints in
New Politics that he knows the culprit but is not letting on.
Who is the mysterious CIA major whose identity would
surprise so many people did they but know it? We understand that he lives not a million miles from Dr Peter Conder,
of Princes' College, Cambridge, guru of the thinking Right.
So is Princes', hitherto considered a respectable academic
establishment, nothing but a nest of spies and murderers?
And can we now expect the New Right to wipe itself out
entirely?

In Herschel Road the Dawes family was having breakfast.
The family consisted once again of four members: Jenny
seemed to be making a remarkable recovery, and had been
allowed to leave Fulbourn. Things seemed, Charlotte reflected, to be in every way returning to normal. The immediate consciousness of impending annihilation was receding,
as it inevitably had to, supposing life was to go on at all.
And the Dawes family was split once again into two halves
—Jenny and John deep in their special complicity, Charlotte
and Esme conducting life on the plane of the practical and
humdrum. Jenny was even beginning to look normal again.

Charlotte glanced down at her *Private Eye* and, thunderstruck, read the paragraph about Conder. She glanced up

feeling almost guilty. Could she show this to Jenny, or would it be too much for her newly restored stability? Well, someone would be sure to mention it to her—that much was certain. Might as well be now.

'Look at this,' she said.

They looked, and leaned back in their chairs. Nobody said anything, but the feeling of relaxation round the table was tangible. It was as if the entire family heaved a great, collective sigh of relief.

'Isn't that amazing?' said Charlotte.

They agreed—singularly half-heartedly, she thought.

'Did you know about this?'

'No, of course we didn't,' said John. 'How could we?' He smiled at Jenny, who smiled back. Charlotte returned to her breakfast, thinking hard. She recalled an occasion some days before when she had surprised her father and sister deep in conversation—a conversation which had ended abruptly when she entered the room. What had they been discussing with such urgency? As she chewed her toast, an idea struck her. It was not an idea she welcomed. But the more she thought about it, the more things seemed to fall into place around it.

She said, for no apparent reason, 'Did they ever find out who tried to do you in, Dad?'

John Dawes looked astonished, then shifty. Jenny blushed deeply and looked as if she might be about to burst into tears. Esme said quickly, 'It obviously wasn't high on their list of priorities. They certainly didn't seem to look very hard, did they? I don't suppose we shall ever find out now.' Her remark feel into a deep silence. Nobody else said a word. Charlotte did not pursue the subject.

After breakfast, Charlotte hurried round to see if she could find Martin in his rooms. She prayed that he would be there, and that he would be alone. Her prayers were answered.

'The thing is,' she said breathlessly 'I'm convinced—oh, it's so awful, I can hardly bring myself to think it, let alone say it. But it's the only thing that fits all the facts. I think Jenny did do it—the actual thing. I think that man King was right. She must have crept out and taken the car and gone up to London and come back before I woke up. We did go to bed rather early—and you know what she was like, there didn't seem a lot else to do. And I'm a very heavy sleeper.'

'So where does Conder come in?' asked Martin.

'Ah well—he put her up to it. She wouldn't have been capable of initiating anything like that. I didn't know she knew him, but she might well have done, when you come to think of it. He was a friend of Paul's. He was part of the Princes' crowd when everyone was up here.'

'But why should she do anything like that for him?'

Charlotte shrugged miserably. 'I don't know. If they're right about him being in the CIA, then he'd presumably do anything. He may have something on her. He may have supplied her with drugs, and then made her do something and threatened to tell if she didn't do this. I don't know. It's not so very hard to imagine. And he could easily have kept up with her in Fulbourn. Anyway, if he knew her that well, he'd know other things—like how close she's always been to Daddy. It's still the same. If she was going to tell anyone, it'd be him.'

'And if she told him, then that was that.' Martin considered. 'So you think Conder tried to wipe him out before any damage could be done. Or in case it had been. Do you think she did tell him?'

'Not then,' said Charlotte. 'I think she told him three days ago. In fact, I think I interrupted the confession.'

CHAPTER 35

Charlotte was not the only person in Cambridge to have noticed the *Private Eye* story. At Princes', breakfasting undergraduates looked with new interest at the vacant chair at High Table usually occupied by Conder. It was agreed that on the face of it the story seemed unlikely. To begin with, the political affiliations of victim and putative murderer were so similar: and it was not suggested that Conder, if it was he, had carried out the killing on anything but strictly ideological grounds. Then it was pointed out that it was hard to imagine the suave Conder doing anything so violent, or indeed physical, as a killing: though one youth, sporting a blue Mohican hair-do, pointed out that as far as he could remember there had been nothing particularly violent about the killing of Silverlight. 'Wasn't it just sleeping pills and a plastic bag over the head? Sneaky sort of way to do it. I can just imagine that creep doing that.'

University habits being what they were, Conder himself did not have to face his compeers until lunch-time. He had been made aware of the story, which normally (for he was not a regular reader of *Private Eye*) he would have missed, by the flurry of telephone calls from newspapers, radio and television asking for his reaction. He fended off all of these by saying that as he had not read the story he could not possibly comment on it, and at the first opportunity hurried to the newsagent across the street for a copy of the *Eye*. The fat lady behind the counter sold him one with the comment that this was the last copy, and she had never known such a run on them. 'So lucky I was in time, then,' said Conder politely, and hurried back to his room to read the worst.

By now, of course, he knew what it said. Even so, knowing is not the same as seeing, and the printed words gave him more of a jolt than he had anticipated. He picked up the phone and instructed the porter's lodge that he was taking no more phone calls that morning. Then he shut his heavy outer door and returned to his chair to contemplate the pertinent question which he had avoided answering twenty times already that morning. What, indeed, was his reaction?

By lunch-time he had decided upon it, and descended to face his colleagues.

By now, of course, every member of the college was aware that Dr Conder was (or was rumoured to be) the mysterious murderer so ostentatiously unnamed by Andrew Taggart in his by now notorious article. Since Paul Silverlight had been a member of the college and a friend, or close acquaintance, of many of its senior members, they naturally took a close

195

interest in the circumstances of his death. Even those who never normally saw a copy of *New Politics* (an irresponsible left-wing rag) had seen that one.

But although the story was at the forefront of everyone's mind, and although they were all dying to talk about it, it was hard to see how they could decently begin to do so.

So conversation at high table (though not in the body of the hall, where Conder was the cynosure of all eyes and a source of unashamed and pleasurable speculation) was stilted. One or two side topics were mooted, but nobody really had the heart for them. The improved prospects for transplants afforded by recent breakthroughs in the immunological work at Babraham, and the effect on grant applications of the new, severe attitude of the planning committee of the Science and Engineering Research Council, did not receive the attention they might otherwise have deserved. Conversation had died away almost entirely when Conder himself electrified the table by remarking, 'Did anyone see the story in *Private Eye* today?'

Silence. At length the Master, possibly feeling that his position required him to give a lead, raised his head from the cheese (a choice of Cheddar and wrapped Camembert: the college cuisine was not what it had been, not at lunchtime, anyway) and said 'I did, as it happens. Most interesting. I was going to mention it, but it slipped my mind.'

There was another pause while people tried to decide how best to carry the conversation on from there. How could they ask the pertinent question—namely, Is it true? At least they no longer had to avoid meeting Conder's eye.

It was a Research Fellow in Modern Languages who resolved the dilemma. He said, simply, 'Are you going to sue?' As a model of tact this could hardly be bettered, implying as it did that the allegation was of course untrue. Yet the reply must indicate whether or not this was the case . . . The College Lecturer in Law nodded approvingly. The man had clearly not found his metier. He could have made a fortune as a lawyer.

All the eyes of the High Table lunchers were now focused on Conder, who was toying with a dish of gooseberries. He said, 'I've thought about that, of course. On the whole I thought probably not, don't you? One doesn't want to make too much of a meal of it all, does one? Libel cases can be so unpleasant, even if one wins.'

Disappointed, the Fellows agreed. As a reply it was masterly, leaving them not a whit clearer than they had been before. Conder glanced at his watch. 'Must rush,' he said. 'I've got a two o'clock seminar. Do excuse me.' And he left.

As soon as he was out of earshot the modern linguist, who was not troubled by niceties, turned to the law lecturer. 'Well,' he said, 'that wasn't very conclusive, was it? D'you think he did it?'

With a mixture of embarrassment and avidity, the law lecturer considered. It didn't seem quite nice to discuss the fellow behind his back somehow, but still . . . 'Of course I can't possibly say,' he said hurriedly. 'But if I were considering the case in a professional capacity, I should have to say things do point in that direction. After all, when you come down to it, he isn't suing. And if he did, and won, then he would undoubtedly be awarded a very large sum of money indeed. If I were in that position and thought I could win, I should certainly sue. I'm not in a financial position such that I can afford to turn up my nose at several hundred thousand pounds, and to be frank, I wasn't aware that Peter Conder was, either. I may be wrong, of course,' he hedged, in a tone that indicated that this was very unlikely.

'So you do think he did it.'

'Oh, I wouldn't go so far as to say that,' said the lawyer. 'What I think is that he can't prove he didn't. That's a very different thing.'

Private Eye, 13 June
Is Dr Peter Conder, Cambridge Reader in American Studies, a clandestine major in the CIA? Did he, in this capacity, do away with the appalling Paul Silverlight a couple of months ago? Dr Conder is, we hear, deriding the very idea as hopelessly melodramatic. However, Lord Gnome still awaits his writ . . .

CHAPTER 36

'On top of everything else,' said the Prime Minister. 'One would have thought they could have prevented that at least. How much do the police get paid these days?'

'A considerable amount, Prime Minister.'

'And some people would say it still isn't enough. But I must confess there are occasions when I think it's a great deal too much.'

'I've heard that the inquest is likely to find that it was suicide,' said her private secretary.

'Yes, but it's too late. The damage is done. And Peter Conder is a man for whom I have a great regard. A great regard. In fact, wasn't he on the luncheon list for next week?'

'Yes, Prime Minister.'

'I'm very tempted to keep him there. If only to show what I feel about all this. To be hounded like that by a dreadful creature like this Taggart . . . He isn't considering suing, by the way?'

'I understand not.'

'We couldn't allow it, of course. Our friends are agitated enough as it is about the state of security in this country. I'm afraid Dr Conder will just have to grin and bear it . . .'

'Is he still on the luncheon list?'

'Oh, I don't think we can, do you? Such a shame, but there you are. Perhaps I'll send him a personal letter, just to make things clear.'

'Do you think that would be quite wise, Prime Minister? If it got into the wrong hands . . .'

'No, on second thoughts maybe you're right.'

CHAPTER 37

Taggart was sitting in a small Italian café in Kentish Town. To the untrained eye it was no different from any of several thousand similar establishments: cheerful, slightly seedy, providing a limited variety of cheap but eatable food and lurid cakes. Taggart, however, held this particular place in great esteem. He had got to know it and its proprietors when he was renting a room in the next street, and now, always conservative, made a beeline for it whenever he happened to find himself in north-west London. He had brought surprised acquaintances to lunch here from as far afield as Euston, Palmers Green and Swiss Cottage, assuring them that it was the best place he knew for lunch for miles around. They did a particularly excellent sausage sandwich (he did not usually divulge this until they were studying the menu: even Taggart had realized that most of his friends were not as keen on sausage sandwiches as he was.)

He was, in fact, waiting for a lunch-date today. He had felt slight twinges of remorse vis-à-vis King and Conder ever since hearing of the possibility that Jenny Chantrey might have done the deed. After all, the thing had never been proved either way. Was it possible that he had hounded an innocent man (for Taggart, always fair-minded, had to admit that even someone he found as unpleasant as Peter Conder might be innocent of the cold-blooded murder of a close friend)? And had he, in so doing, destroyed another man's career? He had heard rumours that King had been demoted, or anyway kicked sideways. Always a generous-hearted fellow, he had thought that the least thing he could do would be to buy King lunch. Might pick up one or two interesting things at the same time.

The door opened. It was King. He looked surprised, as if this was not quite the sort of thing he had been expecting when he accepted Taggart's invitation.

Indeed, it was not. King was fond of his stomach, and if

not the Mirabelle, he felt he was owed something relatively delicious for all the pain and trouble Taggart had caused him. And obviously Taggart felt the same way and was trying, in his ham-fisted way, to make amends. Now King was not so sure. He paused in the doorway, wondering whether this was not some elaborate practical joke on Taggart's part. He had been put to considerable trouble to find this place, which was distinctly out-of-the-way, and had assumed it would be one of those unlikely gastronomic finds which are occasionally to be made in remote parts of London. However, his nose, not to speak of the rest of his senses, assured him that this was not the case. He was about to turn round and leave, scarlet with annoyance, when he saw Taggart waving and calling from a table in the corner.

'This really is the place you meant?'

'Yes, Mutti's an old friend of mine. I come here whenever I can. Here, Mutti, Inspector King's a particular friend. What are we going to give him?'

The imperturbable, blue-chinned proprietor grinned at Taggart: an excellent client, and it was no part of Mutti's job to inquire into his motives. 'The roast chicken's very good today,' he said. 'Or the cannelloni. Like some wine?'

'Wine, Brian?'

'I'll have a beer, thanks,' said King, who hated cheap Chianti.

'Two beers, then, Mutti. And I'll have the cannelloni. And chips.' King settled for cannelloni without chips. The beers arrived. Taggart sat back happily. 'Great place, this.'

'So you said.' King had decided there was no malice in this invitation; it merely confirmed him in his deep distrust of Taggart. Anything supported by such a maniac must be worth fighting against. 'So what's this in aid of?'

'Purely social. Now that it's all over and the dust's settled there were one or two points of interest I wanted to talk over with you—By the way, I heard you were no longer with the Special Branch. That right?'

'I'm leaving the force,' King said heavily.

'Not all on account of—' Taggart checked himself before the word 'me' slipped out. Self-esteem may carry one so far and no further.

King shook his head. 'I'm not devious enough, and it's too late to learn new tricks.'

'So what will you do?'

'I shall teach sociology. Shouldn't be hard to get a job with my experience.'

'Not unless they think you're still an SB mole, spying on them to see where the cuts should come first.'

'Leave it alone,' said King, but lamely: recent experience had shown him that the more unlikely, the likelier.

The cannelloni came. It was very hot, so much so that the temperature effectively masked the taste. They sampled it and simultaneously sat back for a sip of cooling beer. 'The thing is,' said Taggart reflectively, 'do you think Peter Conder really did it?'

'What?' King could hardly believe his ears. 'You were the one who said he did. Isn't it a bit late now?'

'You know what my evidence was. No hard proof. It's just that there was really no reason why my informant should come up with that particular name otherwise. And it did fit. And he hasn't sued—has he? But I heard the other day that there was a confession.'

'Yes.'

'From Jenny Chantrey.'

'Yes.'

'And it isn't impossible that she could have done it.'

'No.' King was staring at his plate: he did not trust himself to look at Taggart.

'And she's much better now—pretty well cured.'

'I didn't know that.'

'I suppose you wouldn't, necessarily. Well, she is. Back in the bosom of her family any moment.'

'I'm glad to hear it.'

'Did you ever consider the possibility that she might have done it?'

King sat unmoving. It was too much. His career destroyed. Fury in high places. Conder's life possibly ruined

—certainly not enhanced. And why? Because Andrew Taggart, sitting opposite him now chewing a chip and picking unspecified crumbs out of his ragged beard, decided to do a little muckraking for the hell of it. *His* career certainly wasn't ruined.

What was more, King realized, he never had seriously entertained the possibility now put before him. He had assumed from the beginning that Jenny must be lying. He had come across enough addicts while he was a copper on the beat, and in his community liaison job, to know that they were compulsive liars, and he had handled enough murder investigations to know that the temptation to confession is often irresistible to the mentally unstable. If, in addition, this death was the fulfilment of a fantasy that had obsessed her for years . . . He had simply dismissed the notion that she might be telling the truth.

'I bet you didn't even take her fingerprints,' Taggart said. King did not reply. It was true. He hadn't. He had shared a Taggart-like resolution to find the culprit elsewhere, to suit his social conscience: not necessarily among the New Right, but not in that room in Fulbourn, either. They had been right all along. The obvious is usually true.

'Of course, I'm just flying a kite,' said Taggart. Now that his shots had gone so painfully home, he felt almost remorseful.

'And may I ask what makes you fly that particular kite? Now?'

Taggart explained about the girl at the party who had reappeared at Clapham and tried to push him under a bus. 'I think it was the same girl,' he said. 'And from what people say, it might have been her. Jenny Chantrey. Pasty, with sort of mousy hair in rats tails.'

'Yes. That could be her. But just because she apparently tried to kill you, what makes you think she did Silverlight? She might just have felt like killing you. I sometimes feel like that myself.'

'Don't be like that,' said Taggart. 'Have another beer while I try to work things out. Let's start at the beginning. I had no particular ideas about it being Conder. All I thought was that it looked like a CIA job. Well, it does, doesn't it? There are too many coincidences. For instance, Brownson died—did you hear? Seems awfully convenient, doesn't it? Do you happen to know what happened there?'

'Natural death, on the face of it. He had a heart attack.'

'Wasn't he awfully young for that? And a health freak into the bargain. I doubt whether cholesterol ever sullied his lips,' said Taggart, shovelling in a large forkful of cannelloni dripping with bechamel.

'He was out jogging. They found his body—I think it was in those woods by that Institute. Where all those brains are.'

'Probably tripped over by an abstracted nuclear physicist. Jogging's awfully unhealthy, you know. Can be quite dangerous. Do you jog?'

'No.'

'Of course, there are lots of ways to induce heart attack,' mused Taggart.

King burst out, 'I don't know how you can just sit there like that. Don't you feel any sense of responsibility? What about Conder? You've ruined his life.'

'Possibly. He hasn't sued,' Taggart pointed out. 'There is that. It's somewhat significant, you've got to agree. In fact, now that I think about it, it's decisive. Think of the cash. He must have been involved.'

'So where does Mrs Chantrey fit in?'

'I've been thinking about this,' said Taggart, and went on to outline the conclusions he had arrived at. Like Charlotte, he inclined to believe that Conder and Jenny had been in it together, and that Conder had somehow been able to coerce Jenny into doing whatever he told her to do. What had set him thinking first was the occasion when he himself had come under attack. 'Now Conder knew I was on to him, or might be. So, supposing he wanted to shut me up—it wasn't much use him trying to do it himself, was it? The very person I'd be looking out for. So he gets Jenny to do his dirty work for him. Again. Or try to. But it didn't work, so here we all are. Except Silverlight, of course. None of us a whit the worse off. Though I don't expect the CIA'll employ Conder any more. In fact, now I come to think of it, they may be paying him not to sue. Had you thought of that?'

'I don't have your imagination,' King said unhappily.

'Then you'll do fine in sociology,' said Taggart. 'I'll tell you something else I thought of. You know that time someone stabbed Dawes. Did you ever find out anything about that? No? I thought I hadn't heard anything, somehow.'

'And you know who did that too. You should be a novelist.'

'Don't get embittered,' said Taggart. 'No, I was just wondering how it fitted in. Well, it had to somehow, didn't it? And I thought—he gets Jenny to do his dirty work for him. And suppose she tells someone—like her Dad? Put yourself in Conder's place. One must cater for eventualities.'

King was silent for some time. There was something at the back of his mind . . . Now, what was it? Then he said, 'Do you know, I think you may be right.'

'Don't sound so surprised.'

'I was remembering something.' said King. 'The first time I went to see the Dawes. He was just out of hospital. I was parking the car—they live in this street with huge houses in huge gardens, not a soul in sight. Except this one man with a shotgun. Walking down the street. I didn't think much more about it at the time. Then later on I went to see Conder. The same day, it was. And I realized he was the chap. I thought of mentioning it, but then I thought I'd wait to see if he did—well, he'd seen me just as I'd seen him, and he knew who I was by then, just as I knew who he was. But he didn't mention it—obviously playing the same game, and he must have thought he'd looked at me harder than I'd looked at him. Well, it was true, I hadn't been that interested at the time. Just a chap out to pot at rabbits, except I couldn't quite see, quite where the rabbits were likely to be . . . Next time I looked, he wasn't there. I reckon I saved Dawes's life that day.'

'Inadvertently, but who's looking at motives?' said Taggart. 'Not for long, though. I heard the news before I came. The Russians have switched to launch on warning. Official. We'll all go up next time there's a computer error. I'm afraid the end may be nigher than you thought.'

They raised the dregs of their beer to the future.